SCARLET ANGEL

ARROW TACTICAL SERIES

ISABEL JOLIE

ISABEL JOLIE

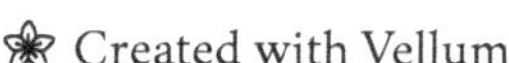 Created with Vellum

The way people come into your life when you need them, it's wonderful, and it happens in so many ways. It's like having an angel. Somebody comes along and helps you get right.
    —Stevie Ray Vaughn

I saw the angel in the marble and carved until I set him free.
    —Michelangelo

CHAPTER 1

NICK

Where the bloody hell is Ash?

Rain lashes the panes with the fury of gods, punctuated with an occasional flash of lightning. In ancient times, men questioned their decisions before such a storm. Weak men perceived lightning as Zeus's anger.

Modern man understands nature has no interest in the goings on of a singular species. Neither do the dead gods.

A bolt of lightning strikes, and the bright reflection draws my eye to the priceless seventeenth-century map hanging in my office, portraying boundaries that no longer align with contemporary divisions. A subtle reminder of the fluid nature of alliances. The faded compass rose yields true north.

Through the rain-pummeled window faint sparks flicker in the distance. A trick of light?

No. Headlights. It's Ash.

I'm off, barreling through the musty, stodgy corridor and never-used formal rooms, reaching the massive oak door and swinging it open before he knocks. The man's absolutely drenched. His mop of straw-colored hair is dry, but everything from his shoulders down is soaked. Rain droplets drip from his Barbour jacket, and there's a field hat in his hand clutched against his stomach.

"Proper nasty out there," he says, stepping inside and dutifully removing his muddy boots.

With the click of the door and one glance around the barren foyer to ensure my sister, Lina, isn't lurking, I ask, "Is it done?"

Ash offers me his mobile. The screen is lit.

I press the arrow and watch as a vehicle slams into a guardrail on a two-lane bridge and careens over the edge.

On screen, a shadow crosses the road and peers over the railing.

"Let's go to my office."

Ash pads along in his socks, following me along the corridor. On the off-chance Lina saw a vehicle approach, it's best we continue our conversation behind closed doors. Once inside the confines of my office, the door closed and locked, I ask, "Who took the video?"

"It's from our man's vehicle." Ash doesn't bother sitting. The fireplace is lit, but Ash doesn't step closer to the heat. He stands at my side.

"Leo's truck? It sank?"

"Right fast."

My part's done. Now we'll see how good these blokes are at their job. Interpol—that's the contact Leo left. The conductor of the arrangement. But the players...I'll wager they're from all over, the unofficial black ops types who break the law on behalf of governments.

"Our man's asking for an additional fee," Ash says while shoving one hand in his trouser pocket.

"I beg your pardon?"

"Cohen. Said he didn't know the Lupi Grigi were a part of it."

Fuckwit. As if he cares about a branch of the Italian mafia.

"Don't tell me the bastard's saying there's extra risk involved."

Ash shrugs. "He didn't know who the girl was in the truck."

I want to keep Cohen as a resource. Ex-Mossad—full name Ashraf Cohen—he's an asset. But coming back and asking for more…it's not a good look. And it's bollocks. The assassin could take out John Wick, if the man wasn't a Hollywood creation. He's got mad skills. I don't buy he's afraid of Italian thugs.

Ash takes the mobile, flicks past the video, and hands it back, set to photos.

I flick through the shots. The snapshots focus on the SUV and the pitch-black river. It's too dark to make out the embankment from the shots.

How far away was the team?

"How's Lina going to take the news?" I slant an inquisitive eye Ash's way. Why's he asking? "Was she close to the girl?"

"Hadn't known her long." Lina isn't one to get close to friends. She keeps them at arm's length. She's rational like that, all thanks to being raised by a stone-hearted scoundrel, *me*. With an exhale, I pass the phone back to Ash.

I'll miss the Texan. The man worked close to me for over

five years. Ah, Leo Sullivan. A mole in my midst, yet I still hold he's a good one. Talk about being good at the job.

"We've got Andrew from Scotland Yard reporting back. With the storm, they're swamped at the moment. Search and rescue called off. Locating the wreck not a priority."

I step up to the window, running through logistics. "If a story develops that may need a burial…"

I let the sentence fall behind the howl of wind. Ash knows the drill.

"When you get confirmation on your end, will you let me know?"

I narrow my eyes at the head of my security. "Getting soft?"

"I liked them, ya know. She seemed nice. Leo…good guy."

Yeah, he was. Turncoat and all.

"You didn't tell Cohen about the second part of the plan?" This is an important piece. If anyone has any idea that Leo Sullivan is still alive, he won't be safe. He violated a code. I'm all right with letting him slink into the night, but others we work with won't agree with my leniency.

Ash's right eye twitches at a rhythmic pace. It's a side effect of a head injury when serving with the SAS.

"Of course not." He sounds both pissed and aghast at the notion.

"These days, I've got to question everyone."

He gives a quick nod of understanding. "Cohen might question why the car drove off the bridge, given he didn't ram it off, but he gave no sign he's harboring suspicions. If anything, he might be wondering if his bullet caught the driver."

The instructions had been to shoot to corral, not shoot to kill. We had a number of routes planned. Cohen believed he acted as a herding dog, but he also believed that after the confrontation, he'd need to dispose of the leak.

A risky fucking plan. But the message I received from an unknown number forced my hand.

The American isn't who you think he is.

When confronted, Leo confirmed.

The question remains, who sent that message? Who else knows?

With Leo presumed dead, does it matter?

Cohen believes he's dead. But he's not likely to talk about it —would be bad for his business. So is asking for money after the deal.

"How much of a fee are we talking about?"

"Cohen?"

I scowl, losing patience. *What the fuck else would I be going on about?*

"Extra hundred."

"One hundred thousand pounds?"

"He's never been cheap," Ash says, looking about like he'd like to take a seat.

"Greedy wanker. Unacceptable." I drop into my desk chair, the spot where I get my best thinking done. "Take care of him. And keep an ear on the accident. We need word to filter."

"Our guys? You want them talking about it?"

"No. We'll crank suspicions if we know more than the bobbies. Need the story kept close, then, in a couple of days, be certain the victims' names are released. If for any reason they aren't—"

"We'll leak them," he interjects.

"We won't." Media isn't Ash's strength. "It's gotta be the proper authorities. It's got to be natural. Believable."

The mobile flashes a flood alert.

"They're saying we might lose electricity," he says.

I won't. I have a generator.

"Why don't you head home? Check on your old man."

He nods, grabbing his coat and hat.

"When your pop's ready, say the word. We've got land, you know. Can set you up with him out here." Ash lives in the village, a stone's throw away.

He grins. "The old man's happiest within walking distance of the pub. And while I love the man, I don't wanna live with him. But I will head on. Make sure the oaf's stumbled home."

I follow him through the house to the foyer, as much out of boredom as anything else.

"Think this is the end of it?" Ash asks after he's donned his boots.

Eliminating the traitor helps. At least, it might satisfy the person who messaged. But that message doesn't sit right. How did this unnamed person know Leo was the leak? What else does he know? Who is he?

The wind blows the front door back, and rain paints the entry.

"Let's ratchet security up a notch."

"You expecting the Grigi boys to come after you?"

I eye my friend. "Always a possibility. But unlikely."

"Possible, though," he says, a touch too argumentative for my taste. "They were after them, too, you know? Might have saved yourself a mint if you let them take care of it."

Ash is wrong. Leo wouldn't leave Willow behind with an ex-Mossad assassin hunting her. He loved his wife. And he wouldn't confront Cohen either. The man's skills precede him. He wouldn't risk a loss to Cohen knowing he'd be leaving his wife unprotected. If it had only been Italian goons in a car, he might've walked outside and blown their brains out. Problem solved. And Leo might've exited, following Interpol's plan—without his bride. No, I needed to act.

Besides, if I didn't act, the mystery messenger might have.

"What's next?" Ash asks.

"You're going home. Tomorrow, when the storm's passed, beef up the ranks."

"I meant the Italians."

He's right to ask. We're not done with the thieving bastards.

"Believe it or not, Willow was the winning sacrificial pawn."

Ash doesn't understand what I'm saying, but there's no need for his understanding tonight. He'll understand soon enough when I bring Willow's charming cousin into my home.

Some plans come together so perfectly, it's tempting to believe in the gods.

CHAPTER 2

My uncle shoots me a disapproving glare as I sidle up to the bar. I return his glower, a subliminal dare. As expected, he frowns—the gray boss always frowns—and follows my mother, aunt, and cousin into the lift.

With an exhale, I raise my eyes to heaven and catch my reflection in the mirror behind the bartender. Wrinkles from travel mar my linen blouse, and unkempt tangles twist my otherwise straight strands. A person could be forgiven for believing I traveled through a wind funnel. I blow a blast of air upwards from my mouth to shift the unruly layers away from my eyes and turn my attention to the leather-bound Savoy cocktail menu.

Winston Churchill, the British bulldog who once redrew Europe's boundaries and freed Italy, infamously frequented this establishment. Did the great man ever feel feeble and dead-tired from the fight? Probably. Funerals try the soul, and the warrior likely attended his fair share.

The funeral tomorrow will be the first I've attended for someone I love. The heavy weight on my chest differs greatly from the funerals in my past. My husband's funeral, for one. On that day, I soared. My memories of my father's funeral are hazy. I'd been too young to comprehend, and the years buried any emotion. This weekend, I fear drowning.

The bartender approaches in a pressed white blazer, oxford button-down, and black bowtie. Straight bangs hang a hairbreadth over her perfectly sculpted eyebrows.

"May I help you?"

I force a cordial smile and, with one last glance at the menu, say, "I'll have the Cardamom Angel Face."

"And you, sir?"

Startled, I shift to see who she's addressing. If it's my uncle…

"The Dandy Beau," Nikolai Ivanov answers, holding a credit card out for the bartender.

The titan's trimmed auburn beard has grown in along the sides, rounding out his angular jawline, but otherwise, little has changed since I last saw him at my cousin Willow's impromptu wedding when he swooped in last-minute to offer his services as best man. He's still got the arrogant angled chin and judgy eagle eyes. He's wearing a custom three-piece suit that declares he's obscenely rich as he stands on a pedestal of his own, expecting that all the little people should admire him on bended knee.

"I'll pay for my drink," I clarify for the bartender, but she doesn't seem to care as she's already busy with our orders.

"Nonsense. I'm the host."

"The host? Pff." I lift my hands in disbelief. "Of a funeral?"

Two funerals, to be exact. I eye the stools across the bar, but moving to another seat would be childish.

"Have I done something to offend?" His cultured Oxbridge accent rubs me the wrong way.

In all fairness, he's done nothing to me. But I know his type, and pompous, self-absorbed men offend me. I'm also in the shittiest of moods, although he's not to blame.

"I'm not in a social mood."

"Are you ever?"

I side-eye him. Given he and I spent less than an hour in the same room at a wedding and had little interaction, he has no ground to stand.

"My uncle and aunt are in their hotel room. Should I…" I bite back my offer to ring them to join us. Sitting with them would be worse than sitting with the arrogant Brit.

This is all Willow's fault. She had to go and die. I pinch the bridge of my nose and scrutinize the bartender, mentally urging her to hurry up and deliver my drink.

"For someone in mourning, you're sporting some tough bark."

Again, I side-eye him. If I'm quiet long enough, maybe he'll move along. I don't get weepy, but it doesn't mean I don't ache. Willow was not only my cousin, but she was also my best friend. My only friend, if I'm honest. I'd been happy for her when she married because she dodged a marriage that likely would've been worse than mine. I wouldn't wish my hell on anyone, especially not Willow. She saw the best in everyone. She shunned the dark side of humankind.

I never expected that she'd be dead a month after her wedding. I can't quite wrap my head around it. None of this feels real. I keep waiting for my mobile to light up with her number.

The bartender slides my frothy concoction across the bar.

"An angel," she says to me, then she delivers a martini glass to Nikolai.

"An angel for an angel," he says.

"And your drink is inspired by James Bond." I, too, can read. The menu declared his drink to be what the modern-day Bond would drink. "Do you think of yourself as a 007?"

"Do you fancy yourself an angel?"

An unladylike snort escapes. "Some say demon would be more apt." I stir my cocktail with the glass straw, evading his pointed gaze. "But you've heard the stories."

"Don't tell me you care what the monsters say?"

Is he calling the Italian mafia monsters? I twist in my seat, slightly more interested in the pretentious syndicate member. "Is that how you describe your own?"

"You think I'm a mobster?" He glances down at his chest as if to ask, do I not see his bespoke suit?

I run the pad of my finger over the gathering condensation on the glass while taking a moment to drink him in. He doesn't look like one of the mafia men. There are no visible tattoos. None of his teeth are gold. There are no rings or thick necklaces.

I know little about Nikolai Ivanov. I never asked and only assumed. The men respect him, and before his death, they respected his employee, Leo Sullivan.

But he can't be a good man. My uncle saw a union between Willow and Leo to be advantageous to his business and therefore approved of the hasty union between his daughter and Nikolai's employee, an American known to be an arms broker.

Nikolai showed up out of the blue minutes before the ceremony with wedding bands and sent the newlyweds off in a limousine he provided to a destination he picked. I presumed he did it to ensure their safety.

If Leo was an arms dealer, and he was Nikolai's employee, then Nikolai is also an arms dealer. My uncle's specific interest of late is submarines, so perhaps Nikolai deals in more than guns.

Assumptions are the province of fools. My uncle loves that saying, and the life philosophy has served him well. If the commanding prick is going to sit here, I might as well verify my assumptions.

"Were you close to Leo?"

Emotion flickers in his dark eyes. Is he hurting, like me? I suppose even arrogant men can hurt.

The titan's lips miraculously bend, pursing. "He was my best mate." He sips his martini. When he sets the glass back down, the perma-frown is back in place. Did I imagine the emotion?

"She was mine," I say.

There's no reason to open up to him, but we are at a bar, and tomorrow, we'll bury our friends beneath six feet of earth. The official cause of death is an auto accident during heavy rains. The brief articles in the local papers refer to unsafe driving during hazardous conditions.

It's a coverup. Leo was running from someone, of that, I'm certain. People don't simply drive off bridges. Besides, Leandro DeLuca, our capo's brother, had been after her. He'd been angry she chose someone else. There's no telling what he planned. Maybe he wanted to kidnap her. Maybe he wanted to kill her. But Leo killed him. It doesn't matter that Leandro was a narcissistic egomaniac who couldn't handle rejection. Rules are rules, so I'm quite certain his brother, Massimo De Luca, the almighty feared head of our ungodly clan, set about getting vengeance for his brother's death. His men or whoever he hired chased Willow and Leo to a watery grave. I hate them all. Every single member of the Lupi Grigi and their fucked-up traditions.

With that thought, anger swells. I could unleash it at the stranger at my side, but he hurts, too. *Maybe.* The jury's still out.

"She's in a better place."

His sympathetic phrase pulls me back to the conversation, but it stirs agitation.

"Because she's not in this fucked-up world, you mean?" I shift away from him, losing the desire to learn more about him. "I thought when she married, your lot would provide her safety."

He keeps his poker face. The bastard doesn't even blink. And yes, I'm blaming him because why not? He was higher in rank than Leo, so it should've fallen on him to protect them. That's the world order.

"Is everything all right between us, love?"

"I'm not your love."

"It's an expression."

I roll my eyes as much out of habit as anything. While I know little about the man sitting beside me, Massimo is the one I hate most. Hate for one doesn't mean I can trust the man to my right, or that I shouldn't hate him, too.

"What's with the anger?"

"Was there nothing you could do to keep them safe? Is the Lupi Grigi that powerful?" My insides churn, dreading his answer.

"What have you heard?"

His elbows are on the bar, and he leans closer, so close I

inadvertently inhale his cologne. The woodsy scent clears the fog of fury and sorrow, and I remind myself that he might have answers.

The bartender is occupied with other patrons, leaving us to our tense conversation.

With the staff far away, and no one seated nearby, I share my reservations in the hopes he will respond with information. "The rain wasn't so heavy that he drove straight off a bridge. There were no other accidents on bridges that night."

"You've heard nothing," he says in a biting tone. "But you're a clever one. Twisting the angles to sort them."

I sip my drink, studying him over the rim.

He doesn't shy away from my blatant perusal. No, he swivels on the stool, opening his chest to me.

It's no secret that criminal organizations have been expanding throughout Europe. It's not a stretch to believe they'd have authorities in their pocket, even in England, to provide cover.

He rubs the side of his neck, digging his fingers into the muscle that binds to his shoulders and releases a guttural, throaty noise. He scans the room and leans closer. "You're correct. It wasn't an accident."

I knew it!

"You didn't expect the interception?" Yes, I'm coming back to placing their deaths at his feet. As Leo's boss, he should've protected them. I may not agree with the mafia traditions, but I understand protocol.

The tables are filling up with patrons, yet we're alone at the bar for the moment. The low hum of unidentifiable conversation lends a dubious sense of privacy.

"Do you want revenge?" His voice is low and deep, and the rumble delivers chills. "Because I do."

Oxygen leaves my lungs. I force myself to swallow and process his words. I want nothing more than to see every single one of those hateful freaks die a torturous death, but...how does the titan fit in?

"Help me understand. How do the Grigi work with your organization? It's called the syndicate, right?"

"First, there is no syndicate."

I shift back on my stool, putting space between us. He's lying to me.

"The first rule of the syndicate is there is no syndicate." His dark eyes sparkle with mirth. He's playing.

"*Fight Club*? I might be Italian, but I've seen the movie."

A maddening smirk flashes across his face. This is not a humorous situation. His lips flatline once again, and all evidence of humor evaporates.

"If such an organization existed, the Grigi would be one of many that exist under its protection."

"You protect the monsters?" My gut churns with wariness. I can't trust this man. I lift my clutch to leave.

My gaze falls to a suited man in the corner. His back is to the corner. He's angled to observe, and he's far too obvious. My skin chills.

Is he here for me? Would they break protocol?

"No." Mr. Ivanov reaches for my wrist, and my gaze cuts to the point of contact and the heat penetrating my chilled skin.

"Do not touch me."

Wisely, he obeys. The sensation of his touch remains after he lifts his fingers, and I stare at the tingling area.

"I want you to help me take them down." His measured words are both preposterous and promising.

I glance over my shoulder, but the suited man is gone. To the restroom, or for good? Am I being paranoid?

The ice clinks against Mr. Ivanov's glass, bringing me back to the moment and his claim.

In a hushed voice, I ask, "Did you not just say that they're protected? By your organization?"

He can deny the syndicate all he wants, but we both know it exists. And he's a member, if not the leader. Is he looking to trick me?

"They targeted someone I love."

"Leo?"

He chuckles and swirls his drink. I raise an eyebrow. My patience is nonexistent. His sexuality is not a concern of mine. He's teasing, but I'm not in the mood. I want to learn his purpose. And if he won't be honest with me, then I'd rather be alone.

"I speak of someone else." He traces the base of his glass with his index finger, giving me a moment to process. "It's my understanding that you possess knowledge that could be beneficial to my purposes."

I'm the bookkeeper for my uncle's business, Titan Shipping, and a handful of other small-scale mafia-run businesses, laundromats, and tours. Understanding dawns.

"Are you amenable to my proposition?" Dark, sinful eyes center on me, and the earlier chills intensify.

"What if I told my uncle about your proposal? Why risk your life?"

"First, I'd deny it. Second, from what Leo shared, you have reason to hate them more than I do. Even more so now. Your logic is spot on. Bad weather was not a contributing factor to the accident."

"Massimo," I whisper, and the name rings of an evil incantation.

"Let's work together, angel." His deep voice drips with temptation.

He can't possibly know how desperately I've wanted to bring them all down, or how I've trained and positioned myself to accomplish the task.

Energy buzzes between us as I weigh the risks. Nikolai has no reason to lie, unless Massimo put him up to it, but Massimo has disregarded me for years. I'm dead to the man. A useless, spent woman. Do I believe Nikolai? Would Massimo risk creating an enemy? Yes, Massimo is foolish enough to forge a dangerous enemy. I am living proof.

When I look into Nikolai's gray eyes, I see determination. He's intent, and so am I. Nikolai Ivanov may be the partner I didn't dare pray would arrive. I've been planning a solo war, and now I've been gifted a powerful knight.

I tap my glass against his. "Let's."

"Would you care to come up to my room?"

"No." I look directly at him, wiping that too-confident and smarmy expression right off his face. My free hand rises in full orchestra mode, insisting he pause. "You may be the ally I've been seeking, but there will be no bedroom visits. Nothing of the sort. That is not what I am agreeing to."

He holds both hands up in a defensive gesture, sloshing his drink with the movement.

"I understand. I meant nothing by it. I was simply suggesting we could talk in private."

Bull.

"Let's talk tomorrow in my office." He lowers his hands, and I slide off my stool and get the bartender's attention.

"Can I carry this to my room?"

"Oh, that's unnecessary," Nikolai rushes to say.

I pointedly shoot him a glare. I am not one of those women who feigns politeness. No, I have zero fucks to give. I ran out years ago.

"Stay. Enjoy your drink with company," he urges.

"I'd rather not."

"What are you going to do?"

"Go up to my room and enjoy my drink with my book."

"Oh, come now. Surely I'm more entertaining than a book."

"I assure you that's not the case."

He laughs.

I depart.

On my way to the lift, I find myself smiling.

Come up to my room to talk business.

What does he take me for? Regardless, he's likely the ally I've been seeking. He's also a pompous, arrogant prick who wields his handsome face and wealth to get whatever he wants, something I'd best remember.

CHAPTER 3

NICK, AKA FALCON

The gravestones date back centuries, or so I've been told. The weathered dates are impossible to read on the diminutive marble slabs. A stacked stone fence marks the perimeter. It, too, bears the ravages of time. Brown dried leaves litter the ground, and a crisp breeze carries an earthy scent.

When I first acquired this estate, I invited a historian to visit. She found the cemetery fascinating. I rather enjoyed fucking her.

The resting place I selected for Leo Sullivan and Willow Gagliano Sullivan affords a view of rolling hills beneath a sprawling oak. Alessio Gagliano wanted to bring his daughter home, but I pushed for my dear friend and his young wife to be buried with my family. Alessio didn't put up a fight.

Timing was on my side. Plus, the old man's heartbroken. He

and his wife's red-rimmed eyes and dazed expressions speak of parents living a nightmare.

The inconvenient truth that his capo's brother died at the hands of Leo Sullivan might have played to my advantage, as well, even if it was self-defense.

Sources claim the marriage of Alessio's daughter to Leo proved to be a sore point with Massimo, the capo, and if the rumors are true, holding the funeral far from Italy is a wise political move.

I permitted the Gaglianos to bring their family priest, an Italian Catholic, who requested a significant donation to travel to England to perform the ceremony. I considered having someone else perform Leo's service to spite the greedy priest, but this isn't the time to wage petty battles. This is a time for grieving and for making amends.

Caskets encased in a watertight steel capsule rest in deep holes, and black folding chairs are lined up opposite them. Lina and I stand in the back to give privacy to the Gaglianos and to ensure we're far enough away that the priest's sermon is indecipherable.

This graveside service follows a lengthy church service. These Catholics could take a lesson or two in efficiency.

Scarlet's fiery strands shift along her back every time she casts a furtive glance in our direction. What is she thinking? If she's reconsidering my proposal, I'll need to sharpen my powers of persuasion.

From what Willow shared, Scarlet doesn't have much of a personal life back in Italy.

I casually asked a bartender back in Italy about Scarlet. I'd been curious after meeting her at Leo's wedding. The man claimed no Lupi Grigi man would marry the ginger widow, given she cut off her husband's dick and let him bleed out. Rumors say when he was in and out of consciousness and unable to fight her off, she placed his dick in his mouth and clamped a hand over his lips, forcing him to die choking on his penis.

Centuries ago, she would've been burned at the stake, possibly accused of being a witch. His death was ruled self-defense—with no mention of a dick in the mouth—so she's free to roam the streets, but the court of popular opinion didn't rule in her favor. Many of the Lupi Grigi men teach their wives lessons, so my source explained that while it is generally agreed that her husband took his lessons too far—breaking her jaw, fracturing her wrist, and slicing her with a knife—the Neanderthals believe she deserved punishment for unruly behavior. Right or wrong, none of the Lupi Grigi trust her touching the crown jewels.

The story of her past draws me to the metaphorical black widow. The beauty is strong enough to play the hand that rights her wrongs. An admirable trait.

Scarlet Gagliano is one avenue I'm exploring in my quest, and she's quickly becoming my favorite. She stands out from the other mourners. Her vibrant coppery hair and pale skin are distinctive, as are her green eyes. Those green eyes are shaped similarly to her mother's blues, but that's the only resemblance I detect. Her father passed away years ago. I'll have to dig up a photo because she looks so different than the rest of the Lupi Grigi with their dark hair and brown eyes; her uniqueness reeks of an affair.

Scarlet's mother hadn't been forced to remarry after her father's untimely death. Sister-in-law status to the wealthiest legitimate businessman in the family might offer privileges. It's also possible that, like her daughter, her marriage activities left her with few willing suitors. I could be off. Any mafia man high enough up the chain desires a young virgin bride.

The mafias and cartels create one fucked-up world. Their seemingly archaic rules and expectations allow them to function in a society that would otherwise lock them up like the brute monsters and drug lords they are. In my world, these vast, organized criminal organizations are a necessary evil—a military for ambitious leaders. Perhaps enforcer is the most apt designation for the protected underworld.

Governments around the world publicly claim to endlessly strive to dismantle organized crime, yet criminal organizations have never been stronger—by design.

Successful strategists deal in solid business fundamentals. But some mergers and agreements need greasing. Moscow rules apply. Old-fashioned kompromat boasts a high success rate, especially among politicians. Even so, all the world's problems can't be solved with persuasion. No, sometimes, people need to die.

I check my wrist, wondering how much longer the priest will drone on.

Security passes in the distance, presumably out for a stroll. I requested no patrols out of respect for the ceremony, but we're on alert. Someone out there knows Leo betrayed us, and until I know who that person is, I can't be certain what else they know.

"I still can't believe this. So surreal. Have they learned anything more about the accident?" Lina dabs her eyes with a folded tissue. Perhaps she grew closer to Willow than I realized.

I clock the small family group. Heads down, dressed in shades of black, lost in the wake of their mourning.

"I've been checking the news," Lina continues. "It's odd, right? That there's not more about two people crashing into the Thames and drowning?"

"More pressing news stories, I suppose. Happened in a crime-ridden area."

"You don't seem particularly distressed."

She's bent on judging me.

"Have you ever seen me cry?" The answer is no, because I don't show weakness.

My sister's teary, but her mascara remains in place. Her dowdy chestnut dress would blend marvelously with pumpkins. It's November, but still. "Is brown the new black?"

"I'm hungover."

Do I even want to know?

"And brown is darkish. It's acceptable."

"Who were you drinking with?"

"Wouldn't you like to know, brother dearest?" Lina has the wisdom to maintain a somber expression, but there's no doubt she's grinning like a deranged lunatic on her devilish inside.

I'll need to ask Ash. As head of my security, he'll know. I spent the night in London and flew the Gagliano clan to our estate this morning.

"Please do me a favor—"

"I'm not abstaining from alcohol."

I release a deep breath to lower my skyrocketing blood pressure. "Please cozy up to Scarlet. Befriend her when the service ends? I need to speak with her uncle."

"The ginger?"

"Yes."

"Pretty sure you can speak to whoever you like. Don't need me to act on your stage."

"Lina." Her eyes flit up to me, giving me a direct view of a mascara clump on her right upper lash.

"You're quite serious." Her eyes widen with realization. *No fuck.*

"Don't get your knickers in a twist. I'll cozy." Her words aim to placate me, but her tone does the opposite.

My mobile vibrates in my outer coat pocket. No one's paying us any attention, so I pull out the device and check it.

Unknown number
Light drizzle and winds expected this evening.

Me
Shall we reschedule?

Unknown number
Your call. You're the one flying.

The family rises and surrounds the priest.

A black sedan rolls into view, parking behind the line of limousines stretching along the lane.

The driver exits, and recognition flairs. Dorian. My old mate from school. An American. What's he doing here? And he's driving himself. He must've showed up at the house and they sent him here.

I gesture with my hand, letting him know he's been seen. Chap has terrible timing. The funeral is wrapping up, and there are things I need to say. He'll need to wait.

I position myself between the family and the limousines.

Alessio sees me and steps away from his wife. Lina, for once, does as I ask and approaches Scarlet.

"The service was beautiful," I say.

He sniffs into a handkerchief. "It's a beautiful resting spot." He lifts his spectacles, wipes below his eyes, and lets the spectacles fall back into place on the bridge of his nose.

"Thank you for flying us out here, but we'll take the car back."

Given his wife was rather green during the helicopter ride, his statement isn't surprising. The hired driver, dressed in a black overcoat, waits by the back of the limousine. Alessio's wife meanders toward the car. His sister-in-law, Scarlet's mother, stands near the folding chairs, watching Lina and her daughter.

"I appreciate your offer for Scarlet to stay back. She's taken the events hard."

I nod, both hands behind my back.

"Catarina agrees it's a good idea to give her time to grieve. This coming weekend will be eventful, and..." Overtaken with emotion, he places the white linen handkerchief over the bridge of his nose and the spectacles slide up to his forehead.

The level of emotion he's displaying is unexpected for a mafia man. Perhaps this is a reason he was passed over for the capo position in favor of Massimo. I had a scout attend Massimo's brother's funeral, and the capo didn't shed a tear.

"I'll arrange a return flight for her," Alessio says after he's pulled himself together.

This weekend, according to a source, Alessio's fifteen-year-old son will become a made man. From what I understand of the Lupi Grigi's methods, this will involve Orlando's first kill of some poor sap and a boisterous party with hookers and whores.

I lack empathy for a man mourning his daughter while planning the death of someone else's son.

"She's welcome to stay as long as she wishes. There's a lot of history in the area, should she choose to explore. And as you can see, my sister and Scarlet are hitting it off."

"Scarlet would like to go through Willow's things. Choose which items to send home."

"Of course."

"Willow sent her photos of her London flat. Scarlet said she wants to see it in person." His gaze never tracks to his niece.

"That can be arranged."

"And her studio."

"Of course."

"I'm not sure her mother or I…" He sniffles, and I clasp his shoulder. I think little of the man, but I'm not a beast.

The reading of the will will be next week. I inherited everything from Leo Sullivan. He updated his will for his estate to go to his young wife, but in the event she was deceased, the estate passed to me. It's crossed my mind to gift the flat to Scarlet, but she might discover some unique attributes that would pique her curiosity. Leo's hidden gun safe comes to mind. Given he had unknown partners, it's likely he equipped his loft with additional features without my knowledge. With proper adjustments, perhaps it can be gifted. I'll need to explore it first. Hire the right crew.

Gagliano wipes his ruddy nose once more and shoves the handkerchief into a coat pocket. He offers me his hand, and I'm grateful for my gloves.

Dorian leans against the sedan, observing. Someone out

there knows Leo was our leak. Did word spread throughout the syndicate? Is Dorian here to verify the funeral? His old man has always used him like a tool. I could see him sending him on an errand. Whatever the reason for his appearance, my mate's in no apparent rush.

Scarlet and Willow's young brother are deep in conversation, and the way her mother is watching, she doesn't approve. Of the family members, Scarlet's mother has displayed the least amount of emotion, and now she's impatient, flitting her gaze between the cousins and the waiting vehicle.

My gut tells me she wants her daughter to return with her. Perhaps Orlando wishes the same. But unfortunately for those two, the brilliant dame is coming home with me.

CHAPTER 4

SCARLET

"Orlando, don't do it."

He looks over my head with a frown, eyes glassy. I wrap my fingers around his wrist to strengthen my plea.

At fifteen, he's taller than me, but he has yet to grow into his frame. He swipes at his eyes while peering over my head, no doubt searching for his father, the man he reveres.

Uncle Alessio rambles, head down, with my aunt. In mourning, the monster appears human. His children love him, as one does with parents, but only because they have yet to see behind the mask.

"There's no choice." Orlando wrenches his arm away, and under his breath adds, "You of all people know that."

"There's always a choice." As the words leave my mouth, I taste the hypocrisy. "For you, there can be. You don't have to commit. You're young. Wait a year. Your sister just—"

"Don't say it." His Adam's apple shifts below two scraggly black hairs he must have missed this morning when shaving. It feels like yesterday Willow and I ran our fingers down his baby-soft skin after his first-ever shave. "I'm choosing my family." Dark brown eyes, so different from his sister's vibrant blue, flash a warning. "You should, too."

With that, he departs, head down, and I watch his sad retreat.

The tall, too-thin woman dressed in clothes that swallow her joins me at the foot of Willow's casket. "It was a beautiful service," she says.

The woman, introduced earlier as Lina Ivanov, inches closer.

I've been told someone will come along and fill the hole with dirt after we're gone. The scent of damp earth permeates the air, and the mostly bare tree limbs add gloom to the grave-yard. Scattered flowers, roses, and a dozen willow branches litter the stainless-steel outer casket, which will keep her remains dry for over a century. Inside the waterproof shield lies an elegant mahogany coffin. I never glimpsed the interior of the coffin, as my aunt and uncle chose a closed casket service. The wreck and river disfigured Leo and Willow beyond recognition.

I don't wish to think of that, yet the insidious thought settles into crevices of my psyche and chips away at my heart until it aches. I've never seen a waterlogged dead body, yet my twisted mind fills in images that I hope aren't correct.

Lina's heels sink into the soft soil, and leaves crinkle as she shifts, seeking firmer ground.

I wish to be left alone, but I can't easily tell this stranger to leave. It's just as well. I'll return later. There are things I want to say to Willow, unsaid things that should've been said, and I wouldn't say those things with family milling about.

"Did the preacher know her well?" Lina asks, breaking the silence.

"Father Francisco has been at our church for as long as I can remember."

Did Willow go to confession and share her darkest secrets with the elderly man? Doubtful. Did she ever have any meaningful interactions with Father Francisco? Again, doubtful. But he serves the *famiglia*.

"Good. I can't stand it when the minister knows nothing about the person and the service becomes a religious lecture."

I have no idea what Father Francisco said during the service. My mind wandered, lost in a haze of sorrow.

"Did you spend time with Willow?" I ask, shifting the conversation away from the service.

Willow talked little about Nick and his sister, but she called me not too many weeks ago, panicked, wondering what to do to help someone who had lost consciousness from drug use. Lina, Nikolai Ivanov's sister, had been the one she needed to assist. Poor judgment aside, I sensed Willow liked Lina.

"I loved visiting her in London. She was a good match for Leo." Lina glances over her shoulder, and my gaze follows hers.

The group is dispersing. My uncle and Nikolai are conversing. My gaze connects with Nikolai's, and the perimeter fades. A heightened sense of awareness strikes. My skin tingles and my eyes burn, and I find myself locked in a trance.

"My brother fancies you."

I blink, breaking the hypnotic state, and focus on her words. Nikolai and I share a common goal, but it's an aspiration that may culminate with a death knell. I'll pay any price to put an end to the cycle.

"Are you feeling the same?" Her teasing tone strikes me as out of place standing next to two coffins.

"I assure you, there's no fancying going on."

"Oh, no. He's a dozen years older than me, but I know my brother inside and out."

An argument brews somewhere deep inside, but I lack the energy to bring it forward. With one last glance at the pair of flower-strewn coffins, I turn.

My mother stands awkwardly, hands clasped, disapproval etched on her face.

"If you'll excuse me, I should bid farewell to my mother," I say, but my heels remain rooted to the damp earth. Too often, I don't wish to do what I should.

"Are you staying?"

There's a spritely happiness to her tone that couldn't be more inappropriate.

"I am."

"Brilliant." She clasps her hands together. "We can go to London. Lunch. Shop. You'll want to go through Willow's things in the flat, yes? She had trunks of clothes. I'm not even sure she finished unpacking."

I place a hand on Lina's forearm. She's making my head hurt.

"I'll be back," I say.

The leaves crunch underfoot, and my heels sink into the soft sod with each step, forcing me to put the weight on the pads of my black leather Louboutins.

Like a good daughter, I hug my mother. Her ice-blue eyes are frigid, but the lipstick she's chosen is a warm rose.

"It's not proper for you to remain behind," she says in Italian. "Please don't do this."

My mother has spent almost two decades as a widow. The proper action in our circle would have been for her to remarry. But in our world, proper is best used as a tool to instruct others how to live.

"Do not worry yourself," I respond in our native tongue. "I'll be back under your watchful eye before you know it."

Her gaze bypasses me, looking over my shoulder. I don't follow her gaze, as it's quite unnecessary. I sense his approach. Heat travels up my spine, emanating across my rib cage.

"It doesn't look good," she says under her breath. "He's not married."

I fail to suppress my snort of derision. "It's too late for my reputation, Mama."

"And whose fault is that?"

"Yes. Whose fault *is* that?"

Surprise widens the whites of her eyes. I've never placed the blame at her feet before, but she's never implied I'm at fault either. I welcome the anger surging in my veins. It's much more productive than sorrow. I'm taller than my mother, and I lengthen my spine, rising inches above her crown. *How dare she?*

"Catarina, come. It's been an emotional day," my uncle says, seemingly oblivious to the ratcheting tension.

He doesn't wait for her but continues on the path to his wife and son.

"Better not let them wait. It wouldn't be *proper*."

Anger flashes in my mother's eyes. I thrust my chin upwards and glower, daring her to make a scene.

Nikolai and Lina step forward, flanking me.

"Return soon," she says in Italian. "Be good."

"Did she just tell you to be good?" Lina asks when the car door closes behind my mother.

The three of us stand in a line, waiting for the limousine to drive away. The tinted windows prevent us from seeing inside.

"Do you know Italian?" I ask.

"I dabble. She did, didn't she? She's like my brother here, treating you like a child."

"Not a child," I say. "An asset."

Given Nikolai's blank expression, I doubt he's listening to us, but Lina leers at her brother. I should've kept my thoughts to myself.

"Is there anything else we need to do?" I ask.

"The caretaker will be here shortly," Nikolai answers. "Would you like to remain behind? Would you like some time alone?"

While I do wish for privacy, I don't care to witness a piece of machinery drop buckets of dirt into the holes. All the same, his thoughtfulness is unexpected.

"No, thank you. I'm good. For now."

"Thank god," Lina says. "I swear the temperature is dropping. Do we need to go back to the Savoy to retrieve your luggage? We can be on the way in—"

"She has her luggage," Nikolai says. "And after an emotional day, I imagine Scarlet would enjoy a night by the fire."

A misty fog blankets the horizon, and the damp chill penetrates my funeral attire. "A fire sounds heavenly," I admit.

Nikolai studies me with an intimate intensity. I'm not sure what it is about those judgmental, stormy eyes, but I swear his gaze lasers every inch of skin he peruses.

Lina looks between us, still grinning, and leaves us, humming a silly tune.

"Tomorrow, the weather should be a touch warmer. You can return any time you wish."

He's perceptive. And, I suppose, kind when it suits. "Thank you."

Nikolai gives a polite, dismissive nod, and heads in the opposite direction to the two vehicles parked further down the lane. A man in a black overcoat leans against a black four-door Audi. He might be security or a driver. He didn't attend the service.

"Are you not coming with us?" I call after Nikolai.

Should I follow him? Or his sister?

"I'll catch up," he says without turning around.

His sister it is. Upon catching up to Lina, I ask, "How far is it to the house?"

We flew to Nikolai's estate in a helicopter this morning. I saw the property from the air, but my bearings were off. We were whisked away into an awaiting processional of limousines, and we drove to the church and then to the graveyard.

"It's about a fifteen-minute walk. Five-minute drive. Would you rather drive?"

"Isn't Nikolai taking the car?"

"Nick. Don't call him Nikolai. He hates it." She taps into her phone, and the black limousine pulls forward, leaving Nikolai and the man with the black overcoat. "On second thought, do. Always call him Nikolai."

She grins like the devil. There's a balled-up tissue in her hand, but that's the only sign she's straight off a funeral.

"Will Nikolai walk?" She looks victorious at my use of his name, but I don't know him well enough to apply a nickname.

"No need to fret. He won't be long."

I'm hardly fretting. "Do you always take limousines?"

"That would be pretentious, don't you think? Nick thought your family would appreciate a traditional funeral procession."

"So, he rented them?"

"Well, he doesn't own one."

Interesting. Nikolai performs the same as my mother.

"But we have hired drivers, so let's take advantage, shall we? I'm cold, and my feet hurt."

Lina scrolls on her phone for the duration of the short ride to the stone mansion. The expansive, manicured lawn, even when coated in fall's yellows and browns, impresses. A fountain in front splatters water over four tiers of stone. Small pebbles in alabaster tones adorn the circular area around the fountain, and cobblestone graces the drive and the courtyard.

"You have a beautiful home," I say.

The uniformed driver's eyes meet mine in the rearview, but he quickly averts his gaze.

"It's not mine," Lina says.

"Do you not live here?"

"Of late, I do. Not by choice."

The limousine parks in front of the house, and Lina opens the door, not waiting for the driver. I scramble out, sliding across the seat to exit through her door.

"What do you mean?" I ask, following her up the stone steps.

The windows of the first and second floors line up symmetrically, but the third floor is styled differently with many small windows, and I can't ascertain if it's an attic or if it's the location of the servants' quarters.

There's a formality to the architecture of the house, and I expect a butler to open the door, but Lina twists the handle and swings the heavy oak door open.

"How long has this house been in your family?" I ask, with one last glance at the third-floor eaves.

"Ask questions like that, and everyone will know you're clueless."

"What do you mean?"

"It's a country estate. The kind that stays in families for generations. Nick bought this, oh, maybe ten years ago. The heir couldn't afford the taxes and sought to sell it to a hotelier. Nick swooped in. Bought it sight unseen and furnished."

The front door opens into a foyer with a grand marble staircase and a polished mahogany railing. The same gleaming banister wraps around the upstairs balcony.

"The house is a Robert Adams, but it's been renovated so many times it's lost the mystique. Or, perhaps, the renovations spanning nearly two hundred years give it the proper countryside mystique. I don't know and don't care. It's stuffy and boring. Give me the city, any city, over the countryside."

She may not care for it, but it is beautiful. There are homes in Italy that are equally as grand, although the most sought-after homes in our area have stunning Mediterranean vistas.

"It's beautiful, but it's not what I expected Nikolai to inhabit." She ignores my comment.

The wood floor shows its age, but a mammoth Oriental rug covers all but the outside edges of the foyer. To each side of the entryway are rooms with quaint antique furniture befitting a museum and ten-foot doors that presumably lead into formal rooms.

I follow Lina's lead and remove my shoes, but rather than kick them up against the wall, I dangle my heels from one hand.

"This Nikolai business. Where'd you get that? Did someone

introduce him to you as Nikolai? Not Leo. Leo called him Nick."

On the day of Leo and Willow's wedding, when he arrived in a tuxedo with a garment bag slung over one arm and a velvet pouch, I don't believe anyone introduced us, but I heard Leo call him Nick. My uncle calls him Nikolai. And Lina did just instruct me to call him Nikolai, didn't she?

Lina looks at me inquisitively, wanting an answer. "I'm not certain we were introduced. I don't know your brother well."

"Eh, well, that'll change." She pauses at a painted door. "I wonder where he'll put you. I should've asked." She snaps her fingers. "I'll call him."

She lifts a mobile to her ear, and I step forward to the window and look out over the courtyard at the gray day. Off in the distance, a man with shears thrown over a shoulder strolls past a line of trimmed bushes. There's nothing in this landscape that's remotely colorful. Even the greens feel muted.

"All right. I got the answer. You want to change those clothes? Your things are in your room."

"Sure."

I follow her down a musty-scented hall and up a back stair-case to another hall with a room that looks out on the side of the property. The lawn extends beyond the shrubbery to a mix of evergreens and hardwoods.

"How big is the property?"

"All told, around two thousand acres. This one was only twelve hundred, but he bought the place next door, too. It was farmland, some dairy cows. The farmer still works the land, only Nick now owns it. Pays the taxes. Win-win for the farmer."

"Why does he want so much land?"

"Country estates are all the rage. Didn't you know?" She

laughs, but it's not a carefree sound. No, it's slightly demented. "Give it time, is what he tells me. I've been trapped here for months, and it blows balls. But"—she snaps her fingers and grins—"now you're here, and we've got business in London."

"You wish to live in London?"

"You've been, yes?"

"I woke this morning in the Savoy."

"Well, yes, but before?"

"No. My mother and aunt like Paris, Madrid, Barcelona. Obviously, Rome. They've talked about London, but…I was supposed to visit Willow." Why the hell didn't I make that happen? I'd been busy, but that hadn't been my true reason. I hadn't wanted to know if she'd married a monster. I hadn't wanted to discover if she'd been hiding the truth about her situation like I had for years. And for that, I missed witnessing her happiness.

"You look so sad." She fingers her lower lip, the long glossy nail scratching the corner. "I suppose it is the day of the funeral. I'll leave you to change, and if you want the fire on in here, just flip this switch. All the upstairs fireplaces are gas. Switches are by the mantle. When you're up for it, maybe tomorrow or the next day, we'll go to London, and I'll show you around. There's so much energy. I'll go plan… See what reservations we can get."

She bends her head to peer at her mobile and shuts the door, closing me in.

The furniture in the room, like the furniture downstairs, is ornate and delicate. I have little knowledge of furniture, but I assume the pieces are antiques. A four-poster bed resides between the two windows on the opposing wall. There's a doorway into a bathroom that is almost as large as the bedroom. I suspect the adjacent room was originally a bedroom, but it's been divided into a walk-in closet and a luxurious bathroom. A clawfoot tub rests in front of one window overlooking the grounds. My suitcase sits in the walk-in closet.

I could take a bath and forget this day, but I'm in a stranger's home, and it would be rude to disappear. Instead, I unzip my suitcase and change out of my black business skirt suit. There's a chilly draft, so I leave my tights on and pull on a sweaterdress. I don't own many warm items. If the temperature in the house falls overnight, I may need to borrow some clothes from Lina or go shopping.

Willow, did you spend time here? You mentioned this place. Which room did you stay in? Do you have warm clothes packed away in your flat in London? This is so wrong. You should be here. Are you somewhere up above, watching?

After resting beneath a blanket on the bed for what feels like hours, drifting in and out of a light sleep, I leave the room and wander through the still halls. I find my way to the stairs and head down. There must be a more lived-in section of the house.

If these walls could talk, I imagine they would speak of years of life with servants buzzing around lit candles and fireplaces roaring in every room. Perhaps there were balls or the family that built this house had the good fortune to host royalty, possibly the queen. The faint musty smell lingering along the halls must stem from the building's age, or perhaps it's the worn, faded Oriental carpets underfoot. I suspect the gilded framed portraits hanging along the walls are original to the home and probably remain in these back hallways because no one cared enough to replace them.

If I lived here, I'd have comfortable rooms somewhere, and I imagine, like my uncle's homes, those casual rooms would be in the rear of the house, so I turn in that direction at the bottom of the stairs. Further down the hall, an enticing, warm light glows from the crack between two stained doors. As I draw closer, I hear murmurs. Someone speaking, muttering, I think. But when I press my ear to the door, the sound stops abruptly, replaced with a loud bam.

CHAPTER 5

NICK

> **Unknown number**
> We're on.

> **Me**
> You're buying. Time?

> **Unknown number**
> 1800

> **Me**
> Affirmative

I open the back of the device, pop out the SIM card, lift the maple gavel, and slam it onto the card.

Movement in my periphery catches my attention.

"Is that a gavel? Like a judge uses?"

Her hair glimmers in the lamplight, like a flame dipped in gold. A soft gray sweaterdress with capped sleeves hugs her curves, from her shoulders, around her breasts, to her trim waist and hips, down to her calves. One hand rests on the door handle.

Ready to take flight. Do I scare her?

"Did you issue a verdict?" she asks, her tone melodic, her presence infusing the space with a warmth the hearth fails to deliver.

I follow her pointed gaze to the wood gavel. "Came with the house." I set it down and sweep the SIM card remnants into my palm. "You going to enter or loiter in the corridor?"

She remains fixed in place, too far away for me to get a good read. *So tentative.*

"You think I'll bite?"

"I've no idea." A cock-sure smile crosses her lips. "But you should know, when bitten, I bite back."

Her hand leaves the knob, and she crosses her arms over her narrow waist and takes a single step into my office.

"I'd expect nothing less, love."

"Don't call me love."

I dump the sharp, tiny pieces in the rubbish and brush my palms against each other. The desire to put the siren in her place brews, but I swallow the temptation.

"Is your room to your liking?"

"I don't hate it."

I bite the corner of my lip, unsure what to do with this one. "Take your pick of rooms, lo—"

A single eyebrow arches, because yes, she caught my near

slip, and damned if that eyebrow raise is irritation or amusement. I haven't a fuck.

"My room is lovely. Thank you. I saw the light on in your office. How shall we proceed?"

"Close the door."

She glances over her shoulder and stills.

For Christ's sake. "Close the bloody door." She pierces me with a glare. "Trust me or not? If you don't, I'm wasting my time."

She closes the door and backs up to it.

What the hell? "I'm not a bloody monster."

Her lips purse, but that's the only movement I clock. What the bloody hell have I gotten myself into?

"Here's the deal. Love." I pause for effect. "If we're talking about something that might get a head shot off, we close the door. And we only talk about it in my study or outdoors." The house holds a lot of rooms, a few with a stuffy old-world library vibe and plenty of locations to stash a listening device. "This room is my study," I add for clarity. "Now, let's get on with matters of import. You do the books?"

"Quicken. And a proprietary program Titan Shipping uses."

Finally getting somewhere. "Can you access them from here?"

"No."

"Fuck—"

"I can tell you where to look. How they do everything."

That's helpful, I suppose.

"I have a favor to ask."

Here we go. Well, she deserves payment. "Go on," I say, curious about the depth of the beauty's greed.

"Help me find a new location to live. Somewhere they'll never think to look."

She's talking about hiding from the mafia. "And where would that be?"

"Greenland? Australia? I don't care. I don't want anything to do with the family. I want to be as far away from them as possible."

If she's a witness, that's wise. "Done."

"Yes?"

"Absolutely."

She stands, eyes wide, disbelief etched on her porcelain skin. She's truly gorgeous. Shiny copper waves and green eyes. Kryptonite for any warm-blooded male.

"Should I select a place?" She sounds impatient.

"You're good here for a bit, right? The bit about going through Willow's personal effects, it was true, correct?"

"Yes."

"All right. Good enough, then. Let's meet tomorrow after breakfast and get a plan together."

"Not today?"

"I've got to head into the city. Meeting. I've a business to run. The meeting was scheduled a while back. Didn't anticipate you'd be here." Why am I rambling? I don't owe her an explanation.

"I understand. Tomorrow."

"Lina will come and find you for dinner."

"That's… I'm not hungry."

"Chef'll have something. Lina will get you."

"I'll rest in my room. Until dinner."

"All right, then."

She fumbles with the doorknob. The door rattles so long she sounds like a prisoner wiggling a lock.

"Need some help?"

A click sounds and the door opens.

"Are you afraid of me?"

"No." She pushes her shoulders back, and the action draws my attention to her breasts. Or hell, it's nothing to do with her posture and everything with me being a horny perv. Her fingers curl into her palms, and her chin lifts, defiant and fiery. "I'm not afraid of anyone."

"I believe you," I say, lying.

She exits immediately.

She's a nervous bird. Is it all blokes? Or just me?

My gaze follows her arse, and I grind my teeth. It's a good thing I'm stopping off at the club tonight. It's been too long since I've had a release. Makes me a horny fucker, which makes it hard to think around the woman, and I need my head on straight with this one.

She's got gumption. I head to the guesthouse in search of Dorian.

"You didn't mention Scarlet Gagliano is staying with you," he says in greeting.

"Saw her, did you?"

"Lina mentioned it." Ah, my sister.

I scan the quaint cottage. "This place okay for you?"

"You know it is."

It's curious he showed up at the funeral. More curious that he wanted a place to crash.

"I'm headed into the city. Any interest in joining?" There was a time I wouldn't need to ask, but Dorian's grown distant. Perhaps we've both grown old.

"No thanks. Like I told you, I've got meetings in Dorset. Reschedule for another night in London. I'm rarely on this side of the pond."

It's true. Last time I saw Dorian Moore was in Telluride. "My meeting's early evening. I'll aim to swing back before it's too late. You sure I can't persuade you to join me?"

"I'll hang here. Have some emails to get to. And I want to catch up with Lina. She's more appealing than you."

I point a finger at him. "Get it out of your head."

He smirks.

"Are you still married?"

His wolfish grin counters the quick shake of his head.

"Exactly. To you, Lina's off-limits."

"The divorce is final. What remains are technicalities. It's with the lawyers." Utter bullshit.

"It bears repeating. She's my little sister."

"Fine. Fine." He sits on the back of the sofa and grins. "Now that Scarlet. She's…" he puckers his lips, and I hold up a hand.

"Up you go. You're coming with me to the city."

"Hmm. Is the ginger off-limits?"

Not happening. I snap my fingers. "Come on. Get your arse moving."

"I'm just messing with you. I'm wiped. I only got in this morning. After those beers we had this afternoon, I'm done."

"Come with me and we'll stay the night at the club. I'll have you back in time for your meeting."

He debates it, squirming in his chair. He wants to. What bloke doesn't?

Leo. Bloody saint, that one. Didn't appreciate the finer points of life.

"Rain check."

His shoes are off, his collar's undone, and his eyes are slightly bloodshot. Looks proper knackered.

"Want me to have your dinner delivered?"

"Room service?"

I lift a shoulder. It's no sweat off my back.

"You really don't want me around your sister. Or is it the redhead?"

"Sod off."

He chuckles. Wanker.

"Chef will be in touch via the landline." I rap my knuckle against the wall on my way out. "Who did you say you're meeting with tomorrow?"

"I didn't."

Fucking wanker. That sly grin.

With that, I head on to the helipad. Chances are he's jostling my chain for kicks. Probably on an errand for his father.

Halston Moore, or Dorian Senior, is one of the most controlling men I've ever met, and given my circle of Type-A's, that's saying something. The man treats his adult son like an errand boy. All the same, I shoot off a text to Ash to have someone follow Dorian in the morning.

Charlemagne prances in high platform heels, a short skirt that poofs out in tiers, and a bustier that puts her voluptuous breasts on display. She holds the door for me as I step inside, scanning the private room. No windows, a plush four-poster bed, glass cabinets with amenities, and a narrow bench at the end of the bed.

"Is this the best you have?"

"I'm afraid so, love." Her red lips are full, and they shine brightly against her dark skin. Her nails could double as daggers.

"All right." I pull out five hundred pounds and pass it over.

She takes it with a gracious smile. "Enjoy."

The door closes, and I take in the room. Nomad offered to provide a location, but I like clandestine clubs.

Built-in secrecy. If someone exits a room, they assume you're fucking, and if they ever leaked it, they'd risk their treasured membership.

I drag the bench away from the bed. The room is tiny, but in the bathroom, there's a stool beneath the vanity. I remove the dainty piece and sit it across from the bench.

If we need to sit, that's taken care of.

I step inside the bathroom, hidden from the hallway or anyone entering, and wait.

Two minutes pass and there's a rap at the door.

There's a faint clicking sound, and the door opens. In the mirrored ceiling, I glimpse the man entering the room. A herringbone six-on-one jacket and matching trousers. Brown wing tips. Classic posh wanker.

The door clicks closed behind him, and I step forward, careful to avoid startling him.

"Nomad," I say. It's the name he gave when I called the number on Leo's card.

The man's name is Tristan Wagner, although he uses the last name Voignier when on Interpol business. In most of his cases, his real identity would hinder his cause.

He first came across our radar when he followed a case to the Caymans.

An Interpol contact equals access. A tool for leverage. He's not our only contact, but a general rule with resources is that you can't have too much of a good thing.

"Falcon." My lips twist at the code name assigned to me. I don't necessarily agree with the code names, but on the off chance anything is being recorded or someone overhears, best to not share names. That's sound advice I can abide by. Of course, the Interpol officer knows my fucking name. Knows everything about me, probably going three generations back.

"I appreciate your agreeing to work with us," he says.

"We have mates in common."

"That we do." His eyes narrow. "You requested this meeting. Do you have something to share?"

"I do." I pass him a dildo and love the fuck out of his puzzled expression. "There's a chip inside." There are photos and maps on the chip. It's everything he needs to track a human trafficking route in Southeast Asia run by a Vietnamese chap who attempted to short-change me on a real estate deal. But it's in my interest to blow his operation anonymously.

"Anything for me?" What I want is confirmation Leo landed safely. I don't know his true identity, but he's not a Sullivan. If I'd pressed on the day of the confrontation, when I considered killing the traitor, he wouldn't have told me.

After all those years, Leo didn't trust me, but I trusted him from the start. He's a good man. A rarity. It's why I knew I had to force him to bring Willow along when he disappeared. He's too selfless. He needed a shove.

My first call to Nomad was to tell him he needed to orchestrate an exit. Have to give credit where it's due. His team pulled it together. Nomad and I worked well together on that first project. Assuming Leo landed safely, that is.

Nomad scratches his jaw as if he's uncertain what I'm asking.

"Did the package arrive safely?"

"Ah. That. Yes. Safely delivered."

His thumb rubs across the curve of the black plastic dildo.

The second he realizes what he's doing, he drops it into his trouser pocket.

"That's a high-end model. Vibrations controlled by a mobile."

"Duly noted." He rocks back on his heels. "When we spoke, you mentioned the need to move quickly because of a burned identity. Any more on that?"

"Unfortunately, no. Traced the message to a burner. The curious bit is the mystery man knew a number only allocated to a specific few."

"If it was someone you knew, why would they use a code name?"

"They wouldn't. I think someone within the group was hacked."

I read his skepticism.

"My friends aren't all as savvy as I'd like them to be."

"So you've no idea who contacted you?"

"None."

"Are you concerned?"

Annoyed is more like it. "If you've done your part, no."

If the whistleblower believes Leo's dead, all's good. At least, there's no grave concern. I still need to identify the leak. If it was a syndicate member, they wouldn't be playing this game. They would've told the group and insisted Leo die.

"You're not worried your communications are compromised?"

"Not mine." I own three different tech companies and specialize in online security. "One of the other blokes, sure. I'm working on it. I'll be careful."

"Our systems… we've been monitoring for any mention of a Prophet."

When I asked the whistleblower for an identity, the prick responded with "A Prophet." Egotistical fuckwad.

"Same. I'll keep you updated on our results."

"Will you?"

He's right to be skeptical. "If it serves me, I'll share."

"I was told you play it straight." He shoves his hands into his pockets, but the one with the dildo quickly withdraws. "Anything else? Any deals in the works?"

"Are there any deals I'm willing to implode? That's your question, right? That's what I gave you on the joy contraption. The ladies call it a pocket rocket. It won't disappoint."

"We appreciate your working with us," he reiterates, sounding like quite the statesman.

I'm not working with them, I'm using them.

"Change of topic. My team tracked a hack into one of my shell companies."

"The two hundred million theft. I heard about it. You found the culprits?"

"Aye. Lupi Grigi."

His eyes widen. "They went after you?"

"Seems they suspect I had a hand in the bust from two years ago."

"Our sources heard the same."

Yes, Leo warned me. "I underestimated their tech capabilities. Won't happen again. I recommend the same."

"We're not in the business of protecting the mafia. We

consider them a threat. It's not my area of expertise, but… appreciate the insight all the same. Others will find the information quite…useful." He clocks the space, his gaze darting about before resting on me. "What're you going to do about it?"

"I'm working on a plan. It should involve quite a bit of useful information for your counterparts."

He connects the dots. "Ah. I see. Well, we welcome it. You know how to get in touch. Is that it?"

"That's all I've got."

"I'll be on my way, then." He holds up the room key. "Do I give this to you? Someone else?"

"On your way to the lift, pick a lovely bird. Hand her the key. Send her my way." I need to blow off steam.

He lifts his shoulders noncommittally. "As you wish. Any preference? Blonde? Asian? Big tits? Small?"

"Surprise me."

CHAPTER 6

SCARLET

I wake to an unsettling quiet. It's as if I'm alone. Do they sleep late in this house? If Nikolai Ivanov earned his reputation as a business titan, then it's doubtful.

On the Gagliano estate, where I spent my teen years and have lived since Vincent's death, the buzz of lawnmowers often passed through open windows, along with the chirps of birds, an undercurrent of waves, and voices. Doors were mostly open, and between the staff and the family, people were almost always milling around. During low tide, I'd wander down the steep, narrow path to the rocky beach beneath the cliff. The arduous climb back up meant it was one of the few solitary stretches on the estate. It's also the location where MI6 first approached me, and realization dawned. Other organizations want to bring down the Lupi Grigi. I'm not alone. Or so I thought. The trouble with being an asset is if you leave your position, you're no longer useful. I thought their goal was to curtail the drug industry, but as time passed, I've grown uncertain. I suspect they want information above all else. And that doesn't serve my purpose.

Glimpsing overcast skies through the windows, I retrace my steps to the front of the stately English manor. A black sports utility vehicle approaches in the distance. I move to the side of the front-facing window, shielded by drapes, and watch as Lina comes up from the side path in riding boots, breeches, and a form-fitting jacket. The driver rolls down the window as she approaches. She hands him something, and he passes her an envelope.

They don't kiss cheeks and speak for less than a minute. He drives away, and she returns from the direction she came.

The interaction strikes me as odd. Perhaps he delivered an item she ordered. Nick said if I needed anything, it could be delivered in town, and he would send someone to pick it up. Perhaps that's all it is.

The quiet of the house agitates. Perhaps that's why it took so long to fall asleep last night. The morning's morose cloud cover feeds the internal discord.

Was it like this when you visited?

If only I could ring Willow and ask.

I could chase after Lina, so I'm not alone, but I'm without shoes, nor do I have a jacket. The hardwood floor chills my feet through my wool socks, and cool air wafts through the glass panes. The forecast is a mild day, but the gray skies seep into my psyche with an ever-present chill.

By a back door, I find Wellies and a Barbour jacket desperately in need of an oiling. I slip the Wellies and jacket on and inhale a faint cedar scent. I bury my nose in the worn collar and pick up hints of cinnamon and clove.

Is this Nick's coat?

I push the door open and step into the chilly morning in search of Lina. Toward the back of the property is a stable, and I head along the brick path, assuming that's where she must be.

As I approach the stable, the mechanical whir of rotors pulls my attention to the sky. A horse in a paddock pricks its ears forward and neighs. The tree limbs sway, and a helicopter appears over the peaks of the trees.

The treetops sway with increasing fervor as the helicopter descends, and the horse enclosed in the nearby paddock trots in a circle. The grass blades on the lawn whip in the wind, and a wayward piece of grit flies into my eye. My palm covers the injury. I keep my head bowed, hands shielding my eyes. The wind and sound lessen.

Cautiously, I raise my head, one hand over the sharp pain. My eye waters beneath my palm. The helicopter door opens and Nikolai hops out.

"Are you all right there? Something get in your eye?" He approaches swiftly. "You shouldn't be out here without glasses, something to shield your eyes."

He reaches for my chin, and I jerk back.

"Let's wash it."

"It's fine. I think it's just scratched." It burns, but it can't be a serious injury.

"Ah. Well, some drops will make it better." He makes a whirling hand motion behind him, and the helicopter blades slowly spin.

"It's going back up?"

"Not going to leave it in the pasture." He places a hand on my shoulder, and I flinch. "Let's go."

The sound increases, as does the wind, and we both take off at a near jog.

Inside the house, I remove the Wellies.

"I borrowed these," I say. "And this." I hang the coat back up on the hook.

"Loads of those around the place. Take what you need. Have you had breakfast?"

"I don't eat much in the morning, but I'm keen for coffee."

"Did Lina not offer you coffee?"

"I haven't run into her, and I haven't come across the kitchen yet." It's a partial truth. There's no reason not to mention that I saw Lina earlier, yet something holds me back.

"Kitchen's this way. It was originally separate from the house. Back when people were redesigning homes and bringing the kitchen indoors, this family kept it in a separate building. It's attached now through a covered breezeway."

"If you hire a chef, I suppose a cloistered kitchen offers privacy to the family."

"And we have a chef. She's here five days a week. Not for breakfast, though."

I follow him through the house, then through a narrow hall that feels like it was built this century with windows along the sides, and into a breathtaking chef's kitchen with a domed ceiling, two spacious fireplaces, stainless steel refrigerators, stoves, and multiple islands.

"If I'd found it, I don't think I would've had the nerve to hunt for coffee," I comment, wide-eyed at the splendor. The kitchen at the Gagliano estate was similar in scale, but not nearly as grand.

"There's room for a full staff if needed. Here's the coffee."

Off to the side is a room with a U-shaped counter with a French press, a La Marzocco espresso machine, and a Balmuda drip coffee machine. White coffee mugs and espresso cups line the top shelf. A small refrigerator with a glass door holds what appears to be a mix of dairy options and sparkling waters.

He sets about fixing us both lattes and I watch, somewhat mesmerized at his dexterity and ease with the equipment.

"You're quite good at this."

"About the only thing I know how to do. I wouldn't venture into the rest of the kitchen if you paid me. I'm quite adept at takeaway."

"But you don't live near anything."

"Hence, a chef. I'm also quite skilled at heating what she leaves."

"Right, then. A man of many talents."

When he passes me my latte, I whiff a strong flowery scent. Perfume.

He stayed away for the night. Perhaps he has a lover tucked away in London.

I could ask, but it's not my business.

He leans against the counter, nostrils flaring as he inhales from the white mug, and then sips. His slim-fitting dark jeans, subdued black tee, and chocolate suede jacket could fit in most scenarios. The everyday casual look works for him. Last I saw him, he'd been in a tailored suit, or what the style icons would call a formal casual.

His hair is slightly ruffled from the helicopter, the skin on his angular jaw up to his goatee smooth and moisturized. He seems showered, so is the perfume from a woman he said goodbye to this morning?

He catches my examination, and I drop my gaze and sip the latte. It's slightly sweeter than I like, but it's good. The warmth coats my throat.

"You have beautiful eyes." I blink. "Lovely shade of green."

"The color can change. In some light, I've been told they're blue."

"I've only seen them green." He turns and messes with the machine again. "Would you like another?"

"You've already finished yours?"

"I've got meetings to get to." He glances over his shoulder. "Would you like another?"

"Can I get it in a to-go cup?"

He lifts a porcelain mug off the shelf. I suppose not, then.

"I've been thinking about this," I say, feeling more courageous with his back to me. "Is there a way to do this where they don't know I'm the source?"

"Depends. What information do you have access to?"

"Shall we close a door?"

"You're a quick study. But I'm not in here enough for anyone to bother bugging the place."

"Right. Well, off the top of my head, I have ledgers showing discrepancies between reported income and actual cash flow, ship manifests, client lists, bank statements, property ownership documents, employee records, shipping routes and schedules, tax returns, and a record of digital currency transactions."

"Gorgeous and brilliant," he says.

A shiver of silly pride lights my skin. This is not a man I should worry about impressing.

"But it's not trapped in that brilliant brain. Where do you have it all? Italy?"

"I've been uploading copies to a private cloud location for years."

I always knew I'd do something like this. Over the years, I've had more than one intelligence officer approach me. It made me wary. If they see me as a potential leak, then so might Massimo or others within the famiglia. Other than the first MI6 contact, I haven't trusted anyone. I've turned them away, afraid it was a trap, a test of my loyalty to the family.

The beauty of Nikolai Ivanov is his background precedes him, ergo he's not fabricated. He's not attempting to trap me. Whether I can trust him remains to be seen.

"Your uncle gave you access—" He's skeptical, understandably.

"Alessio Gagliano carries a low opinion of women. My dear uncle believes I'm skilled with numbers and trusts me more than others he doesn't know well. Most of what he has me doing is data entry."

"Fascinating."

His slow spin on that word…does he not believe me?

"My uncle has known me since I was a child. He—and the entire family—view women as assets to be leveraged. I'm no use to him as a bargaining chip now that I've been married, so he uses me for work he finds boring or cumbersome. Reports and such."

"You"—his lips turn up on the ends and his eyes brighten— "are what we call a jackpot." He leans forward, and I lean back into the counter, knocking into something. The clattering sound echoes through the vast space.

"I was going to kiss your cheek," he says.

Uncomfortable heat climbs my neck. I right the stainless-steel carafe I knocked over.

"You're jumpy," he observes. "I hope you know I would never hurt you."

"I'm an asset. Of course, you won't hurt me." Will he after I hand over the information? That's a question I need answered.

"I don't hurt women."

He steps closer once again, so close the scent of flowery perfume invades my nostrils.

"Of course, I'm not averse to mixing business with pleasure—"

"I am," I interrupt.

He's silent, and I force myself to swallow, then step into the open kitchen to escape the tight alcove and the aroma of a perfumery.

He stays put, leaning against the counter, watching me like I'm exotic prey.

"The stories are true," he says thoughtfully. "Your husband abused you."

I look to the ground, to my cup, anywhere. This man is not someone I wish to share the sordid tale. Not that there's any need to, as my story precedes me. Everywhere, it seems.

"I would never raise a hand to a woman," he goes on. "You have my word. And, unlike your uncle, I value the feminine gender."

"Good to know. Is my second latte done? You have a meeting to get to, right?"

"I hate you endured abuse. That's…" He huffs, and I tear my gaze from the floor only to meet his steady, intrusive focus. "Have you seen a therapist?"

I angle my head, taking him in with a different perspective. In all my years at home, no one asked about my mental health. "Years of therapy. Still jumpy. You should see me around a spider." I force a brightness I don't feel. "You said you have meetings?"

"I do." He offers me a ceramic cup and saucer, and as our fingers brush, I fall into his steady gaze. It's warm and kind and not at all what I need.

"You need to shower."

What the hell possessed me to say that? His brow crinkles.

"The perfume. It's rather strong," I explain. "Unless you're not meeting—"

He smiles, flashing brilliant white teeth, and it's so unexpected and disarming my thoughts fragment.

"Vestiges of where I spent the night." He sips his coffee, and when he lowers it, he licks his lower lip, looking amused.

Why am I watching him so closely? What is it about this man? Frustration churns within my ribs.

"You're quite right. I need a shower. After a certain point, you can't smell yourself. Am I right?" He walks away, taking the perfumery with him. He gestures to the alcove. "Make yourself at home. I'll come and find you when I'm able. I know I mentioned breakfast, but the morning got away from me. If you check the pantry, there should be pastries. Quiche in the refrigerator." He stops in the doorway. "Can't wait to see what you've got. Bloody brilliant."

His eyes sparkle with what? Relish?

Then he's gone.

CHAPTER 7

NICK

A news alert catches my eye. Subsea cables that cross the Atlantic and carry public and private network data for wireless internet are being damaged, sometimes cut straight through. Russian fishing boats have been observed fishing over the damaged areas.

My fucking arse, they've been fishing.

No doubt it's a long-term strategy. The Russians are figuring out how to hamper communications should a war break out.

I should call Dorian. See what he's observed via his satellite network.

Wonder if he's done with his meeting? We can discuss it over lunch.

My Sectra Tiger vibrates. I have ten of the mobiles lined up behind my desk on a shelf. The one vibrating is one I always check.

Halston Moore
It's time we restructure.

Me
I'm not following.

Halston
We're going to lose control if we don't
take a more strategic approach.

Me
Are you a prophet now?

Sure. I'm throwing the word around. It's been on my mind ever since I received the untraceable message from a sender who claimed the word as a name.

Halston
For Obsidian, I am the prophet. Our
members' attention is too fractured. We
need someone focused.

I won't argue with the old man there. Although, of the syndicate members I've spent time with, I'd dare say we all suffer from a level of ADHD and therefore flourish with multiple irons in the fire.

I reread his text. He's the only one of us who loves to use the word Obsidian. Wouldn't surprise me if he named the alliance all those years ago. I pinch the bridge of my nose. This is something else I need to discuss with Dorian. His father. At ninety-two, is he disengaged from the businesses? Is this a bored man who is grasping for relevance?

Me
What do you propose?

Halston
I serve as central command. Monitoring and enlisting services as needed. We meet monthly.

Me
Not feasible.

There's nothing more alarming than someone proposing regular meetings.

Halston
You don't have to attend. This is the right thing to do. I have more time and experience than all of you.

. . .

I roll my eyes and stretch back in my chair. The bloke's ancient and American. An ornery combination.

Halston
Until you replace Leo Sullivan, will you be acting as negotiator?

The reason I hired Leo in the first place is I value experts. I also have time constraints. In some parts of the world, nothing happens quickly.

Me
I lack the social stamina. I'll fill his role.

Halston
Do you maintain contact with your family?

Me
Why?

Halston Moore has a reason for every question.

Halston
Can you send me a list of your contacts?
Those you carry weight and influence
with.

> **Me**
> In writing?

Fuck no.

Halston
It will help with the structure.

> **Me**
> We agreed when issues arise to convene
> and determine who is best situated to
> influence.

Halston
Discuss with Dorian.

> **Me**
> Who is he meeting with this morning?

Halston
Did he not stay with you last night?

> **Me**
> He did.

Why are they being so fucking secretive about his meeting?

Halston
It appears Dorian won't be returning to
your house this afternoon. He's on his
way back to London. But it's your lucky
year. He'll be back soon.

He must have just tracked Dorian, so I believe him, but I'd thought I'd see him this afternoon. Dorian is Halston's only child after a long line of quick marriages. If I remember correctly, the old man was well past the half-century mark when Junior arrived. I was brought into the alliance years before Halston included his son. But I was brought in earlier than I should have by events beyond my control.

Me
Did you read about the subsea cables?

Halston
Sabotage? It's been going on for a while.
Took a while for the press to cover it.

Me
What do you make of it?

Halston

Nothing new. Insinuating Russia's behind
it because of a fishing boat ranks as
ludicrous. Reporters will write anything.
But if this bit is new to you, it
underscores the importance of a focused
command center.

My fingers curl inward. What a bloody wanker. Does it really
hurt me, though, if he steps up?

Halston

A source shared the European Union is
setting up an eagle eye, monitoring the
situation.

Me

But they'll still allow the fishing boats?

Halston

International waters. But if they anchor
along the lines, there will be a reaction,
according to my source.

Me

Imminent action?

Halston

If I expected a shock to the markets, I
would've notified everyone.

. . .

Right.

Me
Anything else I can do for you?

Halston
Dorian will be in touch. A package will
arrive. A device for you to use.

Me
I'm good.

Hell, if anything, I should be sending the old man a secure device. The custom versions we use aren't available to the public. As a rule, I don't use devices others source.

Halston
Use the device I send for our
communications.

That will be a negative. Tell him or ignore him?

Halston
Questions are being asked about the
wreck.

Me
??

Halston
All those who worked with Leo are
concerned. I am, too.

If Halston knew the truth, Mr. Self-anointed Prophet would go ballistic.

Me
There's no reason for concern. He died
because of his wife, nothing to do with a
deal.

Halston
Dorian's helping me smooth things over.
When he returns, answer his questions.
Let's put this behind us.

Me
When is he returning?

Why the fuck didn't he stop back by before heading to the airport?

I wait for a response, staring at the black screen for too long.

It appears Mr. Anonymous ratted out Leo to multiple parties. Damn. Did Halston get the same message? If yes, is this his way of handling the issue? Sending me a device to use and telling me he's taking charge?

I scan the line of Sectra Tigers. I scratched letters into the outer case to help me tell them apart, but I always double-check myself by reviewing the profile in the settings.

Against my better judgment, I shoot an encrypted message to Nomad:

> Questions are being asked about the
> wreck. I need to know who is asking.

There's a rap at the door, and before I get a word out, it opens.

Lina grins wide, like a showgirl presenting a trophy. "Look who showed up."

The slim, brown-skinned man stands behind my sister with a Cheshire grin and his hand on my sister's arse.

"Nooyi, what the hell?" I step around the desk. "What brings you to the country? Did you take a chopper? I didn't hear—"

"You've been locked away for hours. Elephants could stampede the gardens and you wouldn't hear squat."

"Elephants?" Lina's flirty comment is directed at Amir, but the scoundrel's a waste of effort.

"My helicopter is in your pasture. Close up shop. There's a party tonight you shall not want to miss."

"And they're going to let you in?"

He laughs the laugh of an arrogant prick. Amir Nooyi is one of my best mates from my boarding school days, and he's the king of Alliance shipping. Or perhaps heir is the choice descriptor. He's also an investor in a number of lucrative Indian enterprises.

Lina claps her palms together. "I'll get Scarlet. Oh, this will be fun."

Scarlet appears in the hall behind them with an expression that can only be described as deer-in-the-headlights.

"It's a Monday. I can't simply take off." I really can't. I've got to figure out who is sticking their nose up my arsehole.

"It'll be worth your time," Amir says. I recognize his mischievous grin. The fuck is as wily as ever.

"Have you got the paps on standby? Looking for some exposure?"

Lina visibly brightens because, of course, she does. She fancies herself a social media influencer, although fuck me if that's a business.

"Sod off. And you're still coming," Amir says.

Amir's parents want him to settle down in an arranged marriage, following their path, but he'll never succumb. Amir has too much fun playing the field and no reason to cave. His parents have already given him the keys to the empire.

"I'm not coming." I catch Scarlet's gaze, and a sophomoric urge to make a crude joke flourishes but never passes my lips. "Scarlet."

Amir half turns, seeing her for the first time, and judging by his eager expression, he's far too intrigued.

"Hello," he says, reaching for her hand like the gallant gentleman he is not.

"Scarlet, this here wanker is Amir Nooyi. He and I go way

back, and if you're a bright lass, which I believe you are, you'll stay clear."

"What kind of intro is that? Always got to be a prick. A tiny one to match your—"

"And Scarlet is a guest. She recently buried a loved one and is mourning. I doubt clubbing interests her at the moment."

Lina has the grace to appear empathetic. "A little bubbly might cheer you up?"

"No, thank you." Scarlet's green eyes catch mine. The hue isn't as bright as this morning in the kitchen. No, trapped in the hall, it's more of a shaded evergreen.

"Perhaps this weekend we can journey into the city?" I suggest to the room.

I need to spend some time this afternoon with Scarlet to acquire the documentation. If she possesses a fraction of what she says she does, my little Lupi Grigi project will be complete with a simple hand-off.

"I'll be in Turkey," Amir says. "You should come."

"Do you ever work?"

"I work hard, my friend. I also work smart. Observe and learn."

"Get the fuck out of here." I wave him off, knowing I'm not getting out of this without at least an alcoholic lunch.

"I'm going to go pack," Lina says. "Because I'm going." She spins, not giving me a chance to argue. "Chef is preparing lunch and will serve it in the billiard room."

"So, lunch, and then Scarlet and I shall see you off?"

Amir looks between Scarlet and me with a cockeyed grin. The prick practically salivates. "Scarlet, dear—"

"Arsehole. She's mourning. Let her be."

"She's not so distraught she can't speak."

Scarlet smiles, but I'd bet my favorite Macallan whiskey it's a submissive expression she acquired to survive in her demented family.

"It's a pleasure to meet you, and lunch would be lovely."

Graceful. Clever as they come. She doesn't need me to defend her against the likes of Amir. She's a strong one. A far better head on her shoulders than my sister possesses.

I follow behind them, making a mental note to take Amir aside for a serious chat. If he's going to take my sister clubbing, he's going to need to keep a close eye on her. For that matter, I need to get security engaged. And I also need an update from Ash about where Dorian went this morning.

CHAPTER 8

The fire roars in the stone fireplace, and I inch closer, letting the heat penetrate my clothes and mitigate the chill. For the thousandth time, I question my plan.

A caval donato non si guarda in bocca.

Don't look a gift horse in the mouth.

Trust him or not, Nikolai is a gift from above. When I agreed to be an information source for MI6 and INTCEN, the EU Intelligence and Situation Centre, a group comparable to the American CIA, I expected them to deliver retribution. But there were flaws in my expectations. First, they move slowly, and I learned too late they are more interested in information than in actually doing anything to crack down on organized crime. They had more interest in my uncle's meeting agenda than in how Titan Shipping conducted business.

Given how many are on the Lupi Grigi's payroll, I proceeded with caution. Ironically, Willow's death delivered the means to an end. A man who decidedly is not on their payroll and won't be bribed into giving up a source.

Yet there are limits to Nikolai's trustworthiness. Handsome, magnetic men are accustomed to the world bending to their will. Physical attributes are a veneer that gets them far in life. What lies beneath the veneer? Powerful men have gray morals. There's no way he got to where he is in life without stabbing some along the way.

Am I placing too much trust in a stranger?

Willow, did you trust him? You didn't, did you? But if he'd been a concern, you would've shared, right?

I'm in the man's home, yet it whispers none of his secrets. This room, the one they call the billiard room, is the first space I've been in that feels like Nikolai, or Nick, as he supposedly prefers to be called. Instead of portraits of ghosts, hunting scenes, or ancient maps, monochrome abstract art adorns the walls. The leather sofas and chairs feature modern shapes. The thick wool sable rugs are positioned for comfort, not design. There are no window treatments on the windows, but with the press of a button, shades fall from the ceiling, closing us in and blocking the draft.

A pool table resides in one corner, giving the room its name. A widescreen television hangs over the fireplace, high enough above the flames that the heat won't damage the screen, and a round high-top table with comfortable leather stools sits opposite the pool table. We ate lunch there, and I suspect Lina and Nick eat most meals in this room. This is such a formal manor, yet they aren't formal people.

After watching Lina and Amir board the helicopter that was

parked in the pasture while horses milled about, we returned to Nick's office, and I provided him with the promised information. Wise or not, he's got everything now. My life is literally in his hands.

The flames lick the wooden logs, and I inhale the pleasant, smoky aroma. I've stared into the flame so long that when I close my eyes, bursts of red and yellow color my eyelids.

"Are you cold?"

I flinch and turn, arms raised, defensive.

As if my thoughts summoned him, he's there, watching me. Why didn't I hear him approach?

My gaze roves over his relaxed denims and his zippered sweater with the sleeves pushed up his forearms, showing off a bespoke wristwatch and a thick silver bracelet atop sinewy forearms. His attire is relaxed, but his expression is unsettling: intense and purposeful.

If he tries anything, I'm ready. I've trained. I'm skilled. With an exhale, I calm myself. Expect the worst, prepare for the worst, and move forward.

"Did you… Is it done?" I ask.

"No."

"But… What are you waiting on?"

This last step in my plan scares me, and in my life, I've found that when something is scary, it's best to charge into it. Shadows grow into demons if left unchallenged.

"It pays to be cautious. I aim to ensure it doesn't track back to you."

I study Nick's deep-set, intelligent eyes and confident posture. Poised. Strategic. I am not this stranger's concern. "You don't want it to track to you."

"True."

At least the man doesn't deny the truth.

"Can I get you something to drink?" He moves to the bar cart that's against the wall. "The chef will deliver dinner shortly."

I decline with a shake of my head. "What were you doing up in your office?"

It's nearly eight. If he wasn't disseminating the information I gave him, was he squired away in his office avoiding me?

"Tracking Lina."

He pours himself a golden drink in a high-ball glass and joins me on the sofa.

"Tracking her?" *Is he that controlling?*

"I have a security detail meeting up with Lina. It's not her cup of tea."

"Why does she require security?"

"Well, to most of London, she's a well-to-do heiress. If it wasn't for her blasted attempt at being an influencer, she could travel around anonymously. But, in her quest for followers, she highlighted her wealth."

"You worry someone will target her? For ransom?"

"Better safe than sorry, no?"

"She doesn't see it that way." It's an observation that I say more to myself than to him. I assumed the worst about him, but his worry sounds logical.

Back home, my uncle maintains security around the estate. There have been times when relations between other families soured and the security detail increased, but there's a minimum level he maintains, as the world knows him to be a shipping magnate. He shared the same concerns about ransom threats.

"Are you cold? I can turn up the heat."

Why does he keep asking me that?

"The fire is plenty warm."

An older man dressed for barn duty, with knee-high scuffed boots and a flannel shirt, stoked the fire earlier.

"Is that your warmest outfit?"

I glance down at my linen dress. "In Italy, our weather is quite different."

He stands rather abruptly, moves across the room, picks up a device, and taps into it.

When he returns, he carries over a throw and lays it over the back of the sofa. "Are you sure I can't get you something to drink?"

"Gin and tonic?"

"Coming right up."

The clink of ice combines with the crackling fire.

Our fingers touch when he delivers the cocktail. The point of contact stings, drawing my attention to the sensitive skin. Yellow and red spots light my vision because, once again, I've stared too long into the flames. He hovers near, so close I inhale cedar and clove, a scent I assume is his cologne. It's the same as what I'd smelled on the barn jacket. Quite different from the cloying perfume he wore earlier.

"Your hair is ravishing in the firelight."

"Excuse me?"

"It's lovely. You're lovely."

I shake my glass, knocking the ice about.

"Your skin. Smooth and unblemished. It nearly glows."

"What are you on about?" He's full of it. But why?

"I can't be the first to tell you."

"You're lying. I have scars." Annoyed, I lift the glass to my lips and drink. I'm not looking for sympathy, but I won't endure lies.

His fingers lift a strand of hair from my shoulder. My muscles tense, and a prickly sensation trails from the point of contact down my spine.

He twirls the strands between his fingers, and tingling sensations leap from my spine to my scalp.

I force myself to swallow. To breathe. A log crackles and falls, and the flames leap.

His index finger strokes my cheek. I freeze.

I'm caught between pleasure and terror.

Breathe.

Dr. Rosenthal's voice, the American therapist I secretly met with for years, comes to me.

You're stronger than you know. Believe in your strength.

Cold air envelops my side. I blink and am met with red and yellow bursts of light.

The sofa leather squeaks beneath him as he sits.

"You don't like me near you."

"I don't like any man near me."

"Tell me about it." He lifts the throw, gesturing for me to move closer. "I won't touch you. Tell me what he did."

Swallow. Inhale.

"I've been told talking helps."

Dr. Rosenthal said the same.

"You can talk to me."

"Nikolai, you're a stranger."

"Nick. Call me Nick. And am I a stranger? You're entrusting me with your life. And I'm trusting you with mine. Surely that means something."

"How is your life dependent on me?"

"The secrets I've shared with you could get me killed."

"What secrets?"

"I'm unleashing the authorities on an Italian mafia family."

"As a syndicate member, don't you have that right?"

The right side of his lip twitches, and his fingers drum the back of the sofa.

"I'm not sure what you've been told about the syndicate, but it's not a good idea to break rules you've agreed to follow."

"And they would kill you if I let on you're involved? Someone would come after Nikolai Ivanov?"

He answers with a steely gaze. I can't deny strength infuses my limbs with this perspective. It hadn't occurred to me before, probably because I assumed, as a syndicate member, he was untouchable.

With the throw pulled over my legs, the glass in my hand, and enough distance, his cologne doesn't invade my senses, and my heart rate steadies.

"Nick," he breathes.

"Excuse me?"

"We're friends. Call me Nick." He crosses an ankle over his knee. He's not wearing shoes, and my attention falls to his thick wool socks. The informality further calms me.

"Tell me something about you, Nick."

"What do you want to know?"

"I don't know. There's not much of you in this house. No personality."

"I'm not a woman." He lifts his shoulders like that's explanation enough.

"What does that mean?"

"I'm not into sentimental shite."

"You mean, like photographs?"

"That and I bought the place furnished. Had a designer redo

a couple of rooms. I have no plans to waste my time or money on carpets and drapes."

His gaze falls to my lap.

"What about Lina? She doesn't like to decorate?"

"She doesn't plan to stay long."

"She mentioned country life's not for her."

"If she wants me to continue paying her bills, it will be." He exhales. "The crowd she gravitates to in London is…questionable."

"So you're like a parent to her?"

"No."

I pointedly narrow my eyes at him, calling bullshit.

"She's my younger sister. Twelve years younger. And…our parents…"

A log breaks in the fire, and the crackling fills the room. It's peaceful in here. He leans forward and picks up a handheld remote device. With a touch of a button, the shades fall.

I'm about to prompt him, but he continues on with his explanation.

"Our parents died in a car bomb when I was fourteen."

Oh. Wow.

"And she was two?"

He nods and knocks back his drink.

"I'm so sorry." As I say it, I feel the sympathy, and it's an unusual sensation. It's one I would prefer not to experience. When Willow found herself in her predicament, it was like I was watching frames in a movie flick, but I did my best to remove my heart from her drama. I didn't wish for her to live my experience, yet I was powerless to stop her father. And here I am, hurting for Nick and Lina, for a past I am powerless to change.

"Long time ago."

"Who did it?" Bombs are no accident.

"Putin. My father displeased him."

"Is that when you moved to England?"

"We'd already moved when it happened. I was born here. But I suppose there were expectations."

"You were too young to know the details." I'm not sure why, but I sense that from him, in his posture and choice of words.

"I was off at boarding school. Around that time, several of those within Putin's circle were eliminated. My grandfather was still alive and ensured my inheritance remained with me."

"Not Lina?"

He gives a wry smile. "She's a girl."

"My god, she must hate you."

"If she gets her head on straight, I'll fix it. But handing her a sum of money right now would be akin to giving her rope and a hook." He gets up and pours himself another drink. He gestures to me, holding a bottle, and I decline with a shake of my head. "I've shared," he says as he returns to his spot with a fresh drink. "Your turn."

He's correct. "There's not much to tell." I twirl the liquid in the glass. It's not a bad thing to share what happened to me. I'm not embarrassed. There's no shame in being a victim. These are all things my therapist told me. The therapist I sought because I couldn't sleep. "What do you know about the Lupi Grigi? I mean, you obviously know their business, but what do you know of our culture?"

"Conservative customs."

In the firelight, his trimmed auburn beard appears soft and warm, and I have the oddest desire to scratch my nails through it. He leans into the sofa cushion, creating more distance between us and giving me air.

"My uncle arranged a marriage for me. I didn't have a choice or any input. Women in our world often don't." I look to the mesmerizing flames. He has questions and answering them may be therapeutic for me. But there's no need to witness his reaction. "It was a business transaction. Vincent owned a chain of laundromats throughout Eastern Europe."

"Money laundering?"

"Mostly. Vincent differed from the other men. There was a reason he wasn't yet married. He was a little off, and everyone knew it. He tortured the cats in town." A vision of the fountain in the square assaults me. Blood in the water from a stray cat he'd sliced and discarded. "At first, I tried to avoid him. But I couldn't because somehow I became his stray. He'd hunt me, taunt me. Hit me until I balled into the floor and played dead." I straighten my spine and lift my chin. "I secretly sought SERES training. For self-defense," I add as explanation.

"I'm familiar," he says.

"And therapy. I researched poisons under the guise of learning how to treat wounds so I could heal him if he came home wounded. No one else would help me, so I had to help myself." I sip my drink. He must think I'm a monster. Everyone thinks so. "I became pregnant. I hadn't decided if I was keeping it. I didn't want to raise a child to be beaten by him and treated like an animal. But he took the choice away. He beat me so badly that I lost the child, had an emergency hysterectomy, broken ribs, broken jaw." I point to the white line descending from my lip, the scar everyone sees. Scars crisscross my abdomen and back. The worst of my scars are invisible.

"Two days after returning from the hospital, he came at

me again, furious I'd reported him. He had no reason to be angry. They did nothing to him. They didn't believe me, or if they did, they were too scared to admit it. But I expected the worst. I prepared. And when he came at me, I killed him. Shot him first, then I took a knife and saved myself."

"You're the strongest woman I've ever met."

My strength is irrelevant. I shift my gaze from the flames and breathe deeply, forcing down the turmoil building inside. I can't dwell on the past. There's nothing to be gained by unearthing dormant emotions. If Nick pities me, it will twist my insides.

"And that's why you're so willing to help me."

He's got it wrong. "I'm not helping you." Needing him to understand, I look him straight in the eyes. "I'm helping me. This has always been my plan. Your offer provided me with a method of execution. I don't care if I die bringing them all down. My uncle knew what he married me to. So did my mother. If I can do anything good in this world, it will be to stop the cycle."

"Willow knew everything that happened to you? Is that why she pushed Leo to marry her?"

"I told her after it was all over. She's younger than me, but we grew closer when I came to live with her family." I blink against the burn behind my eyes as I'm reminded that she's gone. "I'm happy she escaped my fate. Leandro might not have been as depraved as Vincent, but he wasn't a good man. Death is a better fate."

"They'll pay." He sips his bourbon, and his eyes narrow.

What is he thinking? What is he seeing?

One second passes. Two seconds. And then his steely, determined eyes meet mine. There's no pity. Thank god. I so hate pity.

"When the dominoes fall, all hell will break loose. You'll need to stay here for a while."

"They can't hurt me. Not anymore." I don't fear death.

"Is there anyone back in Italy you need to be concerned about? That we should protect? Orlando?"

"The Orlando you met is my friend. But this weekend..."

"It's his commitment ceremony. And when he kills, he'll change. That's what you mean?"

"The metamorphosis to monster." The flickering fire reminds me of my question. "Are you one?"

"A monster?" His smirk suggests he finds the label darkly amusing. "By your definition, yes. But I'll be the shadow that keeps you safe, angel, while you light up the sky."

CHAPTER 9

"Are you nervous?"

The inquisitive, tenacious beauty at my side assesses the vintage Land Rover winding its way up the drive. Those jade eyes might be assessing me, too.

"Me? Nervous? No, green eyes, I'm not."

I don't miss the look of annoyance that flashes. She's not too keen on the green eyes moniker. I'll come up with something.

Golden highlights frame her porcelain skin. She speaks of scars, but the longer I drink her in, the more transparent her scars become. The freckles along her cheeks and nose soften her hard edges.

Today, she's opted for a button-down that's unbuttoned tantalizingly low and tucked into a body-hugging skirt. She's not aiming to be sexy but fuck me if she isn't. Sadly, I shall be fucking myself tonight in the shower, because she certainly has no desire to do so. Quite unfortunate, that reality.

She's got it all. Intelligence, resilience, and fortitude wrapped in a delectable package. It's best I stick to women I'm only physically attracted to and sidestep a complex woman. Too great a chance I'll cock things up. Besides, I've watched many a mate fall for someone who's more than just a pretty face, and it ends in divorce or a miserable marriage.

Still, the more I learn about Scarlet, she becomes less of a resource and more of someone I wish to protect. She's tough, but those communicative eyes of hers unmask the emotions she restrains. When she shared with me what she'd been through with that bastard of a husband, she stayed calm while fury roiled my veins. Her eyes glimmered with unshed tears, and watching her fight to maintain that shield gutted me. It's a good job she ended the wanker because otherwise, I'd itch to accomplish the task. But she doesn't need a man for protection. She's strong. She dropkicks bastards for sport.

"You trust these men?" She's been standing to my side, quietly watching, but waits until the automobile nears the fountain to ask.

"I do. When they're not investigating me, I do." I grin, letting her know I'm half-serious.

She narrows her eyes, judging me, no doubt.

"You must trust them if you let them come to your home. And you're not armed."

"Home is as safe as anywhere. It's the reason I bought so much land. And I had them park in the village, change cars to one of mine, and sent them the long way."

"I thought you said you trust them?"

"I trust them. They're white-hat blokes. The precaution is

for the less savory parties that might not take kindly to my meeting with Interpol officers."

"Why take the risk?"

"It's not much of a risk. If anyone asks, they show their cards about monitoring me when they shouldn't. And it's easy enough to explain away."

Inquisitive eyes ask for more.

"The smart man plays all sides," I explain. It's an axiom for the modern age. The reason corporations and the well-heeled donate to both political parties in all modern countries.

Her arm crosses over her midriff, below her breasts, lifting the pair rather nicely.

"How do I know you're not playing me?"

"We have the same goal."

I force my gaze upward from her breasts to meet bright green eyes that say she's alert and ready to rumble.

Outside, the Land Rover has stopped and the doors are opening, so sadly, there's no time to play.

"We both want those bastards to pay. Ergo, we're on the same team, love."

She has questions. It's clear from the way she thoughtfully touches her chin. She studies everyone and everything. It's always the quiet ones you should never underestimate.

The two men rambling up the path are dressed for a day in the country, in boots and denims. They've left their jackets in the car. Doesn't appear as if they're carrying, not that I expected them to bring a gun to a friendly chat.

Ash, the head of my security, would've followed them if he suspected anything unruly.

"Shall we greet our guests?" I ask her.

She trails behind me with a deceptively timid posture. She's not fooling me. If threatened, the fiery ginger will turn feral. The meek display may have gotten her far back home, but I see right through the act.

Tristan Wagner, or Nomad or whatever concocted alias he uses, scans the grounds. With his auburn hair, trimmed beard, wire-rimmed sunglasses, and confident swagger, he could be cast as a television detective. His head tilts upward, and I'd wager he's scanning the roofline and perimeter for security.

He won't find any. I value my privacy. Security mans the gate, and there's an invisible red light around the perimeter that sends an alert when anything crosses it. It's not a perfect system, as wildlife crosses regularly. False alarms keep the on-site security hopping.

The older chap with a pouch is Nigel Wilkins. His official Interpol capacity is within the State and Local Police Liaison group, but he manages a group that specializes in gathering intelligence through discreet, clandestine initiatives. It's decidedly impressive he's here in person. Nigel must view me as high-value, as mingling with assets is well below his pay grade. Or perhaps it's the ginger by my side who has lured him out of his office tower.

"Thought you'd have a dog running up to greet us," Tristan says.

"We've got one dog. It's useless. Horses, goats, and god knows what else are back at the stable." I offer a hand. "Welcome."

As Nigel takes my hand, the gentleman's gaze roams beyond me over the hall. It's a rather rundown country house. I should probably do a bit more to it, but I bought it furnished and don't aim to be one of those nouveau riche with a need to trend chase.

As I take Tristan's hand, Nigel steps to Scarlet.

She's a resource, in his eyes, an asset. My muscles stiffen, and I can't break my line of sight on Nigel.

"Scarlet Gagliano," she says, voice feminine yet gravely serious.

"And how will you be introducing yourself today?" I ask Tristan. He's just released my hand and stands quite close. Nigel stands next to Scarlet.

"Tristan," he says to both me and Scarlet.

"Well then, Tristan and Nigel, let's get it done. Shall we convene in my study? If it was a warmer day, we could sit on the terrace—"

"It's nasty," Nigel says. "Quite dreary."

He won't hear an argument from me. It's both nippy and cloudy, one of those days that feels like rain, but there won't be any.

I lead them down the corridor to my study. The plan is for Scarlet to take them through the documentation. I printed a few pages, and some, because of the complexities of spreadsheets and applications, remain online. I had a tech employee mirror the information on a secure private portal and encouraged Scarlet to delete her files.

I might think of the Lupi Grigi as modern-day thugs, but the truth is the mafia and cartels are some of the most technically sophisticated organizations on the planet. That her uncle left it to his niece to perform data entry that could do him in speaks to his place in an older generation that underestimates women and doesn't accurately estimate his risks.

She positions herself at the location we prepared for her. I've set her up at a circular table close to the fireplace, away from the windows, and Nigel and Tristan position themselves at each side.

"I'm surprised you didn't bring an accounting expert with you," I say as I study my Interpol contact and his boss.

Tristan's group skirts laws by gathering intel while undercover. Nigel manages that group, among other things, since officially that little covert, lawbreaking group doesn't exist.

"Accounting's my background, actually," Nigel says, swapping his sunglasses for silver-rimmed spectacles. He smiles, exposing a gap between his two front teeth that instantly abuses any notion he might be a danger. "Quite love it. Don't get to dig in too often."

Accounting is how they catch criminals these days. They might gain intel from surveillance, but it's the accounting that lands the strategists behind bars.

I've waded through it all already and excuse myself under the guise of attending to business.

On my own, I wander back to the front of the house. A couple of crows fly over the front lawn and dip into the tree line. I flip on my mobile and check the video feed. All's quiet. Nothing notable.

Dorian has yet to follow up with dear old dad's missive. Ash confirmed he met with a broker who specializes in the Middle East. Given governments are among his biggest clients for his satellite services, the meeting appears legit.

I could reach out to him now. If he's back in the States, his day is probably just getting going. I could catch up on emails. But instead, I watch the video feed flashing shots of the property perimeter. There's a downed tree on one angle, and I've just shot off a message to groundskeeping when a door creaks.

Tristan rounds the corner.

"Roaming the house?" I ask.

"Searching for you." He scratches the back of his neck. "Nigel's the accountant. Not me."

"And I'm your asset." There's no way he doesn't pick up on my condescension. "Care for a drink?"

"It's not quite noon."

"And?"

"Certainly," he says, but he glances back over his shoulder at the closed door of the study. "My question for you is quite quick."

"Shoot."

"Leo filled us in on significant purchases. Are you planning to do the same?"

If it's in my interest to do so. We went over this.

He scratches at the back of his neck again.

"Have you got the nits?"

"No, sorry. There's a tag on the back of this jumper that's rubbing me wrong."

"Are you wearing a wire?"

"No." He shoves his hands into his front pockets. "I'd never betray the trust."

Hmm. Leo betrayed my trust. Some might say I betrayed Leo's trust. But I did what was best for him. And in this world, we're apt to cross lines.

"As you know, my negotiator died, and I have yet to fill the position."

"So, the deals aren't getting done?"

"They aren't being negotiated on behalf of my firm." The position has been open for under a month. The word firm is rather grand for the operation. We leveraged connections and cut deals. I took a cut on a high-margin business and distributed it to vested parties. The setup allowed the syndicate to have a place at the table and our connections to maintain a reliable source.

"Did you hear about X Shynik?"

"What about it?" As one of the top ten producers in the world, the semiconductor factory in South Korea possesses significant capabilities.

"It was robbed. Four a.m. Security on-site shot. No witnesses."

"Who did it?"

"We don't know."

"No video?"

"Disconnected before the event."

Savvy thieves. "What'd they take?"

"Chips." He shrugs. "The confidence level in the claims is low."

"X Shynik doesn't want what they were working on getting leaked." I get what he's saying. I'll log some calls, see what I can learn. Corporate espionage rarely sanctions killing the security staff, so Tristan's correct. This is interesting.

"And then there's North Korea."

"Trash bombs?" I'm jesting with Tristan, as we take North Korea seriously. Jiang Tu, a retail magnate from China, has several sources within North Korea that serve as levers of influence.

"We have a source that claims one of their silos was broken into. Our estimates are they stole enough nerve gas to kill everyone within a three-mile radius."

"You think the two incidents are related?"

"No evidence to that effect. But we're intrigued."

The Russians? Saudis? Iran? A government had to have

stolen the chemical weapons. Private entities don't aim to wipe out villages, nor do they have the skills to break into North Korea.

"You've heard nothing?" He's dubious. Thinks I'm full of shit.

But I'm straight-up honest, which is troubling. These are the events the syndicate monitors. I've heard nothing from Halston, and the twat campaigned to take the lead.

"I'll look into it." I stare Tristan down, straight in the eye. "To be clear, I don't condone the killing of innocents. You can always trust me to share that kind of intel. I don't know what you expect—"

"Leo told us we can trust you."

Trust is a sizeable word. I'm not looking to let rat bastards rule, but I play hard and fast. I give him a quick, confirming nod. He can trust me in most instances.

"Any information you uncover will be appreciated. It's unsettling to have a cache of chemical weapons go missing. Every ally is on high alert."

"The North Koreans must have an inkling…"

"My source says they don't. But of course, officially, North Korea denies the theft."

"Of course." There's no benefit to admitting a security breach. "If I learn anything, I'll share."

I look over his shoulder down the quiet corridor.

"So, tell me, who did he work for? Which intelligence group?"

I wasn't going to ask Tristan about Leo, as I didn't expect he'd share, given he's Interpol. But I'm coming up with blanks.

"CIA?" It fits. Those bastards will do anything for intel. The corner of his eye twitches. "That's it," I say.

So someone with a source inside the CIA discovered Leo's truth and outed him to me. It could be someone within the syndicate, but why not bring it to the group? Why only threaten me? Why use the Prophet moniker?

Tristan's silent, hands shoved in his trouser pockets.

"Why send me to you? Not to a CIA resource?" The business card Leo handed me led me to Tristan, to Interpol.

"It's not clean cut," Tristan says. "Multiple parties."

"But if I need help, I'm to go to you? Not the other parties?"

"Like you, we have resources. If you ever need something we can't provide…" His lower jaw cracks as he shifts it, thinking.

"Interpol didn't have a team on standby that day, did they?" I think about what was involved to pull off the faked death sham. The mobility. The expertise. "Not CIA. British intelligence?" He's unreadable. I recall a report I pulled on Tristan and a matter in Switzerland. He worked with a private group. "Black ops?" His eye twitches once more.

I can't recall the name of the group, but I'll look it up. I found Leo through Sullivan Arms. There's got to be a connection. An information broker, perhaps?

"And you've had no success in unveiling who blew his cover?"

Tristan's lips purse. His head shakes slightly. "You've not heard more?"

"No."

"We've pulled it off, then."

"Aren't you curious?" It's a loose end. The culprit had access to a private number.

"The matter is closed."

"Is it? Aren't you prodding me to fill the spot?"

He shrugs. Can't deny it.

If someone within the syndicate uncovered Leo's connection to the CIA or some other entity, then why not go to the group? Unless the goal is to step in. Replace me. Reap the benefits. The only member who has pushed me about a replacement is Halston.

"We appreciate what you did." Tristan's comment draws my attention. He's going on about Leo.

"Didn't do it for you." I miss the bloody bastard. He didn't work for Interpol, so who the fuck did he work for?

"Right, but…we owe you."

He's right. They do. As if to underscore his statement, the door opens and Scarlet, then Nigel, exits the study.

"Rain check on that drink?" I ask.

"Right. I've got to drive back."

"You have everything you need?" I ask Nigel. I have questions about Leo, but Interpol's a useful alliance. I trust the chaps to push the case against the Lupi Grigi forward.

"We do. Appreciate this," Nigel says. "Should move quickly."

"Excellent. Remember, they've got people at all levels within the Italian government. Throughout the EU."

"We're aware. Until we have warrants for arrests, only the highest security clearance shall know," Nigel says.

That doesn't mean much, but we shall see if Interpol can do its job. It's a preferable path. If they fail, I'll have Massimo assassinated.

Scarlet carries the cordial, mindless chatter to the front of the house. We stand side by side like the couple from the American Gothic painting, watching them leave. I half wish for a pitchfork to hold.

The vehicle grinds gravel as it rounds the fountain.

"What exactly is it that you do?" Scarlet asks, her high-pitched tone a blend of probing and judgmental.

"You're a curious one, aren't you?"

I don't bother suppressing my smile. She doesn't blink.

"I'm a businessman."

"How does this exchange with Interpol benefit your business?"

It's an astute question to ask any proprietor, although one best asked before she met with the Interpol blokes.

"Darling, it's a little late to ask those questions, don't you think?"

"Why?" She sounds affronted.

"Because you just signed your life over to me."

"I did not." Her shoulders are back, and those bewitching green irises darken.

"But you did," I say, quite aware I'm strengthening the storm brewing within the temptress. "You see, I'm the one who will keep you alive."

I expect a fight. I yearn for it. But those irises brighten, the storm clouds inexplicably blown away.

Her hands flutter at her sides until they settle down over her waist. "I appreciate it. Thank you."

She's rational. Too rational. What's she up to?

"It's my understanding I might be needed in court, and if so, I can avail myself of witness protection. If this happens as quickly as Nigel thinks, I might not need to prevail on your kindness for long."

Trusting one's life with the international community is borderline insanity. But I'll make my case later on.

"I'm having trouble determining which side you're on," she says.

"Are you now?"

"Yes."

"There are no sides, love. Only objectives."

"And what is yours?"

"Same as yours, love. A good life."

"That's a non-answer. You like those. But you also said you want to break apart the Lupi Grigi."

I did say that. I don't need to say it twice.

"And?"

"All right, then. I'm off to the stables."

I only get a glimpse of her backside before she's out of sight, headed through the house to the backdoor and the Wellies.

She may believe I'm evading the truth, but I told her a truth I rarely share. She and I are in agreement on both objective and tactical execution. The world gets complicated because few agree about the best tack forward to achieve a good life.

▭

The sun is lowering in the sky, and there's a chill in the room. I shoot off a message to the house manager to light the fires and a message to the chef to inquire about dinner, then head out in search of Scarlet.

I've spent the day reading reports and reaching out to industry leaders as needed between meetings. I've kept an eye on the news scroll at the bottom of the muted television, although nothing will happen today. In all likelihood, nothing will happen for weeks.

I lob a call to Jiang Tu. He answers, voice groggy.

"Did I call at an obscene time?"

"I'm in the air. What can I do for you?"

Jiang Tu was my first call after Interpol left earlier today.

"Checking in. Curious." Given the nerve gas was stolen from North Korea, it's unlikely Russia or China were the thieves. It'd be a costly heist. Who'd go to that expense? A Middle Eastern country? A terrorist group?

"If I had an update, I'd get it to you."

"Right."

"Received an alert about a car bomb in Rome. Was that you?"

"Haven't left the estate."

"I'll take that as a yes. You're not stopping until they're decimated, are you?"

"No." I'm not responsible for any car bomb, but it's just as well he believes I am. Garners more respect.

There's a pause. It could be Jiang processing, or it could be a technical delay.

"Noted," he says. "It is what it is." Is that resignation in his voice? Nah, flat is Jiang's go-to delivery.

"I land in China in a few hours. All communications should go through the portal."

"Aye, aye."

The call disconnects, and I clomp through the winter garden. Lina sits on a bench, a mobile in hand.

"When did you get home?" I ask.

"This afternoon. Amir sent me back in a car. He had important business."

She sounds...off.

"Did you have fun?"

She gives me her piss-off expression.

"What did you do?" Yes, I'm suspicious.

"That's not your business, is it?"

I pay all her bills, but that's an explosive argument. "Who shoved a stick up your arse?"

"Amir insisted I return home. Because of you. You treat me like a child. Like I don't matter. You don't want me near you, you just want me here. Why? What is it with you and control?"

My nerves go on high alert. I step closer, wrap my fingers around her wrist, and squeeze until she raises her head. Her pupils are blown. Bloody hell.

"Are you high?"

"I hate you," she grits, snatching her wrist from my grip and wrapping her arms around herself like a spoilt child. "You always assume the worst."

Fuck all. I pat my jacket for my mobile. Amir has some explaining to do.

In my periphery, movement catches my attention. It's Scarlet. She scratches Dog's ear, straightens, and slings a stick. Dog's tail wags back and forth, happy as I've ever seen it.

Lina follows my gaze. A good thing. She can't be that wasted if she's aware enough to observe someone approach.

"See something you want to fuck?"

Perhaps sobriety isn't such a good thing.

"Watch it, Lina."

"Why?"

"Show her respect."

"You fancy her."

She's attractive, I'll not deny it.

"Brother dearest has a crush," Lina says. She commences with giggling like a schoolgirl while stifling the noise with her hand over her mouth. She wobbles and loses her balance, catching herself on the bench. "Oh, dear," she says through giggles.

I don't know what she's on, but she's off.

"Lina," I growl. "She's doing me a favor. That's all."

"And it's all about you, right? What favor exactly?" She grins. "Did she—"

"Lina. One more word, and I slice and dice your cards."

"You and your money. It's always about money."

"Christ, Lina. She's my guest. Treat her well."

"Aye aye, big brother."

Scarlet approaches with slow, steady steps. Her gaze flits between Lina and me.

"I'm going to the kitchen. Want me to check on anything?"

"I'm starving," Lina says, popping up off the bench with far too much gusto. "I'll go with you."

I wait for Lina and Scarlet to traverse the garden path. When they're out of sight, I pluck my mobile and locate Amir Nooyi in my contact list. I want to know exactly what he did with Lina. If he gave her anything stronger than weed, I'm going the strangle the fucker.

CHAPTER 10

Quiet reigns in the house, and I hear my every movement. Each step on the floor, the creak of a chair, the brush of my fingers against the velvet drapes. The dreary weather looming through the panes is a far cry from the southern Italian sun, but a week into an English fall, I prefer the clouds mixed with the occasional pitter-patter of rain. Warmth fills the soulless rooms when the fireplaces come to life at night, and the scent of burning wood perfumes the air inside and out. I've also discovered a penchant for cuddling under throws while reading, something I didn't do back home as I was so often sitting at a desk in the office.

A week has passed since Lina and I went to London to go through Willow's belongings. Other than her clothes and art, there was nothing of hers to retrieve. She hadn't lived here long before her past—our family—brought her down. I don't understand all the details surrounding her death. But I understand enough to know our family's sick culture is to blame. Our capo's brother wanted her, and when Leo killed him while defending his wife, Massimo struck out for revenge. Maybe he only wanted to kill Leo. Perhaps in Massimo's mind, Willow is collateral damage. Or perhaps he wanted revenge for her choosing someone other than his brother, a man forty years older with violent tendencies.

A sickness permeates the famiglia. Sure, books and movies romanticize the mafia life, but when it comes down to it, it's a life where women are subservient and treated as a commodity. When I bring the family down, there will be no regrets. A world where women aren't allotted equality is a world in need of change.

I shipped Willow's art—the same art that I packed and shipped to her after her move to London—back to my aunt and uncle. To Orlando, I sent her sketchbooks, as they included her doodles and random quotes and thoughts she jotted down that he would appreciate. And for myself, I kept her clothes. It felt wasteful to throw them away. Her wardrobe sits in the trunks she shipped, stowed in the guest suite's closet. Keeping all of her clothes may not be prudent, but I'm not ready to go through each item. Purging her belongings makes her death feel that much more real. It may be years before I can bring myself to sort the trunks.

While her life ended far too early, the knowledge she discovered love before her death is comforting. Neither of us expected love to blossom from her arranged marriage. Admittedly, her parents didn't arrange the marriage. She begged Leo to help her avoid a forced marriage to a monster. At least,

Willow told me she was happy. She said he told her that he loved her.

Love or lust, it had been new, and her time here was so limited there wasn't anything noteworthy of hers in the condominium. Interestingly, Leo didn't have any photos either. Or perhaps he did, and someone else removed his personal effects before I arrived.

In the flat, I found an empty walk-in safe with the door ajar. Nick mentioned he'd been through Leo's office to remove any business-related documents. It's conceivable Nick possesses more emotion than he lets on and he gathered photographs and mementos. I snapped photos with my phone of their wedding and messaged the photos to Willow on her wedding day, but I assume she hadn't had time to print them and get them framed. Or perhaps she printed them and that's something else Nick grabbed.

Security accompanied us to the flat. Lina wanted to leave, and she wasn't allowed. I get his sister is far younger than him, but she's still in her mid-twenties. His controlling tendencies are reminiscent of my family's culture, a troubling trait given I'm trusting the man. But he hinted there are more serious issues with Lina, so I've remained quiet.

In London, I asked her a bit about it.

"He's a nutter," she'd said. "The way he goes on when I have a cocktail, you'd think I snorted coke."

"Why do you put up with it?" My question had been an honest one.

"He'll cut me off."

"Why not earn your own money?"

She'd smiled like I was the naïve one. "You've no idea how expensive London is, do you? Besides, I am working. I just need a bit more time for it to take off. Then I won't need his money. But until then…" She smiled and took my arm, treating me like a girlfriend. She read me wrong, because I'm not the linking-arms gal-pal type, but I played along. "Let's go shopping, shall we?"

I narrowed my eyes. I can only assume my face relayed judgment.

"I promise you. It's for the job. And it'll make Nick happy. He loves to buy gifts. Makes him feel important."

Those two have some serious sibling issues, but it's not for me to resolve. I've been keeping my distance, eating by myself often. I found a library stocked with historical fiction, and that's where I've been spending my days.

Nikolai leaves and returns without my knowledge. The chef might mention it, or sometimes Lina will. The occupants of this estate are like ships maneuvering through a harbor.

My phone vibrates, and the name *Catarina Gagliano* flashes on my screen. My attention doesn't stray from the device. No, I watch it as if a spider might crawl from beneath the black box. One, two, five seconds later, the screen goes dark. A minute later, the screen lights again. With a swipe of my index finger, the screen displays a message.

Catarina Gagliano
Did you receive my message? When is
your return flight?

Never. That's when.

I let out a sigh and tap out a response.

Me
I'm extending my stay. I don't have a
return flight yet.

Catarina Gagliano
You need to schedule your return flight.
Your uncle has requested your return.

I type, then delete, then type. Her name lights the screen, and I'm careful not to touch the device, lest I accidentally answer. It rings twice, then silence resumes.

While I'm typing a response, a message appears.

Catarina Gagliano
I knew it was a bad idea to let you stay. If
you don't want to end up like Willow,
you'll come home.

I turn the phone off. If I return home, I will end up like Willow. My mother is willingly blind to reality.

Outside, there's a slight drizzle and a mix of fog and cloud cover shrouds the tree line and beyond. I bundle up in Wellies, an overcoat with a hood, and a scarf. I leave in search of the barn dog that is aptly named Dog.

"Dog," I call.

Lina is home, and it's possible she's off riding and the dog followed her. The stalls are empty. A pungent scent of wood chips and manure wafts in the breeze. Outside the stable, there's another small building with a sliding door. The design matches the stable, and it looks like an extension. I haven't seen the door open before, so I wander closer, curious.

I pause in the doorway and blink to ensure I'm not hallucinating.

Nick is shirtless, clinging to a pull-up bar, and lifting himself. Light perspiration coats his skin, highlighting the corded muscles along his back. In the mirror on the wall, I visually trace the line of his pecs, the ridges lining his firm abdomen, and a dusting of dark hair trailing down to the pair of sweats that hang precariously low on his narrow hips.

With each rise over the bar, he gasps for air. His jaw flexes with determination, his lips in a set, firm line.

The second he catches my reflection in the mirror, his movement slows. He drops from the bar, slaps his palms against his thighs, and addresses me in the mirror.

"Did you come to work out?"

"No." I look like a fool. "I...ah, I was looking for Dog and didn't know what was out here."

He bends, picks up a white towel, and wipes his face, neck, and shoulders.

Back away, Scarlet.

My legs don't move. My throat and mouth are dry.

The hair along his brow is darker, damp with sweat. Light shimmers along the curve of his biceps. The shirts and coats he sports reveal the breadth of his shoulders, but they don't do justice to his taut, muscled abdomen.

"Scarlet?"

I bring my hand to my nose and pinch the bridge, snapping my brain back into functioning mode.

"Is everything all right?"

"Yes. Yes." *Tell him something. Anything.* "Yes, ah, my mother wants me to come home."

I shift my attention to the pasture.

My reaction to a shirtless man defies logic. I can't remember ever being attracted to a man, at least not since school. A flash of Vincent naked comes to mind, his hairy chest, bulbous belly, and thick, gnarly curls. There it is. That's the reaction I know. Revulsion. I can swallow again, but I don't dare look Nick's way.

"My family will probably become insistent. You might get a call."

"Won't be a problem."

"Has anything happened yet? Any progress?"

His footsteps warn me he's approaching, but I start when pressure befalls my shoulder.

"Wheels are turning."

I risk a glance, and he's donned a long-sleeve thermal.

"It's my understanding several businesses were notified this morning that an investigation has been opened into their accounting practices."

My mother's phone call makes sense then. "If they are asking questions about the books, my uncle will want me to return home to assist him."

"You look tense."

"I'm fine. I was quite aware that when I handed the evidence over, it would point to me. It might be best if you tell my uncle I'm not here. He'll send men here to retrieve me if I refuse to return."

"I'd like to see him do that."

Goose bumps rise on my skin. I'm dressed warmly enough, but the damp air cuts through the fabric.

"Come on. Let's ask Chef for a tea service. Get you under a blanket."

"I'm not cold." The rebuttal falls flat. He's close, and his scent clogs my senses. It's molten. Sweaty, yes, but also dangerous and irrationally enticing.

"You're tense. There's nothing to fear. You're safe here. Come on. Let's get you warm."

Inside the billiard room, the fire crackles. My skin heats beneath the heavy blanket.

The chef isn't on the property, so Nikolai pours bourbon and drops a square ice cube in the glass for me.

"More effective than tea," he says with a wink that flips my tummy. Inexplicable, as I haven't yet imbibed. "Sip. It's good. Like candy."

In a trance, I do as he suggests. The bourbon burns a trail down my throat, and my muscles loosen. Nikolai—Nick—is a handsome man, but he's not a good man. And I'm not in the market for a man at all. I married once and murdered the man. From here on out, I'll stick to vibrators and plants. Things that don't cause a stir when they meet their maker.

I set the drained glass down and lie back against the pillows. My eyelids burn as I close them, a reminder that I haven't been sleeping well. I'm not sure why. I prepared for this moment for years. Gathering evidence on the sly. Waiting for the moment to end their corrupt little kingdom. Willow's death freed me. I hesitated because of her, but now I've acted. If there's a god, the destruction will occur before Orlando sells his soul irrevocably.

"Better?"

"Yes, it's good." I observe him watching me, and a question that has repeatedly appeared and disappeared in my mind surfaces. "Do you have Willow's mobile?"

"No." His index finger taps against his glass. "If it was recovered, I imagine it's nonfunctioning."

Right, because the vehicle she was in sat meters below the surface of the river. Based on the location of her body when it was recovered, she and Leo escaped the vehicle, but the current had been too strong for them. I squeeze my eyes closed. I don't want to think about what her last moments would have been like, what she went through, or her fear.

Redirect.

"Where's Lina?"

"Off pouting somewhere, I'm sure."

He's freshly showered, something he must've done when he went off in search of the chef. Damp, his chestnut hair is darker, and when he nears, I inhale soap and sandalwood.

I'm noticing too much about this imperfect man. He treats his sister abysmally.

"Why?" *What did you do to her?*

"I said no when she wanted a yes."

"Why don't you let Lina live her life?" *What gives you the right to control her?*

"You think I'm holding her back, do you?" I open my mouth, but he speaks before I launch a word. "She's free to leave and do as she pleases. But as long as I'm paying her bills, she's not going out clubbing. Is that the life you like to lead?"

"Me?"

"Do you live to party?"

"No."

"Did you ever?"

"When you're forced into an abusive marriage at eighteen, you skip that stage."

"Noted. Well, you might not have picked up on all the signs then, but my sister loves getting high. I'm not granting her free use of the heli to party with her friends."

She said he blows everything out of proportion. She didn't get high with me. But…the man and the envelope. Huh.

"Is she an addict?"

"She'd say no. I'd say yes."

It makes more sense now. He's controlling, yes, but with reason. Whether his fears are rational or not, keeping her under lock and key strikes me as misguided. "Does it work? Forcing her to stay home?"

He narrows his eyes, and I'm struck by the stormy blue. When he's commanding and forthright, he's gorgeous.

Keep the conversation flowing. "Is she following your path?"

"Hardly."

"You never went through the partying phase?"

"When your parents die in a car bomb, leaving you with a toddler to raise and businesses to manage at the ripe age of fourteen, you tend to skip that phase."

"Right." I might've just met the first person who one-upped me on a shite life. "But you do party." He shakes his head in disagreement. "You stay the night in London. You've a bar cart in multiple rooms in your house."

"Scooch."

"Pardon?" He's standing beside the sofa, looking down at me, tall and divine like the Archangel Gabriel.

"Slide over." I do as he commands, but I do so while eyeing all the space on the other end of the sofa.

"You're tense. I'm going to work those shoulder muscles of yours."

"I don't need—"

"Come now." He sits behind me and tugs on my jumper. "Have you got something on underneath this?"

It's been years since anyone touched my skin. This is not necessary.

The jumper pulls as he lifts it from the back, not waiting for my answer. There's only a cotton tank beneath the itchy material, and the removal is welcome.

In the absence of the heavy outer layer, my skin chills. He lifts my hair off my neck and drapes it over one shoulder. The fine hairs on my arms rise in unison. The backs of his fingers skim slowly from my elbow to my shoulder, dragging warmth as they climb.

The heat from his touch soothes. I breathe out air I hadn't realized I'd been holding. My neck bends forward, pulling the muscles along the spine and the base of my scalp.

I am allowing him to touch me.

The thought comes out of nowhere. If it didn't feel so good, I'd push him away. But his touch feels divine. The pads of his fingers dig into sore muscles. He kneads, playing me pliant.

Be careful, my inner voice cautions.

A moan escapes in response to his thumb flattening against the corded shoulder muscle.

I went to therapy to face my fears. A determination born out of a stubborn refusal to let Vincent win, to let him take any more from me.

The past is behind me.

Strength and warmth cover my shoulder blades, and pressure kneads my spine, melting years of carefully constructed barriers.

A lone tear slips down my cheek, and I swipe it away quickly, surprised by my own vulnerability.

"I like your tat." His voice is low, miraculously both rough and syrupy.

I aim for a mild acquiescence, but what comes out is another mottled moan. I hadn't realized how tight and sore my muscles were. More than that, I hadn't realized how deeply I'd buried my need for human contact. His fingers spin magic, awakening sensations I thought I'd forgotten how to feel.

"Angel wings? What's the meaning?"

Tattoos don't have to have meaning. Mine cover scars, but I was thoughtful when I chose my body art. "The wings remind me this isn't the end game."

He digs into a tight knot, and my spine curves into the pain.

"When I close my eyes, with a little effort, I feel myself flying high above an ephemeral planet. I suppose that's another reason I chose wings. It's a reminder that I can close my eyes and travel anywhere."

Another tear escapes.

"Am I hurting you?"

He must think I'm such a freak. "No, it's just…"

"Does touch frighten you?"

"I'm not scared." My muscles tighten as my spine straightens. He removes his hands, and…that's not what I want. It's not what I need either. Dr. Atherton's kind, wrinkled face flits before my mind's eye. A brave soul. She met with me for years, knowing someone from the mafia might knock on her door.

I exhale, swallow, and admit, "It's the first time someone has touched me in years. There's just… It's my body's physical reaction. I am not afraid."

"Hmm." He shifts. "Lie down. Flat on your belly."

Is that wise?

I close my eyes to quell the torrent of tears threatening to swell. I haven't cried in years, and I'm not sad. It must be the bourbon.

It's not the bourbon. It's your body's reaction. It's not your fault. None of this is your fault.

Dr. Atherton's kind words reverberate deep within. Nick's palm warms my shoulder blade, and I settle into his suggestion and arrange myself flat on the sofa. He sits on the edge, and I close my eyes as he kneads my spine.

His fingers span my sides, and I inhale, expanding my rib cage and clearing my mind.

Warmth accompanies the pressure, and my core tightens as my muscles release. Needs and desires stir, and I force those sensations away, pushing everything out of my mind until my skull is a void.

His palm warms my buttock, over my clothes, but the intimate placement snaps me out of my meditative trance.

"I can do more for you."

My thigh muscles tense as my pulse quickens.

"No…" I breathe out, blinking my way back to the room. "You've done plenty. Thank you." I'm too weak and spent to lift my head, but add, "That felt amazing."

"Anytime, angel." I sense his presence hovering over me, and my eyelids open in time to see him descending. His lips brush my forehead for the briefest second, and he departs.

CHAPTER 11

NICK

The faint line along her luscious lips speaks of a split lip. The angel wings cover what looks to be a burn scar. I'd wager the Milky Way tattoo on her arm covers another brutal attack. There's a thin scar near her ear along her jaw I suppose is from surgery. The line is clean.

When I first met her, I'd seen an eye-catching lady who stood out among a sea of middling villagers. Fiery red strands and captivating green eyes set off by creamy, porcelain skin. My field of vision centered on her, and the periphery blurred.

Leo is one lucky bastard.

That was my first thought. My second was that I could see why he so-called rescued her by agreeing to marriage. But then she ushered us to the church, and I wondered what the fuck was wrong with Leo that he chose a bleached blonde when he could have pursued the fiery dame.

Leo said she killed her husband, and sick chap that I am, the tidbit intrigued. So I asked around. The bartender at my hotel in Rome had not only heard of her but shared gory details of a severed dick placed in her husband's mouth and his death by asphyxiation.

My bullshit detector rang. But here's the thing about tall tales, there's usually a kernel of truth from which they sprout.

When I learned she was the bookkeeper for her uncle's shipping company, I set aside my desire to fuck her and my curiosity about her torture techniques. She's a resource. Sex can be procured with ease. Access to the Lupi Grigi's Achilles' heel is rare.

And now, I don't know what the fuck is going on in my head —why I'm noticing every damn inch of her.

She's handed over everything useful, but she needs to remain alive. If I had my head about me, I'd send her far away like she asked. Greenland. Australia. Some place they'd never look and that I possess zero association.

Yet the thought of flying her anywhere, even a quick jaunt to London, twists my insides. When she went to London, I tripled security for her and Lina.

And then I go and touch her. Fuck, how I wanted to curve my hands around her ribs to her chest, to cup her breasts, to tweak her nipples.

The little moans that escaped as I worked on her back went straight to my cock and fed my brain a constant stream of pornographic ideas. Visions danced of her naked before me. Her long legs spread wide. Tasting her, sucking her, memorizing every tattoo, every curve and ridge, and god, sinking into her tight heat, slamming into her. Over her. Behind her. Quite the daydream.

Where I got the strength to walk away without trying something when I had her pliant, I'll never know. But I'm at the door, and it's time to exit.

My heart thunders in my chest, and there's a light coat of perspiration around my temples. I brush it away with my palm. It's too bloody hot, an inferno of temptation and the ultimate forbidden fruit.

I pull open the door and am met by a cool draft.

"Wait," a wily, feminine voice calls. I've one foot in the corridor and one too close to temptation. "Would you like for me to return the favor?"

Erotic visions blast through my filthy mind.

Her fiery strands glow crimson in the firelight. That scrap of cotton reveals the dew drop shape of her breasts and a hint of color…

Christ, her nipples. Shapely. Aroused.

"I've got to go." I don't bother closing the door behind me. It's way too bloody hot in that room.

On the way to my office, Lina crosses my path. "Chef said you made her come back."

"Do you need something?" What the fuck does Lina care about the chef?

"What's up with you?"

"Lina." I exhale frustration and suppress the desire to push my fist into a wall. There's no need to be angry. This is sexual frustration, and I fucking know how to handle it.

"Did someone take a piss in your cornflakes?" she taunts.

I don't bother with an answer. I've already worked out today, but I might go for a run.

I leave my sister in the corridor, round my desk, and skim a flurry of updates. Two cartel leaders captured in the United States. El Paso, Texas.

It's just what I need. I set about investigating. A glorious coincidence. Perfectly timed. When the authorities descend on Titan Shipping and those involved within the Lupi Grigi, it won't stink of me. Especially if Scarlet leaves to return home and mysteriously doesn't arrive.

CHAPTER 12

Touch.

It's important to our sense of wellbeing.

That's what my therapist said.

What I felt on the sofa? The tremors. No, *vibrations*. The low hum. An unwavering buzz. It had nothing to do with him. The sensations had everything to do with healing.

I was able to hug Willow. And I hugged Orlando on occasion. That counts, the therapist said.

My muscles feel weak, like I completed a draining rendition of one of my trainer's workouts. My therapist introduced me to Maxine for self-defense techniques. She's former military and SERES-trained, and she taught me more than self-defense. With her, I grew strong. In a ninety-minute routine, she propelled me through running, pull-ups, push-ups, and sit-ups, and then she'd send me into the ocean to swim until my muscles burned.

After a session with Maxine and a hot soaking bath, I didn't want to move. I'd lie in bed, bone-tired. It's no wonder the memory surfaces as I sink into the couch cushions. Only I didn't lift a finger.

When he touched me, warmth rained over my skin, penetrating to the bone. Tears spilled, bewildering me. I do not cry. I haven't in years.

I am not weak. I am strong.

After such an emotional release, my muscles feel like water. I'm not sure I could have steadied my hands enough to return the favor had he accepted my offer. But I offered, because otherwise…

Otherwise what? Would that be him doing me a favor?

I force my emotionally spent limbs off the sofa, leaving the warmth of the hearth, and meander through the halls, arms wrapped around my middle.

Flashes of heat strike with the velocity of a thunderbolt.

I'm flustered. That's all.

I should've listened to my therapist and sought massage therapy for post-therapeutic continuity.

In my room, I stand by the window, taking in the drab countryside cloaked in fog. If I let myself, I would unravel.

But I've come too far. I've done everything I said I would. Revenge has yet to be delivered, but I've done my part. The wheels of justice grind slowly, but I've pushed the cart, and eventually, it shall gather steam. All that is required now is patience. Living—no, thriving—will exact a deeper revenge. If I get wrapped up in emotion, if I succumb to the pain, they win.

I press my forehead against the cold windowpane and think

of Willow. My cousin, my best friend, the only good in a world of evil.

I miss you, Willow.

"I'm still here."

I shake my head at the response that comes through in her voice. *If only.*

There's still Orlando, but his evolution has begun. He's only fifteen, but Uncle Alessio raised him to be one of them. His kind, empathetic soul will be crushed, and a heartless, greedy spirit will rise. One day. But today is not that day.

I pick up my mobile and dial the one person I care about in that world.

He answers on the fifth ring. *"Ciao."*

"Orlando." A wave of warmth crashes within as I say his name.

Static-like sounds crackle through the connection. Heavier noises cross the line, possibly footfalls.

Click.

"Orlando? Are you there?"

"Now I am. I didn't want anyone to hear. Why haven't you agreed to come home?"

"What's wrong?"

"You should hear what they're saying. What's going on?"

"What's being said?"

"Massimo was here earlier."

"At the—"

"Papa wasn't at the office, so he came here. To the house. He's furious. He'll send someone to retrieve you if you don't return."

"Why?" A sense of dread coils in my stomach. Have they

launched an investigation? Does Massimo know what evidence they possess?

"I don't know. Papa's away on business, and Massimo won't talk to me."

That's because Massimo is an ass. Sure, he's capo, but he's a narcissistic jerk who won't deign to talk to those at the bottom of his organization. Our old capo wasn't like that at all. He knew everyone's name. I wouldn't say he was friends with everyone, but his strength was in building unity. Massimo derives strength from fear.

"You need to leave. Get a flight today."

"I'm not coming back there, Orlando."

"That was your plan all along, wasn't it? It had nothing to do with you being distraught over Willow." There's a pause. "Or my ceremony."

"Orlando, come on. You have to see that I don't belong in the *famiglia*."

After I killed Vincent, my friends disappeared, proving they weren't friends at all. The only ones who speak to me are those within the Gagliano estate or at the office.

"If you don't come home, Massimo may send me to get you."

"I'm not an object to be retrieved."

"Scarlet, you'll be lucky if it's me he sends."

The Lupi Grigi grows cruel men. I should know, I married one of them.

"Orlando, tell me something good. That's why I called."

"*Ma sei fuori di testa?* Your mother isn't saying much, but she's walking around like she's already attended your funeral."

"No, I have not lost my mind, and I assure you, her sorrow is not for me."

"Well, mine is. You're one of the good ones. Don't force Massimo to make an example of you."

"Why does he want me back?" Is this territorial, or has he gotten wind of the evidence?

"If I were to guess, I'd say he doesn't like you hanging out with the people responsible for his brother's death."

Ah, so Orlando knows nothing.

"Scarlet, please. Come home. If he sends men to get you, it won't go well."

"Why do you want to become one of them?" At least his sister had the guts to get out, although that didn't work out well for her either.

Silence descends. I check the mobile to see if he's ended the call. He hasn't, so I wait. There could be someone around him. Or maybe he simply doesn't have an answer.

"Why do you think there's a choice?" His voice is so low, I barely hear the question.

"Because there's always a choice."

"You should've played chess more."

"That would have required spending time with your father."

"Contrary to what you believe, Papa's not a bad man."

"That's where you're wrong. They're all evil."

"No. Everything my father does, he does with our community, with our country, in mind."

"Remind me, what's his net worth?"

"His shipping business is legitimate. You're the bookkeeper. You know that." He half snorts, and then there's silence. A different silence. He just figured it out.

"Scarlet. They will not let you leave. If you blackmail them, they'll kill you. You might as well put a gun to your head and pull the trigger."

Oh, I know.

CHAPTER 13

NICK

My business line rings. It's one that I use for all business calls, and it's the one that would be most likely to undergo surveillance.

I read the name. *Bloody hell.*

"Massimo," I answer. "To what do I owe the pleasure?"

"Your employee murdered my brother, yet you've been quiet."

"Please let me express my deepest condolences for your loss."

"Fuck you."

Goddamn Neanderthal. "Massimo, I had no involvement in your brother's death. Be rational. Your brother was certifiable. An unstable twat. Yes, my employee killed him, but in self-defense." I pause for effect. "But I am sincerely sorry for your loss. I hope you received the flowers I sent and the donation to the church." *Quiet my fucking ass.*

"Your contribution is most appreciated."

Doesn't sound like it.

A beat of silence passes. I wait. He called. "And Willow? You held one of ours."

What the fuck? "First, we didn't *hold* Willow. She married Leo, and that marriage, as I understand it, received your blessing."

"Yet I wasn't invited to the ceremony. Did you not find that odd?"

"Bloody hell, mate. What do you want? I had jack shit to do with that marriage. If I were to guess, she married Leo to avoid marrying your psychotic brother who was also what, forty or fifty years older? Look, you do you, but to me, that's cocked. If you're seeking to cast blame, look elsewhere, mate. I had fuck all to do with it."

"Yet you now have the cousin. Are you looking to marry her?"

"Why the hell would you think that?"

"You'll send her back?"

"Massimo. Let's be clear. I do not work for you. As for Gagliano's niece, she's not your property. She is a guest in my home. If you have an issue with Scarlet, call her. Not me."

"You're innocent in this, are you?"

"Innocent in what?" *Bloody fucking wanker.*

"Harboring her."

"She's not a refugee. She's a woman with free will."

"Send her home. She belongs with us. Send her home, or there will be retribution."

He did not just threaten me.

"Massimo, I don't permit threats." My fingers tap out a beat on the desk. These fuckwads don't get it.

"Send her home, and we'll be good."

"Will we now? Because you see, that also sounds like a threat. Do you really want the weight of the syndicate crashing down on you?"

"All for a girl?"

"All on principal. Do not threaten me. Ever."

I end the call. That won't be the end, but I bought a few days for him to stew.

If Massimo called me, does that mean Gagliano has called Scarlet? Has she told her uncle she's not returning? It's one thing to defy her mother, but has she defied her boss?

I leave the office in search of the strong-willed beauty. Obviously, Scarlet will remain under my protection from the thugs. It's a good job we're cutting those bastards off at the knees. Threatening me. The chap's not the brightest.

Of course, he's unaware I've traced his theft. I don't want it getting out. Makes me look weak. But when I visit him in prison, I'll be certain to let him know he didn't pull off the perfect heist. Bastard thought he could hack one of my shell companies and walk away unscathed. He's no idea I've traced it to him. But he will.

I find Scarlet in the stable, head bent, talking to a stable hand who came with the estate. He's in his twenties, fit, and loves horses more than money. The chap's name is Thomas or Ben or something ordinary. His head is bent, and her hand is on his shoulder.

I slow my steps, watching. Their voices are low and indistinguishable.

He brushes a hand over his forehead, and as he does so, he

picks up on me in his periphery and jerks straight. He nods and sods off to a stall, pitchfork in one hand, like an unruly boy caught red-handed in the ginger snaps.

A smile brightens Scarlet's face upon seeing me, and she joins me in the breezeway.

"Making friends?" I shouldn't ask, but I do. It's my fucking property.

"I overheard his phone conversation. Ben's going through a tough spot."

"How so?"

"He's overdrawn on credit. His wife's worried they may lose their flat."

"Is that right?"

"He might not want me telling you that."

"Mum's the word." That's a phrase I haven't used in eons. The guy told her he's married and broke. He's not hitting on her. I guess I read him wrong. And what about Scarlet? She's empathetic to someone in a tight spot. I suppose I should be, too. I'll have Ash look into his situation, see what we can do.

Scarlet looks at me expectantly. I did come out here to find her, but I don't want to talk where we might be overheard.

"Fancy a walk?"

She nods, and together we stroll toward the garden by the main house.

"Got a call earlier," I say, side-eying her. *Can I trust her?*

"I imagine a man like you receives many calls."

"From Massimo De Luca."

She comes to an abrupt stop and scans the grounds like she expects men to leap out of the shrubbery and tie her down.

"Are you sending me back?"

"I told you I won't." *I keep my word.* "You've gotten a call, too. Who?"

"Who called me?" she asks, wrapping her middle with her arms. She drops her head and resumes the forward motion. I barely nod in response. Scarlet understands the question, and this is her buying time. "My mother called a couple of days ago. I told you."

"She the only one?"

"I spoke to Orlando today, but I called him."

"What have you told them?"

"They both know I hate our life. They suspect I'm hoping to never return home."

Never, huh?

"Has the investigation started?"

"No."

Questions and worry fill her deep green eyes.

"If Massimo had any inkling of the impending storm, our conversation would've gone differently." Might not've been a conversation at all.

"Right," she says.

"He sees you as his property. But if he knew what you were about, I don't think he'd bother with a call."

"Orlando said someone would be sent to retrieve me."

"Is that right?"

I need to meet with Ash and review plans for further increasing security on the grounds.

There's a bench up ahead, and I gesture to it, asking her to sit for a bit. It's a cloudy day with a nip in the air, but there are blue patches between the clouds, and the faint scent of burning wood lingers from some cleanup work the grounds crew did earlier this morning.

Scarlet takes a seat on the bench, quiet. Intriguingly so.

"So what else did the young Gagliano say?"

"That he's committed to the family."

"Did he question your loyalty?"

She snorts. "He knows I'm not loyal. When the investigation begins, he'll be the first to pin me as the culprit."

"Have you asked him to leave? To join you?"

"Many times. He won't. He's his father's son."

"Can't fault a man for being loyal to his father."

Her nose scrunches as if she's tasted something rotten.

"You disagree?"

"You don't know these men."

"Don't I?"

Her eyes narrow with pointed evaluation. In this light, there's a blue tint.

"Are you dangerous?"

What a question. "I pose no risk to you."

"I meant, are you a bad man? Do you kill when it suits you?"

So that's her biggest issue with the family she was born into. Not the drugs. The tendency to murder. I lean forward, letting my forearms rest on my thighs, and risk a side glance when I answer. "I'm no different from you."

"Earlier, when I offered to return the favor, is that why you said no?"

Now it's my turn to snort. "You think I'm afraid of you?"

She arches an eyebrow.

"It's not fear I was feeling back there."

She dips her head.

"Did being touched…did it bring back memories?" That's how I interpreted her tears.

"Are you asking if your touch reminds me of being raped?"

"Well, if you're going to be straight up about it."

"There's no shame in being raped, and I won't be made to feel that there is. Ask me anything you want to know."

"All right." Didn't aim to get her riled. A tiny ant passes by, climbing a blade of grass, then dipping lower out of sight. "Did he rape you often?"

"No." She looks off to the horizon. "Vincent got off on scaring others. He wasn't a particularly sexual person. Our wedding night..." She closes her eyes and shakes her head as if she's having a conversation with herself. "It didn't take me long to realize that what he got off on was fear. If I didn't show fear, he didn't get aroused. There would be no rape. But then, depending on what he'd had to drink or god knows what else...that would turn into rage. I suspected there was someone else because he would go months without paying me any mind. And then, out of the blue, kabam. I expected he would kill me one day, so I acted."

"Good on you."

"Exactly."

"I have zero tolerance for a man hurting a woman. Abuse is a no-go for me. I'll never hurt you. You get that, right? While you're under my protection, no man shall hurt you."

"Human."

"Come again?"

"Another human. The women in my life haven't been particularly wonderful. Except Willow."

We sit there, silently on the bench, watching the occasional bird flying overhead.

"I miss Willow."

I raise an arm and catch her eye, sure to gain her approval

before I wrap my arm around her slender frame and pull her snugly against me.

"She's in a better place," I tell her, then place my lips against her crown. She shifts, and I place my lips against her temple, then her forehead. It's like I can't bloody stop.

"Have you ever lost someone you loved?"

"I have," I admit, not wanting to think about my family.

"Your parents. Is that why you're so protective of Lina?"

"Lina's not well. She seems right, I'll grant you. But I fear she's not. She needs protection."

"From herself?"

"Obviously. I've got security for anyone else."

"You can't protect someone from themselves. She's the only one who can do that." She peers up at me. "You get that, right?"

"Good way to play my words right back to me."

"You know, you're not what I expected."

I chuckle. "I'll take that as a compliment."

CHAPTER 14

SCARLET

I read the message. That's typical of my mother. She ignores that which displeases her and assumes that by insisting something happen, it will.

When she saw my bruises, broken bones, and stitches, she told me to be a good wife and refused to see the truth. She avoided me, as if putting me out of sight would eliminate the issue. And perhaps it did. Avoiding me eased her guilt. She could tell herself I was living a good life as the wife of the enforcer, and in her mind, it would be true.

I could respond and tell her I won't be on the flight, but that might expedite plans to retrieve me.

I set the phone down and look outside the window to judge the weather. It's overcast with a weighted melancholy I feel in my bones. My sundresses and skirts don't work in this climate. I peruse the assortment of clothes Lina ordered for me at her brother's request. He asked her to ensure I had a full wardrobe suitable for an English winter, and she delivered. Tags remain on many of the hanging and folded items. If I don't use them, they can return them. At least, that's my thought process. I locate a pair of denims and a thermal. It's not particularly fashionable, and most definitely casual, but I'll be warm, and there's no need to dress for business.

I head to Nick's office to locate him. He offered me his protection and his home, but it's better if I leave. Tristan Voignier mentioned Interpol could protect me, and it's better if I pursue that option rather than bring Massimo's retrievers to Nick's doorstep. Each attempted contact from my mother drives that point home.

An angry voice coming from the office halts my steps.

"You don't believe that for one minute."

A brief silence follows.

"Bullshit! I want to know everything. Every detail they discover at the crash site. You hear me? They're going to spin it. I want the truth."

I step to the doorway as Nikolai hurls a glass against the wall. Crystal shatters.

"Bad time?"

He startles, a reaction I didn't expect. I took him to be a man who is never taken by surprise.

"Come on in," he says, running his fingers through his hair and turning to the window.

"Did something happen?"

"I don't know." He's thoughtful, eyes narrowed, his mind somewhere far from his study.

I stand there, torn between taking his time or exiting and leaving him be.

"Don't just stand there. Enter. Sit. What do you need?"

"Was that about Willow's wreck?"

He blinks, and the hard lines around his eyes soften.

"No. A plane crash. What did you need?"

"Ah, I…" I swipe my palms on my front and step forward. "I plan to ask Interpol to place me under their protection."

That gets his attention.

"Why?" He looks like he needs a smoker's pipe to hold. Something to do with his hands. Maybe it's the stuffy room. "What makes you say that?"

"My mother booked a return flight. When I'm not on the plane—"

"Didn't you tell her you weren't coming home?"

"Yes. She doesn't care. I could fight her. Message her back and tell her I won't be on the plane. But Orlando said Massimo is threatening to send someone to retrieve me. If I fight her—"

"Right. Well, here's what we're going to do."

I take a seat and cross one leg over the other. My fingers twitch, wishing for a notepad.

"You'll stay here." His tone brooks no will for argument, but I open my mouth. "You're safest here."

He can be as firm as he wishes. "This isn't your fight. It's mine."

"Massimo won't send his thugs to my estate. If he does, retribution will be swift."

"You mean, you'll send men or—"

"We'll fuck his distribution chain."

"You're already—"

"But he doesn't know that. If he sends men, I'll shift demand to one of the other families that are still in favor, and he'll find his routes getting busted one after the other." His lips spread into a slow, conniving grin. "Massimo fucked with me once. He won't get a second chance. It's probably why they're using your mother."

"If that's true, then it's best to tell her I won't be on the plane, right? It will just be a quarrel between my mother and me."

"Are you close to her?"

"No."

When I was younger, we were close. I've lived lifetimes since those days.

"Who raised you?"

What's he on about? "That's an odd question."

"You're resilient. Confident. Those things don't come about when someone grows in the wild."

"Are you sure about that?"

With a grin, he sinks down into the chair across from me. "No. I'd imagine some kids would fare better in the wild than with their parents."

"Were you close to your parents?"

"I was." The grin disappears, and the room is noticeably draftier without it.

I'm sorry is on the tip of my tongue, but I bite it back. "And they raised you?"

"Yes." His gaze lifts from his lap. "They were exemplary parents. The best, truly."

I sense there's more, but he doesn't want to talk about his past.

"It's not fair of me to say my mother didn't raise me. She did. She was very present in my life as a child. But, as I grew older, and after my father's death, we grew apart. And I became an asset. Something to be bartered."

"In marriage, you mean?"

I lift my brows and nod at the bizarre notion. It shouldn't bother me so much, as it's what I grew up with, but it infuriates me that I'm not seen as human and worthy. Less so now, given I've got a broken hymen and can't bear children. What a screwed-up world.

"But now"—he lifts his shoulders—"how does that play out? You're not on the marriage market—is that what they call it?"

"Have you watched *Bridgerton*?" I stifle a laugh.

"Do I not look the type?"

A girlish giggle escapes, and I clamp it down.

"I live on an English estate. I love a show with spice."

My fingers cover my grin. I can't imagine this man watching a romance.

"Lina," he explains, grinning. "She's fond of the telly."

His shoulders lift, a nonchalant shrug, and as his shoulders fall, so does the mood in the room.

"In our world, we don't have a marriage market. It's not really given a name. But that's what it feels like. Only it's not so much about choice; it's rather strategic. And there's this idea that you always want to climb higher, the next level in the organizational hierarchy, so you want to be matched higher and higher." I hold my hand up, visualizing a tiered cake with only the tip top being delightfully rich.

"How's that work out for everyone?" He slouches in the chair and kicks one leg back over the other one on the ottoman.

"Horribly."

He chuckles and I grin. It's not a cheerful topic, but it's a relief to talk with someone who will not counter with all the benefits of such an archaic system.

"Your English. It's as good as Willow's. Mild accent. Is that part of the social climb?"

"Oddly enough, no. At least, not how you mean. Uncle Alessio requires everyone to speak English on his property. He considers Titan Shipping to be a family-run operation, and speaking English is important for interacting with clients around the world."

"If it was all about his business, I'd think Russian."

"They don't expect us to speak Russian. For a long time, Russians were competitors. It's relatively recent that they've become clients, and only for my uncle. Many clients don't speak Italian. English is an intermediary. Plus, given we're a coastal family, many of the Lupi Grigi own businesses that cater to tourists. English is an asset."

"Do you meet the clients?"

"Yes. Uncle Alessio likes to introduce family to clients when they visit. The meetings are always brief, but it's the image he sells."

"He's a smart man. It surprised me that they didn't pick him to be capo."

"Massimo has the time. Uncle Alessio doesn't. And Massimo also had the desire."

"Your uncle didn't want to reign?" He's rightfully skeptical.

"I'm not close to my uncle. I can't tell you exactly what he's thinking. But from what I've observed, I'd say he's been steadily working to separate himself from the Lupi Grigi."

"Which is why he was open to his daughter marrying outside the family?"

"Marrying her to Leandro would've been cruel." Leandro was almost as horrible as Vincent. Almost.

I glance up to find Nick's gaze on me, studying me like an art exhibit. I can't blame him for thinking I'm an odd one. Our world is bizarre. And I killed my husband. Can't quite forget that eccentricity.

"Alessio Gagliano arranged a cruel marriage for you."

"That he did." *Bastard.* "And that's why I'm working with the authorities to bring him down."

"But he didn't do that to his own daughter."

"Don't grant him grace. Willow made an alternative path for herself. Her father didn't lift a finger to make that happen. All my uncle did was agree, and the choice played into his desires. Hierarchy, remember? Syndicate over Massimo and his demented brother."

"Even after what happened. The accident. You think it's better she married Leo?"

"A marriage to Leandro would have been a death sentence, too."

Nick's a well-to-do man in his thirties or early forties who is handsome yet single. Admittedly, he lives in the modern world, far removed from our traditions. But there are still expectations. "What about you? How are you not married?"

This earns a prideful smirk. "First, my parents passed when I was far too young for them to push a union on me. Second, where I'm from, if one locks himself down, it's for love. At least, the perception of love."

"Do you not believe in it?"

"I'm not an ogre. I've seen *Bridgerton*."

I'm not really the smiling sort, but he's beginning to make me do it quite a lot.

"My parents loved each other." The tentative way he lifts his gaze, he reminds me of a young boy with a shy admission. "But marriage isn't in my future. I quite like the life I've laid out."

"Roaming a quiet country house with a sister who hates you half the time?"

He chuckles. "She's twelve years younger. We had nannies, but in many ways, I'm the only parent she's known. So, I suppose that attitude she shows me… It's not so different from your feelings toward your mother."

"It's different." It's absolutely different.

"How?"

"You would never marry her to a known psychopath. Vincent hunted feral cats and killed them as a child. He was cruel and disturbed even as a child."

"What did your mother get from the marriage?"

"My uncle acquired Vincent's father's shipping business on favorable terms. Vincent wasn't only an enforcer. His laundromat business performed well. And what does my mother get? To live at the Gagliano estate in perpetuity."

"Wouldn't she get that, anyway? She's your aunt's sister, right?"

"My father was my uncle's younger brother. Still, one would think Uncle Alessio would look out for her."

All she told me was that we owe Uncle Alessio and that we need to do what's best for him. The old proverbial *we*.

"What did your father look like?"

He's cautious, tentative even with the question. He's not the first to ask.

"I'm adopted. At least, I hope I'm adopted and not stolen."

"Pardon?"

"I've searched. I can't find a record of an adoption."

Now he understands.

"Have you asked your mother?"

"The first time I asked in a fit of fury. I knew I didn't look like her, but people would say things like the shape of our eyes were the same or they'd comment on the remarkable recessive genes and so I didn't really believe I'd been adopted. But, when I shouted it, her expression gave her away. But I've been unable to uncover a record of the adoption."

"Did your mother ever admit it?"

"Years later. She said it was a closed adoption, and she didn't tell me because she didn't want others to know. She wanted people to see me as a blood relative, although obviously my aunt and uncle know. It was more… I don't know what she and my father were thinking."

"What was your father like?"

"I don't remember him well. He was a Lupi Grigi. Died for them. That says it all."

"And then they married you off to a monster."

"A 'good' marriage," I say, the sarcasm thick on my tongue.

I'll never forgive my mother, my uncle, or any of the bastards. But there's no need to dwell on it. They raised a serpent, and I struck. Now, I've only to wait for the poison to take hold.

"Are you sure you want me to stay here?" That's what I came here to ask. "I have options."

"You're safest here. I don't trust Interpol."

"Why?"

"Too many countries source intel from them. If you want a secret distributed broadly, tell Interpol."

"I don't want to put you or Lina in danger."

"I'd like nothing more than for Massimo to give me a reason to go after him. He sends someone to my gate, and that's reason."

"You're already going after him."

"Covertly." He stretches his neck and scratches his throat. "Which is frustrating as fuck, given the process is achingly slow."

"You're not worried it won't happen, are you?"

"No. It was always going to take time. Your smoking gun isn't the garden-variety murder weapon and photo routine. It's accounting. It's numbers. It's the Achilles' heel of all criminal organizations. The reason billionaires back crypto and love untraceable currency flowing between countries in the EU. Anything to make catching them harder. But you handed over the keys to the deceit machine. The crimes cross borders and are bound to incriminate powerful players in the Lupi Grigi's pockets, so the case has to be ironclad. But it will be. You'll get your revenge."

I stiffen at the word, accurate as it is.

"What is your business? Not shipping. What do you do exactly?"

"I'm a hotelier and real estate investor. I'm a majority owner of three different tech enterprises. Security. My businesses are quite legal."

"Industries associated with organized crime."

"Association doesn't equal guilt."

"But you're also an arms dealer."

"I bring together suppliers with buyers. Nice margins. It's not a core business."

With dark, hooded eyes, he examines me. I want to believe him, but I'm not sure I can, which is why I keep asking questions.

"Why did the plane crash upset you?"

His eyelids flutter closed, and it's as if I've caused him pain. He rubs his face and sits forward. "Eighty on board." He lifts his eyebrow for emphasis. "Eighty."

"And you had—"

"No, no." He dismisses the notion with a wave. "But I suspect I know who did." He rubs the tip of this thumb, his gaze down at his hands. "You may think of me as a bad guy, and I'll grant that I bend laws. But a lot that I do...it's a balancing act. It's meant to keep things level."

His hand cups the back of his neck, and he flinches as he stretches his head to the right.

I push off. "Is it tight? Let me."

I come around behind him and tap his jacket. "Take this off."

He does as I ask.

"Why do you wear business attire at home?"

"It's a mindset." He sounds tired, like he's taken on too much.

I attempt to reach over the seat, but I'm too short to do so, so I have him shift and stand behind him from the side. I dig into rock-hard muscle.

"Christ," he grumbles.

"Too much?"

"No, no. Feels good."

"You're stressed." I've read about knots in muscles, and have them, too, but his shoulders feel like a steel rod. He bends his head forward, and I dig into the firm muscle along his neck. My fingers drift of their own accord into his thick hair at the base of his neck, eliciting a groan.

"Do you like that?"

"Fuck yes."

As I work his muscles, a thought comes to mind. Or rather, it's a vision that flies to me from the skies. It's of me kneeling before him, taking him into my mouth. I imagine he'd be shocked. Pleased, but shocked.

I've never willingly given a man oral sex. I doubt I'd be any good. Buried memories threaten to spring forward, and I force my gaze skyward.

I am strong. I beat him.

"Oh, my word. You have magic hands. Has anyone told you that?"

He brings me back into the moment, but this time when I smile, my eyes threaten to water.

"Can't say they have."

"It's a crime."

Is that why I'm here seeking revenge? Because I haven't been valued? No, I'm here because I've been underestimated. They thought they could treat me as a disposable asset, my only value tied to my virginity and ability to birth children. They have never been more wrong.

He catches my hand and presses his lips to my palm. The pressure radiates through my body, a sensuous pulse that awakens every nerve ending.

"Thank you."

Blithe, casual commentary circles in my head. Standard quips for civilized society.

Anytime. No problem. Of course.

But my throat is too tight and my mouth dry, so I back away and retreat to my room.

CHAPTER 15

The scroll on the silent television reads like an apocalypse.

Worldwide outages.

London Stock Exchange closed.

SIX Swiss Exchanges closed.

Frankfurt Stock Exchange closed.

Fears in the US triggering a sell-off.

Cyberterrorists expected. Authorities investigating.

On the screen, a reporter approaches a woman leaving a Starbucks. She smiles and says her office let out early.

My satellite phone rings and I answer immediately.

"What the hell's going on?" Paolo, an old Oxford chum, leads one of the biggest tech companies in the world. When he didn't take my call earlier, I knew we were in a shit storm. "Have you got a handle on it?"

"Aye." There's a flurry of noise in the background. "Damage being assessed."

"What happened?" There's a click, and the background noise mutes.

"Officially? It'll be blamed on a security network update or a solar flare."

"Who did it?"

"If I didn't know better, I'd say someone within the syndicate."

"What makes you say that?" Unease hits, and I push off my chair to look out the window.

The theory doesn't fit. Anyone who joined the syndicate did so to avoid markets crashing. High-handed morals and dreams spout around the table, but it all comes down to a concerted effort to avoid a market meltdown. Our mandate is to preserve global market stability despite prevailing political parties or factions.

"It was a one-two hit," Paolo says with chatter in the background. "Transatlantic wires cut at the same time three satellites were taken out by what may have been a conventional munition in the atmosphere. And cyberterrorists attacked."

He's lost me. "An attack on western Europe. That sounds like the Russians or Chinese, but China's a stretch."

"Based on appearances, I'd agree with you." A door closes and quiet replaces chatter. "But the tactics follow a risk assessment the syndicate created two years ago."

"Didn't you implement protections?"

"Aye. And they worked around them. It's early days. We're still figuring it out. But my gut says the coordinated attack was a pilot program. Testing systems before a full-blown attack. Might not have hit their targets."

"You think they wanted to hit the US?"

"If they're following the risk assessment, the US is next. Ah, there. London's back up."

"You'll let me know if I can do anything?"

"You still own a collection of hackers, right?"

"I own three technology companies, yes."

"We may need them. Stay put, mate. It's likely this is round one."

"You really think so?"

"It's my best guess. I've got to jump."

The call ends, and I set the device down. Movement catches my eye. Scarlet stands in the doorway.

She's in a luminous off-white dress that covers her from wrists to ankle and gives her an ethereal quality, casting light along a shadowy corridor. It's those green eyes that draw my attention, giving life to a knowing and inquisitive expression. *So fucking beautiful.*

"How long have you been standing there?"

"A bit. Who were you talking to?"

"An old Oxford mate."

"Part of the syndicate?"

"He's a part of our network. His business is technology." I glance at the telly and consider shutting it off—turn my back on it for a needed break.

"Your family must be expecting you to arrive any moment now. Are you nervous?"

I haven't seen her since yesterday when she wordlessly departed. The flight her family booked for her lands shortly, assuming it left before the outages.

She's hovering in the doorway. The blackout is enough to unsettle anyone, but she's got more on her mind. Ash and I met yesterday evening and increased the perimeter security and refreshed the bunker.

The way she's looking at me, so still and observant, unsettles me more than the news.

"What?" I ask.

"All flights are grounded."

Ah, of course, they are.

"My phone doesn't have a signal. How does yours?" She pointedly looks at the array of mobile devices spread across the credenza.

"Satellite phone."

"Ah. You've got one of the fancy ones that will work anywhere?"

"That's what I've been told." I cross my arms and sit on the edge of my desk.

"Are you done working for the day?"

Is that why you're in my doorway in a dove-white gown?

I answer with, "There's not much I can do at the moment. Everything's down."

"And you aren't part of the team working to get everything back up?"

"No."

"What did you say you do?"

Why does she keep asking? "I'm an entrepreneur."

"The tech companies?"

"As I told you."

"How do you own so many companies at your age?"

"The old-fashioned way. I inherited my wealth. And grew it."

"Shouldn't you be in the offices?"

"No. I hire well."

"And those hires man the offices?"

"Yes."

She steps into the room, toward the bar cart that sits near the window.

"Care for a drink?"

"I could use one." That's an understatement.

With her back to me, she pours us drinks. I can't see what she's pouring. Has she observed me closely enough to know my preference?

Her dress marks a distinct departure from the casual styles she's worn since arriving. It clings to her body, sharing her silhouette, and my gaze falls to the curves of her waist and hips. If this is a dress Lina picked, I must compliment my sister the next time I see her. Red tresses glimmer down Scarlet's back, and I have the urge to step up behind her, weave my fingers through her loose strands, and breathe her in.

But I'll suppress the urge. Last night proved she's beginning to trust me. No need to cock that up.

She hands me a highball glass. I lift it to my nose and take in hints of orange, chocolate, and nuts. *Glenfarclas*. She poured the same for herself.

"Scotch?" I raise an eyebrow. "Wouldn't have picked that for you."

"Then you don't know me well."

"That's true." I hold the glass up to the light, taking in the caramel hue before sipping and savoring the burn down the back of my throat. "I believe you were more generous with my pour than your own. Are you trying to get me drunk?"

Her eyes widen and her cheeks flush.

Bloody hell. Is she?

"If you want me, you don't need to get me drunk." I take a large swallow, nearly emptying the crystal highball.

"Shall we sit?" She gestures to the chairs by the fire.

"Let me get a refill." The liquor is already working its magic through my veins. The world's amok, but there's not much to be done until we've got a better grip on the situation.

"Let me. You sit."

I do as she says. If Paolo is right, and someone within the syndicate is behind today's events, then we've got a much bigger problem. But it fits. The plane explosion was definitely a ground-to-air missile. No one took credit, but plenty of doubt was cast. Doubt seeds instability.

"It doesn't take long for your serious face to take over."

She's before me, serving me a refilled glass. She's a vision before the fire.

The room spins, and I rest my head against the back of the armchair.

"Come sit."

"On your lap?" She releases a girlish noise of amusement. Not a giggle, but delightful all the same.

"I won't bite."

"No, you won't, will you?" She's introspective.

"Only if you ask."

To my delight, she steps forward and sits on my thigh. She's perched tentatively, and I shift, letting her fall behind my thigh, so her arse is planted on the chair, with her thighs draped over mine.

"That's better," I say.

She smells of soothing eucalyptus and mint. It's probably the shower gel in the guest bath, but having her near is like stepping into a spa.

"Was I hurting you?"

"No."

She raises a skeptical eyebrow.

"Well, your arse bones were digging into my thigh bone."

She laughs out loud. It's a beautiful, relaxing sound, and I knock back a little more of my scotch.

"This is more comfortable, though, isn't it? It's better than sitting across from each other."

"Well, I do want to get to know you."

"What a gorgeous coincidence. There are things—"

She places her finger over my lips, shushing me.

"Let me ask you questions. And then you answer me. Can we play that game?"

"Is that the only game we're going to play?"

"That depends on your answers."

"Hmm. It's like a high-stakes poker match. Or strip poker. I'm down for that."

"Are you attracted to me?"

"Give me your hand." My cock is rock-hard. Sadly, she doesn't comply, but her pupils enlarge when she glances down.

"I don't think that's necessary. My vision's quite—"

"I've wanted you since I first saw you. But you know that, don't you, love?"

"Since you first saw me? At Willow's wedding?"

She can't exactly be surprised. Even Leo noticed, on his wedding day, no less. He raised an eyebrow. He saw it. No need for admonishment. I was in the coastal village for only a few hours.

"What do you like about me?"

"Your bravery. Strength." She narrows her eyes, but her fingers reach my shirt, and she undoes a button. *Christ.*

"Are you being honest with me?"

"Those were the first attributes that came to mind. But, of course, there are other things, too. Your perky tits. Slender neck. Porcelain skin. Fiery strands. Eyes I see when I close mine. You're like a siren."

"You want to shag me?"

Her fingers are on my chest, right over my sternum. The soft pads of her fingers burn like fire. My cock is probably dripping cum.

"Well, if you want to do that, I need to get to know you, and I need you to answer me truthfully." She sounds like a primary school mistress.

"I don't suppose there's any way I can convince you to give me a hand job while we're playing this game?"

She smiles like I'm being funny. I'm not. That was the worst fucking pickup line. My brain's gone rogue. But I really want her hands on me. I love them on my chest, but fuck, I want them lower.

"Tell me about your childhood."

All I want is for her to sit on my lap and sink down on my cock, and she's—

"Where did you grow up?"

"London, mostly. Summers in Greece."

"Did you have a good childhood?"

"Yes. Until…" I don't talk about this.

Her palm flattens on my chest. She's undone my entire shirt. *Lower.*

"Tell me. Here. Let's shift." She gets out of the chair. *Fuck.* "Sit in the center." I do as she says, and she straddles me, one thigh on each side, and her center covers my groin. *Lord, yes.*

She rocks her hips, and the pressure and heat on my length is out of this world. "Does that feel good?"

My hands fall to her hips. My breaths are coming quick and fast, like I've run miles. "You know it does."

"Every time you answer me, I'll do that."

I swallow.

There are too many clothes between us.

"Now, were you close to your parents?"

"Yes."

She rocks against me. I close my eyes, luxuriating in the motion.

"Was your father in the syndicate?"

"No."

I open my eyes, willing her to move.

"What is the syndicate?"

She settles against me, and a swell of dizziness hits.

"Is it like the Lupi Grigi?"

"No. It's a collective."

My breathing is… I swipe a hand to my forehead. It's damp with perspiration.

"A collective of what?"

"Influential individuals. A global alliance."

"Men and women?"

"At present, all men. But in theory, women could be included." *If they sat like this…*

"If your father wasn't a member, how—"

"My grandfather was a Russian oligarch. My father, too, but he was one of many sons, and he ventured to Europe. And our family, we made our money in oil. My grandfather was a member of the Russian Bratva, much like your uncle is a member of the Italian mafia. Membership allows your uncle to grow his otherwise legitimate enterprise, but he's not the leader, and he likely doesn't approve of their ways."

"My uncle's enterprises are not strictly legitimate."

"Neither were my family's."

"So, is the syndicate Russian?"

"No."

"How did you get into it?"

"My parents were among many of the wealthy who rallied against Putin's regime. He had them eliminated. My grandfather's influence allowed me to keep my inheritance. Plus, my parents had become UK citizens. It was too complicated for Putin to reclaim my father's businesses. And me. I was already off at boarding school with friends with influence. A friend approached me. Given my wealth and background, they deemed me a perfect fit."

I close my eyes and let my head rest while I drag her hips forward, then push her back, then forward. *Heaven.*

"When were you approached?"

"My third year at university."

"What was the pitch?"

"Influence."

"What does that mean?"

"The world's too complicated to control. There are too many disparate factors. But the collective includes leaders in all powerhouse industries. They own politicians and statesmen. Police. Esquires. Control is elusive. Influence obtainable."

"And what do you use that influence for? To grow your business?"

"To maintain market stability." My hand travels along the curve of her waist.

"How do you control the criminal organizations?"

"Again, there's no control. It's influence. We scratch each other's backs."

"But Uncle Alessio viewed the syndicate as powerful."

"We have more connections than the Lupi Grigi. Across more industries on a global scale. More government leaders."

"And you sell arms?"

"I facilitate deals. I told you this."

"You're a broker?"

"Of sorts."

"Do you deal in drugs?"

"No…" The answer is automatic, but it's not true. "I have a small marijuana business. An investor, really. I have my fingers in many businesses. I'd like to have my fingers in you."

She grinds her hips willfully against me, and my eyes flutter closed. Christ, dry-humping never felt so good. She takes my hand and places it over something soft. My eyes snap open, and I can hardly believe what I'm seeing. She placed my hand on her breast.

"Do you break the law?"

"When necessary."

"Do you kill?"

"When necessary." I squeeze her breast, but she's in this contraption, and there's too much material…

"Why do you want to bring down the Lupi Grigi?"

"They targeted Lina." My nostrils flare as I snarl, "My sister."

"So, you're like Massimo."

"I'm nothing like that Neanderthal. He goes after individuals with a short-sighted end. I'm going after the organization, and they'll rot in prison, a fate worse than death."

"When you finish, what do you intend to do with me?"

"Shag you as often as you'll let me."

She giggles. A lovely sound. I can't seem to look at her face because I've got my hand on her boob and I'm struggling with the brassiere so I can tweak her nipple.

"Seriously."

"I'm quite serious. Can I?" I move my hand, and it seems to take so much effort, but I lower it and reach up under her dress, and there…ah…skin. Smooth, satiny, heavenly skin.

"If put to the wire, would you turn me in?"

"Never." Fuck, my dick aches to be inside her.

"If it was your life—"

"I'll let no one hurt you, love. Saint's honor. Can we shag?" *Please tell me I've answered enough questions.*

"You've no idea how desperately I want to be inside you."

She bends her head, and those radiant coppery strands cast about like a halo. I glimpse eyes so dark they're almost black, and then her lips fall to mine.

Soft and gentle.

Oh, thank god.

My thumb finds her nipple, and as I brush over the tender peak, her hips coax my cock, and we both moan.

And then she's up. I want her so badly, but my limbs are heavy.

"Where are you going?"

"To get you some water."

"But you kissed me," I whine.

"I wanted to know what it felt like."

"But there's more we need to feel." I've never wanted a bird to bounce up and down on me more than I want this one.

"I'll be right back. Stay there and wait for me." Her lips curve into a smile as she adds the endearment, "Love."

Is she mocking me? Why do I feel so groggy? *Bloody hell. The vixen drugged me.*

CHAPTER 16

SCARLET

I wake in the middle of the night.

Alarm filters through my pores. A chill infiltrates the sheets.

Silhouettes form in the dark.

Someone is in here.

I scramble, reaching for the handgun beneath the pillow.

Smooth linen glides beneath my fingers. I stretch, grasping.

Where'd it go?

The pillow lands on the floor.

"Looking for this?"

I scream.

Silence.

Breathless, my vision adjusts, sharpening the shadows.

A dark figure reclines in the armchair.

"Nick?"

My throat constricts. I force myself to swallow.

Is he... "Are you angry?"

"Why would I be angry, love?"

I scramble from the center of the bed to the edge.

"You didn't need to drug me. You could've asked, and I would've answered, and I wouldn't have woken with a pounding headache and blue balls."

"I needed the truth." I dry my clammy palm on the silk sheet. "I needed to know you were telling me the truth."

"Trust an issue, eh?"

"I'm sorry, I—"

"Gave me an erotic memory for the record books. Trouble is, I don't know what's real. Don't remember what I told you."

"Not much."

"I have a bad feeling that my memory of sinking inside you isn't real and that perhaps I shot my load without ever entering heaven."

I restrain my smile. "I don't believe that happened."

"Thank god for small favors. Let's see...I felt your breast. True?"

The feel of his rough skin on my breasts hits with intense vividness. "Yes," I breathe out.

"Perfect size. Fills my palm. And your hips...you ah..."

"Wanted to keep you talking."

"Did it work?"

"Yes."

"What'd you give me?"

"The men call it Mind Eraser."

"Rohypnol? Date rape drug?"

"Version of it."

"You packed it?"

Her slender shoulders lift. "Best to be prepared. I carry aspirin, too."

I scratch my jaw. *What's important here?*

"Do you trust me now?"

"I suppose."

"Explain."

"As long as our needs align, I believe I can trust you."

"Quid pro quo. Can I trust you?"

"Yes." My weak response reveals the truth. I shouldn't have drugged him.

"Planning to drug me again, or did you learn everything you need to know?"

"I…won't do it again." *Unless I need to.*

"But you still have questions?"

"I thought of other things I want to know."

"Why didn't you ask them?"

Because my body's reaction surprised me. I wanted you.

"Did you kiss me? Or is that an apparition?"

"It happened."

My mouth is dry. I wet my lips, and it's as if they are once again touching his. When our lips touched, I felt it through my core, and my hips involuntarily rocked against him as my center clenched.

"Here's the thing, love, anytime you want to use my body, I'm game. There's no need to drug me."

"Does your head still hurt?"

"No. I took the aspirin someone left beside the chair."

He sets the handgun, my handgun, the one he must have somehow known I keep beneath my pillow, on the side table, and flicks on the lamp.

"I'm sorry I drugged you."

"Are you?" His brow crinkles. His lips… I swallow. It's amusement. I swear that's what I see.

"No." I slink back, awaiting a blow. But he remains seated. Distant. "I needed to know."

"Now you do. And I meant what I said. Anytime you want to use my body, I'm game."

It's too dark to see his eyes; I can only make out his shape. The rolled sleeves on his arms. His unbuttoned shirt. The watch is missing from his wrist, as if he began undressing for bed and stopped.

My nipples tease the thin fabric of my nightgown. Need and desire strum every delicate nerve ending.

My heart palpitates in my chest. Being with a man is my last hurdle. It's one I haven't attempted, in the interest of self-care. But I want him. There's no denying the physical urge. And I do not shrink from fear.

"How about now? Are you game?"

He's silent. One second. Two.

I shouldn't have said anything.

"You want me? Right now?"

The chair creaks, and he rises.

"You're not teasing, are you, love?"

That word. It's so British. One he bestows on all, yet my insides flutter every time he says it. It's why I hate it.

I shake my head as I search the dark.

He steps forward, and the details of his face emerge. His roughened goatee and angular chin. Ruffled hair. Deep-set eyes I can't see, but I swear I feel.

"Shall I get a condom?"

"Can't get pregnant, remember?"

"I'm clean."

"I figured, or you would've just gone to get the condom."

"Right."

He steps forward, and I slip off the bed so I'm standing before him.

"So you do trust me then, eh?"

In answer, I lift my nightgown over my head and let it drop to the floor.

I hate fear, and running head-first into the source is how I attack what I hate.

"My god, you are lovely."

He steps closer, close enough the energy between us is palpable. He tenderly tilts my chin upwards, and his lips fall over mine.

Soft, at first. A flutter.

His hand cups the back of my head, holding me, gently asking.

I open, and his tongue slips inside. Tentative.

His tenderness throws me. I expected him to throw me on the bed, to slam into me, and yet…I'm bared to him, and his interest is in my lips.

His kiss is slow and sweet. Exploratory. Soon, it steals all thought.

CHAPTER 17

NICK

She's fierce. Strong. I sensed her spirit in the chapel.

I've wanted this one since I first spotted her on the threshold of a sanctuary. Hair aflame, magnetic green eyes atop a divine figure of milky smooth skin and curves.

Finally, she opens, and her sweetness is everything I dreamed of. As heavenly as she tastes, as intense my cravings, I will myself to maintain control.

She needs to gain her footing.

The agreement isn't for me to do as I like with her body. No, she wants to use my body. And I'm game.

My body begs, eager, but I must take my time. Appreciate her swollen, wet lips, so full and plump. Her chest rises and falls slowly, as if she, too, fights for control. And fuck, her breasts. Those eager peaks beg to be suckled.

"How do you want me?" I'll let the goddess direct this play.

Uncertainty flashes in her eyes.

Please don't fucking change your mind.

My cock is so fucking hard. It might be a remnant side effect of whatever drug she dosed me with, but I jacked off earlier, dreaming of the sex we didn't have. And yet you'd never know based on how badly I ache.

The pads of her fingers touch my unbuttoned shirt. The material falls off my shoulders. Her thumbs brush my skin, and my muscles tense with restraint. I want nothing more than to lift her, throw her on the bed, and take her.

I visualize the heat of her pussy so vividly my cock jerks. Likely weeps.

Her fingers fumble with my belt, and I close my eyes, inhaling deeply. But I'm not missing this. My eyelids lift, and I fixate on her slender fingers working the buttons on my trousers and the length of the unbuckled leather belt dangling in the air.

"You slept in these clothes," she says as the zipper descends.

"Is that what it's called when one passes out? Sleep?"

My trousers fall unceremoniously to my ankles. She's not touching me, but I swear the heat from her skin imbues my briefs.

"You will not let me forget that, will you?"

Those hooded, yearning eyes are going to do me in.

"Does it matter? I'll let you do anything you wish."

Her lips curve upward, and her knees bend. Her grip on my briefs tightens, and cold air meets my arse. My dick protrudes, hard and needy.

She lightly strokes me, tentative.

I wish I knew what that fucktard of a husband did to her, but now is not the time to ask. I only wish I knew so I could avoid doing anything that reminds her of the past. Like cup the back of her head and push until I hit the back of her throat.

Her touch is so light, too light, really. But with her kneeling before me, I wouldn't change a damn thing.

A slip of her tongue appears, wetting her lower lip.

God, I want that mouth on me. My knees and even my bloody elbows quiver in anticipation. But she rises and points to the bed.

"Lie back."

"Yes, madam," I quip.

If she plans to straddle me, she might need… "Can I do something to you first?"

She doesn't speak, yet with the tilt of her head, and the drop of those strawberry strands over the perky nipple…I close my eyes and swallow. Focus.

"Can you lie back? Or sit on the bed? Let me pleasure you. I want to taste you. Bring you to an orgasm with my mouth."

Her fingers brush over my chest ever so lightly, her gaze lowered.

"I won't come." It's an admission. And a challenge.

"I'll only do what you like. If it gets to be too much, tell me, and I'm on my back."

With a slight nod, she crawls onto the mattress, giving me a splendid view of her behind and an earth-shattering vision of her on all fours. And with that comes a vision of my bruising grip on her hips as I pound into her.

Focus.

She twists on the bed, lying across it sideways, and spreads those lovely thighs.

Deep red trimmed curls surround her glistening pink pussy.

I crawl closer, eager, nipping my way up her tender skin. I brush my finger over her, verifying that yes, she's quite ready.

She's ready, but I won't deprive myself of her gift. I slide a finger inside her heat, studying her. She tilts her head back, eyes on the ceiling. I shift forward and taste. Her thighs tighten around my shoulders. Her arms lie by her head, uncertain, in limbo.

I close my eyes and lick, working my tongue and fingers in tandem. I can't see her eyes, but I feel what she likes through the tension in her thighs and her soft mewls. As her knees rise and her hips buck, I know she's close. I let my teeth graze that sensitive bundle, and she jerks.

Right on the edge, but she didn't fall.

"Can we…"

She doesn't have to say it. I understand.

"How do you want me?"

She blinks.

"Missionary? Or do you want me on my back?"

What will make you feel the most comfortable?

"Missionary…I think."

It's counterintuitive to me, but again, there's so much I don't know about her experience. Perhaps she never climbed on top of a man. If her husband was always forceful, then that's not a position that would have likely happened.

I crawl up the bed. Cum leaks from my tip. I slide it up and down her silky entrance. Those green eyes watch.

Good.

The milky skin of her breasts pleads for touch, a reminder I have yet to plunder them. I pause, kneeling before her, and push up. The mattress dips with the weight of my balled hands on each side of her. Unsure eyes meet mine, and I dip my head, sucking a nipple, twirling my tongue around the nub. Her legs tighten around my thighs, and her fingers find my hair.

That's it.

I alternate to the other breast, delivering the same treatment and receiving the same in return, with possibly slightly more intensity.

When I lift my head, she breathes out, "I want you."

"Oh, you'll have me."

But first, I claim her lips.

This isn't my normal. Kissing a woman isn't something I crave during sex. For that matter, pleasuring with my mouth isn't something I often offer. But Scarlet's different, in so many ways. And I fucking love kissing her.

She wraps her arms around my back, and my cock buries itself in her hip. I haven't claimed her yet, but it fucking feels like I have.

Her nails gently scrape along my ribs, and I break the kiss, panting, arm muscles quivering.

"Please."

Does she want this to be over?

Her hips buck beneath me, and I focus on aligning myself. I watch as I enter her heat. Her tight cunt practically strangles my cock. It takes every bit of control not to slam into her.

But I take it easy, working myself into her slowly. When I'm balls deep, I can hardly breathe. She feels so fucking good.

"Is this okay?"

She opens her eyes. And I don't know what I see. Fear? Determination?

"Move," she gasps.

So I do.

"Fuck. You feel good." It's a confession, but one I'm not certain she hears.

We move in tandem, like lovers who have done this a million times and plan for a million more. But it's not until I claim her mouth once more that I lose control, lose focus, and empty everything inside her.

I collapse beside her. A light sheen of perspiration coats our skin. Our breaths, once short and fast, slow. Her lips curl upward, smiling at me. Is that relief?

"Did you…" I don't think she did, but there's no point in putting her on the spot. Next time I'll do a better job, pay closer attention.

Her fingers touch my skin, graze through my beard, and tug. "I enjoyed it. That was…freeing."

I tug her to me, into my chest. The beating of her heart penetrates my chest. And then I do something highly uncharacteristic of me after sex, but it's the only thing I want.

I kiss her.

CHAPTER 18

SCARLET

In the bathroom, I study my reflection.

Reddish pink splotches scatter across my normally ghost-white skin. Deeper red marks dot my neck. I strain into the light. *Did he mark me? Or is that beard burn?*

My palm covers my nipple, and I'm hit with the feel of his mouth and tongue. My core tightens in response.

I did it.

I took the last step to recovery. I had sex. And I enjoyed it. I wanted it.

Vincent is no longer my only.

I can honestly say I'm now glad I didn't force myself to have sex with just anyone to get it off my list. Nick…it's like he understood what I needed and could handle it.

He was gentle, and what just happened in there…in that

room…it's so unlike any of my prior experiences. Even before Vincent turned vile, it was never like that with us. He was—

Knock. Knock.

"You okay in there?"

I reach for a towel hanging on a knob and pull it to my chest, then crack the door open.

"I'm going to shower."

One eyebrow lifts and he smirks. "Want company?"

I giggle. The ridiculous sound bubbles out, and the sound is unnatural and freakish.

"I'm not sure I'm ready for that."

He narrows his eyes. "Why?" His gaze lowers to the clutched towel. "You know, that's quite unnecessary."

I look to the ceiling, smiling like a loon.

"Let me shower. I'll see you in a bit."

He sighs and runs his fingers through his hair. "Fine. I suppose I should shower, too. I've got a slate of meetings. But for the record, I don't care to shower alone."

"How sad for you."

He narrows his eyes and wiggles a finger at me. I lean forward and snap my teeth as if I'm going to take his finger off, but he gathers me up, towel and all, pushes me right up against the doorframe, and kisses me thoroughly.

When he breaks away, he taps my nose. "You are a tease."

"I am not," I shout at his retreating back. We had sex. He can hardly call me a tease.

I don't know why I wasn't ready to shower with him. I stood before him naked, but I felt… I'm not sure. Exposed. Raw. I need time to process. One thing I learned in therapy is that listening to yourself is important. I don't need to understand all the whys, I simply need to hear myself. Or maybe it's not simple at all.

Who am I kidding? None of it's simple. But I don't regret standing up for myself. And his reaction to me saying no? Well…a smile keeps breaking free.

After I shower, I wander through the house with that silly smile popping up at random. Walking down the hall. Pouring myself coffee. Passing Nick's closed office door.

I need fresh air. Some exercise. The day is overcast, as it has been since I arrived. I hold a finger up to test the air—it's dry. The absence of drizzle is an improvement. Wearing an old pair of Wellies that sit by the side door, I cross through the garden and down the path to the stable.

Dog comes trotting up, tail wagging.

"Hello there."

He jumps up, his front paws landing on my front.

"Down, boy." I can't imagine that's approved behavior.

Obedient, his paws hit the ground, his lolling tongue saying he's not in the least bothered by my reprimand.

He trots ahead and pauses, waiting for me, tail wagging.

"You must want food." Or no, he wouldn't look to me for food. I've never fed an animal on the premises. "Don't want to be alone?"

A horse neighs, but Dog's attention doesn't stray.

I reach him and scratch behind his ears. His tail wags back and forth. Lina told me Dog showed up one day and never left.

"We're both strays, the pair of us," I tell him.

He trots ahead, tail wagging, and I follow.

The breezeway door is open, which it always seems to be. I suppose on bad weather days they must close it to keep the animals warm and dry.

I've never ridden a horse and have no intention of saddling one up, but I'm growing fond of the scent of leather and hay, and even the earthy smell of manure. I can see why Lina spends most of her time here.

It's interesting. I've perused her influencer posts, and they are all about clothes, cosmetics, and nightlife. But I bet she could have some fantastic videos of the animals, or even of her trail rides. Perhaps those videos wouldn't resonate with her target market.

Lina's horse's head hangs over the stall door. I reach up to pet him, but he jerks, and I back away. He's a beautiful boy. Ebony eyes, glistening black fur. A light coat of dust reflects the sun when it hits right. If I had the nerve to reach over the stall door and pat his neck, I bet a cloud of dust would rise.

His nostrils flair, and I back away, heeding the warning. Lina said he's friendly, but all the same, I won't risk those enormous teeth clamping down on me.

Dog trots ahead, out of sight.

I move on, intent on reaching the trail. There's a chill in the air, but once I strike out on the path, I should warm right up.

A dusty black boot pointed skyward atop the shavings in an empty stall catches my eye.

Odd.

I circle back and see Jodhpurs.

My heart kicks up a notch.

"Hello?"

I round the corner.

Lina lies in the shavings. But it's her pale arm that slows time. A needle juts from it. Her eyes are closed.

I reach for the wall to steady myself and blink off the wave of dizziness.

"Christ. Lina."

I possess medical training. I trained as a nurse until accounting became far preferable to mending Lupi Grigi men.

Pull it together.

I bend beside her and place my fingers against her throat, searching for a pulse.

Her lips are dark. As are her nail beds. My index finger digs into her still-warm skin, and I examine the protruding needle.

It must be heroin. Has to be.

Beneath my fingers, there's a pulse.

I yank out the needle and scan the stall.

She's overdosed.

Think.

"Helloooo!" I scream. If anyone is here, I need help. I can't carry her back to the house by myself.

A horse neighs. Dog runs in, tail wagging, nose in my face.

I brush him away from my face and stand. "Stay with her. I'll be right back."

I take off running as fast as I can in the unwieldy Wellies. It's possible Nick has Naloxone. If he doesn't have the drug on hand, he'll have to help me load her into a car. How far away is the hospital?

I sling the door open and let out a blood-curdling scream. "Nick!"

CHAPTER 19

NICK

Shrill shouting penetrates the glass.

Bloody hell.

I towel off and snatch trousers and a shirt, dressing like there's a fire.

I sprint through the back of the house.

What the fuck's going on?

An attack?

Where's Ash?

If they sent someone, so help me...

I burst through the back hall.

Scarlet's hands cup her mouth like a megaphone. Eyes wide.

"What?"

I scan behind her. There's nothing. No one.

"It's Lina."

Fuck.

Dread explodes with the force of a land mine.

No. Please no.

"She's overdosed. Do you have medication?"

I blink, processing. *She's alive?*

"Naloxone?" Scarlet yells, breaking through.

Right. I have it.

I turn, yelling back to her, "I'll get it. Where is she? In the stable?"

"In a stall."

"Go back to her," I shout.

I slip into autopilot and grab the unopened box from the medicine cabinet. The one a doctor recommended I keep around.

It had to have been Amir. I should've never trusted him to keep her safe. She must've found her old mates and brought drugs back with her. Shit. This is my fault. I should've had security around her. I shouldn't have trusted she was okay. I should've spent more time with her. Watched her more closely. Hired more staff.

Where the hell is the stable hand?

When I reach the stall, I freeze. The unnatural deep blue hue of Lina's lips arrests me.

Scarlet's over her, rubbing her sternum, talking to her.

"Give me that," she says, holding out her hand.

It takes a second to register. She's pointing at the box in my hand.

"Is she...is she alive?"

She can't die. Not Lina.

"She's alive." She pops open the box, removes the dose, pushes it up Lina's nose, and presses the plunger. "Can you bring a car around? This should work, but let's bring her in. How far is the hospital?"

Scarlet's focus is 100 percent on Lina. She hovers over her, attending to her, and her words hit me with a velocity I can't grasp in my shock.

The trip to the hospital blurs. I drive. Lina lies in the back seat, and Scarlet kneels on the floorboard.

Lina gains consciousness before we arrive at the hospital, but she's high. Spacey. I can't tell if she sees me.

The doctor asks what she took, and it's Scarlet who hands him a used needle. I should've thought of that…looked for it.

It's Scarlet who takes my hand and leads me to a waiting room. They've admitted Lina but have asked us to wait. A nurse comes out with information on rehabilitation centers. They'll keep Lina here until she's stable, but they recommend we admit her for drug rehabilitation.

It's my fault. I should've been more on top of this. More vigilant.

Scarlet brings me coffee. Holds my hand. An angel.

"Are you okay?" She touches my jaw, and I grasp her wrist, pressing her palm against my cheek.

"Thank you." It's the only phrase that fits.

"How long has she struggled with addiction?"

What's the answer to that? The excessive drinking during her university years—was that addiction or the slide into it?

"She'll tell you she's not an addict. She'll tell you I'm a control freak."

"Has she ever overdosed before?"

"Not like this." I force myself to swallow. She's going to be all right. "I walked in on her once. Shooting up. I lost it. Ape shit. Drove her to rehab. She claimed she was experimenting. It was nothing to get hung up over."

I release Scarlet's hand. Lina had been so angry at me for doubting her. And I'd begun to think I overreacted. Too protective once again. Trust me to cock it up. Too protective. Not protective enough.

"Willow mentioned a club. Said she had to be carried home. That wasn't like this, though, right?"

"No. That time, I had her blood tested. Leandro De Luca had her drugged. Date rape drug. He knew I was out of the country and I'd send Leo in my place." My molars grind against each other. "He wanted to find Willow, so he used Lina to track her."

When those fuckwads drugged her, I should've asked the doctor if that would increase her cravings. Is that what did it? Leaning forward, I place my elbows on my knees and rub my temples.

"None of this is your fault."

I side-eye her. She doesn't know shit.

"You can't fight the disease for her."

I clamp my eyelids closed. This day sure went to hell.

"I'm sure it's hard for someone like you to hear, but you can't control everything and everyone."

It's the same as what I'd told her last night when she'd drugged me and asked me about the syndicate. I can't control, but I can influence.

I've spent billions engineering the tide. And fuck, this happened right under my nose.

Did all this start with Leandro's stunt, or was it before?

Amir. He'll know. I pat my coat, searching for a mobile. Left it in the car.

"I'll be back," I announce.

I'm in the hallway when I glance over my shoulder and glimpse her concern.

In three strides, I'm back to her. I lift her and pull her to me, burying my nose in her floral-scented hair.

"Thank you."

An old chap peers over a magazine from the corner of the room.

Choking back emotion, I press my lips to the top of her head. "I need to make some calls. I'll be back."

Alone in the car park, it's as good a place as any to call Amir.

"You on the lam?"

I flinch at Amir's carefree tone. Fucking twit.

"I'm at the hospital."

"Christ. Who'd they send after ya?"

"Lina overdosed."

"Christ. Is she okay?"

"She will be. Did you go clubbing with her?"

"You know I did."

"Did you shoot up with her?"

"Bugger off. I don't touch it."

"Did she? Were you watching, or—"

"She's not a little tyke, is she? I think she might've done some blow. But…what'd she OD on?"

"Heroin."

"Mate, no. Scout's honor. Didn't see that shite."

I pace the lot. The lights at the nearby intersection flick red.

"Christ. But thank god. I thought you were calling me, saying you'd been shot up."

"What are you on about?"

"Have you not heard? There's a hit on Scarlet Gagliano. Official investigation opened. An open hit's been placed. If you don't want to be collateral, I suggest you send the ginger packing."

CHAPTER 20

I've seen men with grave expressions like Nick's before. My gaze drops to his waist, searching for the telltale bump beneath his jacket.

"Are you ready?" he asks.

"The nurse left for the wheelchair," I answer.

"Can't you walk?" He's derisive and surly to his sister, but she's not flustered by his gruff tone.

We've been tucked away in accident and emergency all day. The doctor recommended she stay, in an abundance of caution, overnight, but Nick declined. He's been in and out all day, presumably sorting business.

Curious about her perspective and with little else to say, I asked Lina what he does, and she gave a half-hearted, "What doesn't he do?"

She drops her head, looking down at her legs. She's in the

clothes I found her in, and there's a dark stain on her Jodhpurs that looks suspiciously like horse manure.

"Let's wait for the wheelchair," I say to Nick, meeting his eyes.

It's hard to believe this morning he was inside me and we were in sync. At the moment, he has the wild, harried look of a demented serial killer.

"I can't wait to crawl into my bed," Lina says, rubbing her temple.

"Have you still got a headache?" I ask.

"I don't feel good," she mumbles.

"You're not going home," Nick says.

"What?" Lina and I ask simultaneously.

"I found a program that's going to take you in."

"I'm not going to rehab." Her gaze is down, shoulders hunched. "I don't need it."

"It's not up for debate." He pulls a mobile out of his pocket. "I'll be outside."

"He's such an arsehole," Lina says when he's no longer in earshot.

"He cares for you."

She has to see it. I don't know that I agree with his decision to force her into a rehabilitation program. She needs it, there's no doubt. But from what I understand of them, they don't work unless she wants to get help. But I've spent my life around men like Nick. He's used to calling the shots. He won't accept this isn't his issue to solve. He also won't accept that he's powerless.

The nurse, a young Black man with a cheery smile, arrives, pushing a wheelchair. "Here we are, love." He comes around to help her from the bed to the chair. "Know it's not my place, but the doc's right. Staying the night—"

"You're right. It's not your place," Lina snaps.

The nurse meets my gaze over her head. I'm not an expert on these things, but I suspect she's still high. If there are stages, I'd say she's becoming lucid and grumpy. If she's truly well and addicted, withdrawal symptoms will descend.

Lina settles into the chair, and her head lolls back, and her eyelids close.

"All right, love. Let's get you out of here. But you've got to promise me we won't see you back, you got that? Fly straight."

I follow behind them and can't see Lina, but if she heard him, I'd bet she's not at all pleased.

The nurse wheels her out below an overhang. There's a black Range Rover with the back door open. And parked behind it are four more SUVs, and in front, two more. A group of men stand on both sides of the exit, all in dark clothes and overcoats.

Nick sees us and drops his mobile into a pocket. I give him a questioning look. I'm no stranger to security, but we didn't have this before.

What's going on?

This can't be good. Something has happened.

"Hell," Lina says. "Did you hire a goon squad?"

Nick bends to help his sister, but she pushes him off.

"I'm fine," she growls.

"Thank you for your help," I say to the nurse.

"Are all these folks here for you?"

I shrug, having no idea how to answer.

"We've got it now." Nick slides a bill into his palm. "Go on," he instructs the nurse. To me, he asks, "Up for a ride?"

I nod and go around to the far side of the vehicle. There's a man driving, and Nick gets in the seat beside him.

"Are these men going with me?" Lina asks. "Is your idea they'll watch me around the clock? A dozen sitters for your precious, silly sister?"

Nick's gaze meets mine in the rearview. If Lina wasn't high, she'd see he's not in a jocular mood.

"If they're bisexual, I'm game. Could be fun."

Nick's scowl is the only sign he heard his sister.

I wish to be anywhere but in this vehicle. I don't have siblings, and for the first time, I'm inordinately grateful.

Lina's poor jokes aside, I don't think our additional company has anything to do with Lina, and my stomach roils with uneasiness. He's been stepping outside because today of all days, the investigation began. Call it a sixth sense. The knowledge seeps into my bones more solidly than the November chill.

They'll be seeking revenge. He doesn't need to deal with this, with me. He's got his hands full.

It's time for me to disappear.

CHAPTER 21

NICK

The private facility housing Lina has been around for over fifty years and has seen dozens of dignitaries and celebrities pass through its doors. She's been here for two hours. Dropping her off presented no issues. Surprisingly, she remained mute through the process.

With Scarlet safely ensconced on my property, now, I'm back.

Technically, I'm not supposed to see Lina this early in her stay. But she'll go mad if she picks up she's got a security detail. Tough titty. You can't have a family history like ours and not prepare for the worst.

On the way over, Nomad called and confirmed he's got a team assisting. Nomad doesn't know the players, and I told him as much, but he said he's got a resource. A private party. I'm skeptical, but it won't hurt to let his wheels spin.

The only source I can think of that would know all the players is one deceased Leo Sullivan, and ironically, if he still breathed this air, he's the one I'd go to now. But he's breathing air in another land under a different name.

The car park is full, so I leave it in a no-parking zone on the side of the street leading up to the stone mansion. Given the rates to stay here, it's doubtful they ticket visitors, given the visitors are likely the ones paying the exorbitant rates.

The young woman at the desk has big blue eyes etched in black, a nose ring, and enough silver in her ears to set off security at Heathrow.

"It's not visiting hour," she says.

No shit. "I need to meet with Lina's doctor."

"He's not here."

How the fuck is that possible? "Where is he?"

"He's only here three days a week. He's at Gramercy Hospital the other two, but today, I believe, is his day off."

"Who may I address?"

"What's the problem?" a middle-aged woman in a stodgy suit asks.

"And you are?"

"Dr. Jergensen. I'm the facility director."

"Then, Doctor, you are exactly who I need to see."

I look at the men I left outside monitoring the entrance. She follows my gaze.

"Are they with you?"

"Yes. Is there a place we can speak in private?"

"Mr…"

"Ivanov."

"Mr. Ivanov, I hope you can understand that we follow protocol for the good of our patients—"

"I'd like to talk with you about my donation to your facility. Fifty million pounds. Anonymously, of course."

Her eyes widen an appropriate amount.

"Betty, can you reschedule my next appointment?"

After I finish with Dr. Jergensen, I'm granted time to meet with my sister in a private room that reminds me of an elementary school art room.

Her heather gray sweats hang loosely, covering her from wrist to ankle. I can't recall the last time I saw her with a freshly scrubbed face and no trace of blush or lipstick. She looks younger and more vulnerable. Skin and bones. Can't say I fancy the model schtick. Why didn't I see it earlier? Is she that good at hiding it, or am I that obtuse?

"How are you?" I ask as Lina pulls out a chair.

"Dandy."

"Pissed?"

"What gave it away?"

I exhale, tired of this game she and I play. "What would you have me do? If the shoes were reversed, and you found me with a needle up my arm, what would you have done?"

She has the wisdom to look away. She folds her arms over her middle and pouts like a teen.

"You nearly killed yourself." *Bloody hell. What the fuck should I do?*

"I would've been fine," she mumbles.

"Would you now? Is that what you've been doing with your days? When I've thought you've been riding, you've been in a stall shooting up and coming inside when you come to? Rolling around in the horse dung? That's your idea of a good time?"

I close my eyes because I can't look at her. I shouldn't have come here. It's too early in the process. She's at the angry stage. *We're* in the angry stage.

But I don't have a fucking choice.

"I'm sorry."

The words are so faint I can't quite believe she said them. "What are you sorry for?"

She wipes a palm across her face. Is she crying?

"I think I do… I'm…" She tilts her head and looks up to the ceiling or the heavens… Anywhere but me. "I have a problem."

She sniffles. I don't move. Don't speak.

"The urges are strong. I've been…doing it alone."

Christ.

She sniffles. "So you don't need to kill anyone."

I keep her out of the business, so what's she going on about?

She smiles, but her eyes are a teary mess. "Anyway, if that's what you came to hear, I'm tired. I'm in this time. I want to stop."

Before, she'd been adamant. Claimed I'm too old. I didn't understand. She'd been full of accusations. My throat tightens, and I sniff, fighting the urge to pull my little sister into my arms. I practically raised her and did a shite job of it, but it doesn't mean I don't love the pain in the arse.

"I don't wanna die. Is that what you want to hear?"

"That you want to get better? That you'll put the work into doing so? Yeah, that's what I want to hear."

"You couldn't wait to hear it. You had to break policy? Couldn't give me space to get my head on?"

Oh. That. I fidget a bit. Damn.

"Did someone else die?"

"No." Her question snaps me out of whatever bog I fell into. "But you'll be having security here." I can't read her expression.

"I know it's not your favorite, but it's…" I lick my lower lip because it's dry as fuck. "I've pissed off some people, and I… You're going to need to be careful. Smart. It's not inconceivable they'll come after you to get at me. You know what I'm saying?"

"If someone shows up telling me you've bought me a pony and do I want to go see it, I shouldn't climb in the van. That's what you're saying?"

"You're a bright one."

We both fight smiles as we look at each other.

"You thought this bit would upset me? I'm an Ivanov, too, you know?"

She's right. And hell, I'm going to blink, and she'll be thirty. It's about time I stop treating her like a kid.

"Is this to do with Scarlet?"

Her question hits like a dagger to the heart. I dig two fingers into my temple over the raw pain.

"No." I force a casual smile. "Scarlet's going away."

"Is she coming back?"

"I'm leaning toward no." I meet my sister's gaze, and it's a bloody delight to find her focused and intent. "It'll be safest if she goes off the grid."

Safest for her, safest for Lina.

"But once this blows over, you'll bring her home, right?"

"Won't be wise." Knocking out one mafia family is one thing. But this is about to blow. The syndicate won't approve. There's a good chance I've already got an enemy within the group. If the syndicate turns against me, I'll be going up against some of the most influential men in the world. If they don't come after me with guns, they'll unearth skeletons, paint me as a monster, frame me for crimes.

If I come clean about the message, about Leo and the so-called Prophet, they might back me. That's what I should do. But other than a lone message, I've got no proof.

And if I call a meeting, make my case, they'll want me to hand over Scarlet. The Interpol investigation won't incriminate any of them, but the reverberations will be felt by their connections. It's an incestuous fucking world. And I won't give them Scarlet.

"Nick?"

I meet my sister's gaze.

"You deserve happiness."

I rub the back of my neck, taking my little sister in. "Well, get clean."

"When I do, it'll be for me. Not you. You've got to do you, boo."

"Look at you being smart."

She rubs the inside of her arm. It might itch.

"You can't trust Amir."

"Curious thing to say. Why?"

"I overheard him on the phone."

"If he spoke in front of you, he meant for you to hear whatever he said."

"I don't think so. He thought I was high."

Bloody bastard.

"And I was. But I remember."

"What did he say?"

"He said Ivanov won't be an issue."

"That's all he said?" That doesn't mean squat.

"After the call ended, he saw I was awake and told me to unzip his pants and suck him off."

Yep. Not a friend.

"Did he get high with you?"

"He stuck with alcohol."

There's a knock on the door, and a guy in scrubs peers in, looking between the two of us with all kinds of suspicion.

"Lina, the physician's ready to meet you. And a physical therapist. They want to do an admission workup."

"Ah, celebrity treatment. A team awaits." She stands, rolling her eyes, but readying to follow the chap.

"You get strong, yes? Kick this."

We embrace, and she tightens her grip around me. She pushes up on her toes and whispers in my ear, "Keep Scarlet around. She's good for you. I don't want you to be alone."

"Aye." My sigh's a long one. "You'll be back before we blink."

"I'm not so sure." She squeezes my arm. "It's too early to say, but I was so unhappy out there. I think…I need to go on my own. I think. I don't mean it as an attack."

The man at the door clears his throat.

"You take this time," I tell my sister. "You focus on you. Heal. Get your head on straight."

"I love you." She gives me a final hug, and I watch as she shuffles to the door.

Christ. I want to believe her. Believe she's going to find her way straight, but for today, I'll have to settle with knowing she's safe.

CHAPTER 22

SCARLET

I opted to hole up in the upstairs library, as the billiard room downstairs opens onto the lawn, and every time the security personnel pass by the window, I startle. The dusty smell in the library bothered me initially, but I've warmed to it. The leather-bound volumes on the shelves probably haven't been opened in generations, and many of the titles aren't at all to my taste, but I love sitting amongst the volumes. The gas fireplace flickers orange with hints of blue, creating a warm ambiance that's particularly desirable against the clouds shrouding the skyline.

I should find a book to read, but instead, I've wasted hours scrolling through TikTok on a random mobile Nick said I could use. I keep replaying a video of a Spanish guy saying, "Hello, gorgeous" over and over. It's not what he's saying as much as it is his tone, and comments are cracking me up. I wish I had someone to share the video with, but I've got no one.

Orlando, possibly, but I'm on Nick's random device so no one can track me. Reaching out to Orlando would defeat the purpose.

Footsteps sound in the hall and Nick appears. Relief flashes across his face.

"I see you found the library."

"It's a lovely room."

The cushion on the sofa sinks as he takes his place next to me, looking over my shoulder at the screen in my hand.

"Who is that?"

"Listen to his voice," I say. "I'd love to have his voice on my Siri. Some are saying he needs to be installed on the car nav."

"Where's he live?"

"I don't know." I toss the mobile on the sofa. "How's Lina?"

"Hand me that phone."

"Why?"

"Need to find that bloke. See who I've got in his area who can take him out."

My mouth gapes, and I flail my hands about, somewhat certain he's joking—hoping he's joking.

He cracks up, laughing at his own joke, and I slap his chest.

"Seriously." I roll my eyes, waving my hands about in exasperation. "For a second there, I truly thought you might be mad enough to assassinate a TikToker, Mr. Jealous," I say, shaking my head.

"Not normally," he says, growing quite serious. "It's you."

He's playing, but I've been over here worried about his sister.

"How's Lina?"

"She's good, I think. I mean, what do I know?" He rubs a hand through his hair. "I've thought she was in a good place before. But she isn't in denial. Accepts she has a problem. For the moment. She was worried about you."

"Me?"

He brushes his fingers across my face, circumspect.

"And me. It's good to see she's thinking about someone other than herself, if I'm being honest. This place she's at now, it's got good reviews."

"They'll allow the additional security presence?"

"Aye. They're working with me."

My mobile screen lights, and we both read the text.

Unknown number
My flight's on schedule. I'll call when I
get in.

"Who's that?"

He's right to ask. In theory, no one should have this number. The country code isn't Italy. Will he recognize it? Of course, he will. This is Nick.

The coded message is meant to avert suspicions, but it couldn't look more suspect to Nick.

"Wrong number," I say, looking across the room instead of at Nick.

I'm lying. Why? What am I doing?

I sense Nick stiffen. He picks up my mobile and pecks away at it. I've no idea what he's doing but…oh, Christ. He's going to track the number.

I glance down in time to read his message.

. . .

This is Nick. Get me everything you can on this number and a log of all calls made from the number I'm messaging you from.

If I weren't guilty, I'd be furious. Should I act furious? For survival, yes. I should be affronted and storm out. Only, I can't quite force myself because I am guilty and he's right to investigate.

"I lied," I say, head bowed.

"You don't say." A chill crisscrosses his tone, but it hasn't dropped to deadly.

"I had a plan. Before you." I lift my gaze from my hands. "A member of British intelligence approached me. They wanted information on Titan's shipping clients—I presumed to curtail the drug trafficking going on through the EU—but it became clear they also have an interest in tracking shipments to and from Russia."

"Go on."

"I haven't given them much. I haven't told my contact what I provided to Interpol. Honestly, my contact seemed more interested in information than in actually bringing them down. And I hadn't yet decided if I could trust him."

"Why is he reaching out now?"

"He keeps up with me."

"Via mobile?" There's disgust in his tone.

"He tracked me to the Savoy. That night you approached me in the bar, he was there."

"And?"

"After you approached, he disappeared. The agreement was he wouldn't approach me when I was with anyone."

"Right." He waves the mobile back and forth.

"I reached out today. Figured he'd be worried. I didn't want him sending anyone to rescue me."

"You think they'd do that?" His eyebrows lift, and I can't tell if he's amused or dismayed.

"I'm an asset."

"A gold coin is an asset."

"You don't think—"

"There's nothing to think. I'll verify you're talking to who you think you're talking to, and then we'll go from there."

"Are you mad?"

He tugs at his chin, considering, and huffs. "Annoyed. Why would you keep that from me?"

"Wasn't sure how to tell you."

"How about, 'Hey, Nick, by the way, before you came along, this chub asked me to give him the nitty-gritty on the drug smuggling business, and now he's sniffing my tracks, hoping he doesn't lose his source. Think I should tell him I've gone and shot the load with Interpol and I'm no longer nearly as valuable of an asset?'"

"I should've trusted you."

"What was your plan? Using the chub as a backup should things go awry?"

"Wouldn't you have a backup?"

He narrows his eyes. "Aye, I would. But let's circle back to the trust bit."

"You're right. I should've told you."

"Can't blame you, I suppose. I don't trust anyone."

"Not even me?" *Why would he?*

"Did you not just see me send off the request to my team?" My gaze falls. "Truthfully, I had an idea what was going on."

"You did?"

"You were the perfect target. The intelligence folks spend their days searching for people just like you. Folks who've been slighted but maintain a presence in whatever—a government, a business, anything that might have information of value. Was that the only one who approached you?"

"No. Someone from Italy did, too."

"You're an asset for—"

"No. I didn't trust him. Seemed too likely it was a setup. My uncle feeling me out to see if he could trust me."

"Likely it was." He yawns. "But you trusted me. Why's that?"

"I trusted we had a common goal."

"A common goal," he repeats.

"Aye, we do," I say, using his words.

"Are you mocking me?"

"Never."

"Good. That would require a punishment."

That gives me pause.

He holds one hand up, flat like a paddle. "Of the delightful variety."

A surge of energy connects the two of us.

"I must say, you've handled this remarkably well."

"Might not if there's a second time." His eyes are heated, but there's a threatening undertone. But he doesn't need to worry.

I straddle him on the sofa, sitting back on his thighs, and reach between his legs, cupping him through his trousers.

"Perhaps I can make it up to you."

He groans as I stroke his erection.

Oh, he likes this idea.

CHAPTER 23

NICK

I should be livid. Furious.

But it's been a shit day.

And her hands are over my cock, and she's straddling my lap, so I'll go with it.

She fumbles with my belt buckle.

Adorable.

I'd say my brain's lust scrambled, but it's more than that.

There's something about her I'm drawn to. If I were to guess, it's her scars.

Closed, healed wounds.

Symbols of strength.

Character.

I've spent my life trusting my gut.

Right more times than wrong.

In all things that matter, I trust her.

Like Leo.

If she burns me, I'll have one more scar to blend with the mix.

She succeeds with my trousers and releases me.

Pride flashes in her determined eyes.

Her thumb slides over my crown, but I reach for her, lifting her, and cup her jaw.

"You don't have to do this. I'm not angry."

If she's with me, I need her to want it. To want me.

She dips her head. I glimpse a flicker of green, and then her lips cover mine.

I could lose myself in her kiss. Her tongue toys with mine, teasing, pulling me with her.

It's been a fucked day. The shittiest. Yet her kiss feels like the heavens have opened.

All too soon, she slides from my lap, kneeling on the floor.

I lift my hips, helping her tug my trousers and briefs down.

Once again, she takes me in her hand.

My head tilts back, eyes rolling in my head as her tongue flattens against my base, and she licks my shaft.

"Holy fuck."

She smiles through glossy, wet lips, then bends to take me.

Her hold is loose, and my fingers cover hers, tightening her grip, showing her what I like.

"You fucking me with your mouth has to be one of the hottest things I've ever seen."

There's a pop when she comes off me, but it's her devilish smile that kills all patience.

I grip her wrist.

"Come here."

She stands before me, and I pluck at the button on her denim.

"Where'd you get these?"

"You bought them for me."

They fall to the floor in a pile around her ankles.

"Off with your shirt."

"Do you not like these clothes?"

"I prefer you in dresses or skirts."

I pause, staring up at her. "Why is your top still on?"

"Because yours is. You take off yours, I'll take off mine."

Such a temptress.

I work the buttons on my shirt, gaze locked on her as she lifts her shirt over her head.

I toss my shirt on the nearby chair as she reaches behind her back and unclasps her bra.

I push up from the sofa and step out of my trousers as she does the same.

Her fingers wrap around my shaft. Tighter, like I like it.

"Show me what you want." Her voice is soft.

"You really want to know what I want?"

She gives a quick, short nod. And that tongue… *Fuck.* It licks her lower lip, and I swear I feel it on my tip. So sweet, but that's not what I want.

"I want you to lie back, hands above your head. And I want you to tell me what you want. What feels good to you."

I'm not certain she's breathing. Too much? It's not like I asked to handcuff her.

"You'll be in control. Just—"

"My hands out of the way."

"Right. I'll give you a safe word. You say it, I stop. Whatever it is I'm doing, I stop immediately."

"A safe word."

"That's right."

"What would it be?"

"Angel."

"You want me to lie here. On this sofa?"

"We can go in the bedroom if you like."

"Okay, handsome. Let's try this."

She lies back on the sofa, completely nude except for a slip of panties.

"You are so fucking gorgeous."

She raises her arms over her head, stretching her pert breasts and her flat stomach and the faint tattoo along the side of her ribs.

"And you think I'm handsome?"

Her teeth sink into her lower lip, and she nods with the slightest of smiles.

I kneel before her, much as she did with me, only my legs are on the couch. She bends her knees, making room for me, but I reach around her thighs to clasp her panties and drag them over her hips, down her thighs, over her joined knees, then down her calves, before I send the unwanted scrap of material across the room.

I glimpse the rows of stately shelves with dusty leather-bound books.

"Do you think the Kama Sutra is on one of these shelves?"

"Probably. It doesn't look like anyone has added to the library in some time."

I return her legs to the sofa, one on each side of my thighs, and I lift one slim ankle and press my lips to the side. She shivers.

With her legs wide, I take her in. Her glistening pussy, her red curls, her erect nipples. My fingers stroke my shaft, and her gaze watching me pleasure myself is almost enough to tear me from my mission.

But no, that's not my purpose.

The couch sinks on one side as I crawl over her, hovering above her, lowering my head to suck in one of those pretty nipples, teeth grazing slightly.

She gasps, and I lift my gaze.

"Pain or pleasure?"

"Pleasure."

I mimic the action on her breast. She squirms, and my dick presses against her thigh.

I nibble my way down, stopping to suck on a tattoo, and she twists, hard.

"Pain?"

"Ticklish."

"Hmm. Good to know for later."

She bends an elbow, and I tsk.

"Keep them out of the way. If you don't like something, tell me."

On another day, I'll find out if it's that one area or all her ribs that are ticklish. But for now, I'll focus on my mission.

I cover her mound with my palm, watching to see how she responds to the warmth. Her hips roll against me.

"You like that? Want friction?"

She nods.

I slide a finger into her wet center and press down on her

clit with my thumb. Her knees rise, and her hips buck once again.

She's fucking drenched. Silky smooth. Her body wants me. But her eyes. I read her uncertainty.

Perhaps I'm too tall. Too high above her.

I slide back, grateful I replaced the dainty furniture that had been in this room with oversized leather seating, and replace my fingers with my mouth.

She squirms again.

I lick her seam, lap her. Pulse my fingers inside her.

But where does she respond the best?

Where do her breaths get shallow and rapid? When do her thighs squeeze together like the pleasure is too much?

It's when I lick her sensitive bundle…and so, that's what I do. Taking my time. Working her into a frenzy.

Her toes curl, and if it weren't for my fingers in her channel, I might not be sure, but she comes.

Her closed eyes open, and I kiss the inside of her thigh, hiding my grin.

Fuck, I want her.

I lunge over her, positioning myself at her entrance, ready to thrust.

"Angel."

I pause, uncertain I heard her. My biceps strain from my weight, holding me suspended in the air. Her fingers find my shoulders, pushing me.

Fuck.

I freeze.

She said Angel.

Did I scare her?

I fall back on my knees. My hand grasps my cock. I just need time.

"You stopped." She sounds incredulous.

"Are you okay?"

"I'm sorry."

"Don't be sorry."

"It's just…it all happened so quick. It was perfect, and then you were over me."

"Hey…no worries. I told you. You're in charge. We don't do anything you don't want to do."

Her eyes glisten.

"Are you crying?"

Holy fuck, what did I do?

"Sit back."

I don't understand.

She slaps a hand against the back of the couch.

"Sit."

It's awkward, but I reposition myself, back to the cushion, feet on the floor.

She crawls over me, her thighs cradling mine, and my thumb wipes a tear away.

Her pale teardrop-shaped breasts are inches from me, and I rub my face over her chest. Her fingers tug at my hair, directing me, rubbing my rough jaw over her tender skin.

She lifts up, brushing her wet center over the tip of my cock. We both watch her tease, dragging me through her center.

"What do you want?" It takes all my control to refrain from gripping her hips and slamming her down over me.

"Your dick inside me."

That wasn't the expected response, but fuck if it isn't flaming hot.

My fingers dig into the cushion, controlling my urges.

The green of her irises turns bottomless, and her mouth opens as she lowers onto me.

My head falls back, and pin-prick lights swarm as my periphery darkens.

"Your pussy is so goddamn amazing."

She keeps going. Hot. Wet. Tight.

All on her own.

"That's it."

She lifts, pushing off her lower legs, and a whimper escapes.

Then she slams down on me.

"Fuck."

Her breaths are tight and shallow.

My dick pulses. Stretching her. Filling her.

A tight fit. So fucking good.

The urge to take over is so fucking strong. To claim. To ensure tomorrow she's so sore that with every movement she thinks of me.

And why would I want that?

Because I can't get her out of my head.

What's fair is fair.

She rocks her hips back and forth, rubbing herself over me, bringing herself to the edge. A fucking wondrous sight to behold.

When her head tilts back, gazing up to the heavens, she pulses around me, and I let myself go.

Do I want more? Do I want to flip her onto her back and drive into her like a wild, rutting animal? Yes, but this isn't about me. It's about her.

She collapses against me, and I sit straighter, holding her against my chest, the two of us still joined.

"You listened to me."

The words are so soft. She presses her lips to my chest, and I tighten my hold.

"I'll always listen."

She pulls back. "Was it all right for you?"

I'm still inside her, softening yes, but god, still in her, and she asks that?

I answer her with my lips, and a kiss that sparks another round that's somehow more intense.

CHAPTER 24

NICK

"You have a visitor."

Scarlet stands in the doorway. It's been the two of us in the house since we left Lina at the rehabilitation center four days ago. Heightened security remains at the perimeter.

"The guard waved him in. He's the same man who appeared at the graveside service."

Ah, fuck. Dorian. Post-blackout, we've been crazed, and in my nonworking hours, well, I've had Scarlet. If I'm honest, the nonworking hours have been plentiful. I've operated in a state of denial, locked away on my estate. He must've been dispatched to hound me.

"Where is he?"

"At the front door, I imagine."

"You didn't let him in?"

She wraps her arms around her middle.

"Are you scared of him?" I push up from my desk.

"No." She lifts her chin, defiant. "If he tried anything, I could handle him."

"If he tried to hurt you, I would kill him." She rolls her eyes.

Headstrong.

I step past her, but my gut hollows. I loop an arm around her waist and pull her against me, pressing my lips to hers.

"What's that for?"

"Needed it."

Her arm snakes behind my back in a full embrace, infusing me with a sense of calm. She pats my back. Once. Twice.

"Go on. He's going to think you're not home."

"I'm sure the guard told him I'm here. It's more likely he'll canvass the house in search of an unlocked door."

I reach for her hand, interlocking our fingers, and together, we head to the entryway.

Dorian's face presses against the window to the side of the entry, one hand blocking the sun, his black mop of curls sticking out every which way. The agitation on his face when he sees us is priceless.

I release Scarlet's hand and rub my palm against the curve of her rump. "Care to take a stroll through the garden?"

"Is he dangerous?" She cocks her head, evaluating me.

"He's a nuisance."

I caress her cheek. She's so fucking gorgeous. If said nuisance wasn't at the door, I'd properly enjoy her. "He's American. If he's here, he's on business. Let me get that bit out of the way, and if he lingers or asks for the guesthouse, we'll all dine together."

She presses up on her toes.

Knock. Knock. Pound. Pound.

She grins. "He lacks patience."

"One of many attributes he lacks."

"I'm going to go outside and give Orlando a call."

"You sure that's wise?"

"They know where I am. What harm can come from a call? I'll use my mobile. They already have my number."

I let out a slow, calming breath. I've got a massive amount of security working the perimeter and multiple balls in play. The only intel they can derive is her location, and that's a known fact. "True enough. Don't go far."

"What's too far?"

Pound. Pound. Pound. "Nick! Come on, man."

"The stable." My men patrol the grounds, but I don't want her close to the perimeter. Yes, surveillance monitors the perimeter, but she needs to stay out of range of any snipers.

Dorian stands in the window, arms spread out to his sides.

"Go let him in," Scarlet says.

Once she's out of sight, I turn back to the window. Dorian's hands are on his hips, knickers twisted full circle up his tight anus.

Why is the bloody wanker here? Is it as a friend or syndicate business? The last syndicate member I spoke to was Amir. I've been waiting.

I swing the door open and step outside. "What're you doing here?"

"What kind of welcome is that?"

He pushes past me, scraping his feet on a nonexistent doormat. "You Brits could take a lesson in southern hospitality."

"You're not Southern."

"My mother is. Makes me half Southern."

"You never knew your mother." I close the door behind him, huffing in exasperation.

It's like he's forgotten he shared his muck with me. We were best mates at university. His mother is MIA. His father claims she's an alcoholic, so he wrote her a check and cut her loose. Kept his son, though, if one counts shipping him off to boarding school at the first opportune moment keeping.

I follow him inside. "Are you staying? Should I prep the guesthouse?"

"Why do you always stick me in the guesthouse?"

I scratch an itch on my jaw. "It's nice…."

"You let her stay in the main house."

"I've no desire to shag you."

He chuckles. "Yeah, that's what I thought." He heads down the corridor, and I follow.

"You never said, are you staying—"

"No. I've got a flight out of Heathrow in the morning. Staying the night in London."

"Right, then. To what do I owe the pleasure of your unexpected visit?"

"You haven't been answering your phone."

I knew it. Syndicate business—

"And there's a lot of shit that's happened."

I pause at the entrance of my office. He sinks into a chair.

"Sorry about Lina, by the way."

I've kept that shit out of the news. I close the door and click a button on a panel by the door. The shades drop, closing us in.

"Did you hear from Amir?" He's the only one I've told. Wasn't so much telling him as conducting an inquisition.

"I watch out for you."

My skin tingles with unease, but it's just Dorian. "Do you want a drink?"

"Only if you're pouring the good shit."

I roll my eyes and lift the bottle of scotch.

"What news do you think I've missed?" It's true my priorities have muddled, but I haven't been under a rock.

"Well, let's see. Car bomb outside of Rome."

"Terrorists."

"Explosion in an office building near Atrani."

"Gas line."

"Anton De Luca shot in a drive-by shooting outside his villa."

I don't bother with a response and offer him a crystal highball glass.

"Didn't realize Americans monitored international news so closely."

I sit and swirl my drink.

"Cocksucker." He leans forward, holding the glass but not sipping. "You think we don't know what you're doing? Lupi Grigi have been dropping daily ever since they threatened Scarlet. The woman you're shagging."

"What the fuck do you care?"

"It's against the rules."

"Pardon?"

"Don't give me that shit. Within the syndicate, there's an understanding, and you know it. We don't attack our own."

"Fascinating. Anyone scold Massimo De Luca when his brother had my sister drugged?"

"Your sister is an addict." He drawls it, implying I'm the problem.

"De Luca had her drugged." To get to Leo. There's no benefit to raising that point.

"Huh." He slides the glass onto the coffee table. "Here I thought you were on a rampage to protect the ginger."

That, too.

"There's an investigation into Titan Shipping." I study him to see if this is news to him.

He swirls his drink, unaffected. As expected, he's aware.

"There's blood in the water. Those attacks could be from anyone. And what do you care, Dorian? What does the syndicate care? Did you miss the bits about a blackout, cyberterrorist attacks, and an EMP blast? Isn't that a higher priority?"

He stands and strides to the window, which is now shaded.

"We go way back," he says.

"Yes, we do," I concur. "Is that why you're hopping to London so often? You miss me?"

"You haven't replaced Leo Sullivan."

"Told you. Other shit's been going on." Clearly. But both he and his father have asked.

"Well, I'm here to tell you there's no need." *Fuck me.* Dorian does have an expanding satellite business. Contacts within the CIA. The highest echelons of the US government. If he's the one who discovered Leo's role, why go at it with a covert message?

"Why?"

I eye my mobile sitting on my desk. A handgun is in the drawer below it.

"As your oldest mate, I'm the selected messenger," he says.

"And?"

"You've broken the rules."

"You realize the syndicate or Obsidian or whatever the fuck

you want to call it doesn't own me. You've got nothing on me. Is this your father's doing?"

I can't see his face, but I swear the bastard stiffens.

"A notice went out. You're no longer the selected negotiator for the alliance."

"Under whose order? There hasn't been a meeting." *His fucking father.*

"I'm here as a friend."

"Fucktwat. You just said you're here as a messenger. Is your father trying to pull his seniority prophet bullshit? He wants to lead?"

"If you drop this half-cocked attack on the Lupi Grigi, we'll look the other way."

"Really?"

"You have my word. I'll make it happen."

"My mates won't go against me, no matter what dear old pappy tries to pull. How old is he anyway? Shouldn't he retire? Pass those reins?" His father's age resistance to passing the reigns used to be a sensitive topic, but there's no visible reaction.

"The syndicate is in agreement. There have been discussions." *Fuck his father.* This is utter bullshit.

"Why does your father care about Italian organized crime?"

He sighs like I'm a bore. "It's the rules. Without order, there is chaos."

I sip my bourbon, contemplating his presence. Something's changed. I cut the Lupi Grigi off at the knees two years ago and didn't hear squat. And now he's looking to step in and fill Leo's role. Coordinate sales between countries. Is his father driving this, or is this all about business expansion?

"Are you going to stop?"

Two hundred million gone. If I came clean, the syndicate would drop this. But my companies keep other accounts secure. I don't want to cop to being hacked. And I won't be bullied.

The glare I give Dorian says everything.

"Thought you might say that."

"I said nothing."

"Oh, you spoke." He points two fingers at my eyes. Dorian picks up the glass, swirls it, and knocks it back.

"You should sip that." It's not my best scotch, but he just chugged a couple of grand.

He wipes his mouth with the back of his hand and stands.

"You're going to be targeted."

"By whom?"

"You've broken the rules. An example must be set."

"Are you here as executioner?"

"Messenger. Dammit, Nick. You should listen when I speak. I wish it hadn't come to this." He steps to the door, and I glance back at the drawer in my desk. "Don't bother running. Or holding services. They won't buy it."

He and his father were suspicious of Leo Sullivan's funeral. That's why he showed up that day. Why the suspicion? What do they know? Dorian wouldn't come at me unless his father pushed him.

"Are you ever going to stand up to your father?"

He fumbles with the lock on the door. With a huff, he turns. "You locking me in?"

"What would Caroline think of you now?" I step to the panel and press the button. The shades lift, and the door unlocks.

He shoves his hands into his pockets and swivels. "Mentioning my ex isn't the slam dunk you think it is."

"I liked you better when she was with you."

He steps into the hallway and holds up his hand, his middle finger noticeably higher than the others.

"Perhaps I'll give Caroline a call. Check in." It's a bluff. Haven't talked to her in years.

"Do what you like."

"What do you think she'd say about you selling me out?"

"She never liked you."

"That's punchy. And false." Caroline loved me.

He stops at the front door.

"Why are you doing this?" If I'm reading him right, he's exasperated. "Let the Italians have Scarlet Gagliano. Bringing in Interpol was beyond the pale. None of us welcome an investigation. Call it a day."

"You mean a man up for chief of staff shouldn't be associated with an international drug smuggling operation?" His calculating expression says he's trying to determine my information source. "Yes, I track American politics."

He's on the shortlist to replace the current chief of staff who is reportedly on the outs with the current president.

"There's no connection to me," he insists. "As I told you, I'm here as a messenger. The others, they don't like it."

"By others, you mean your father."

"If you thwart the investigation, that will suffice. The investigation will pull in too many. Multiple stakeholders. If this keeps going, it'll set off more investigations. No one wants it. Just hand her over and call it a day. You made your point. The Italians are permanently weakened. No one's going to fuck with you from here on out. If you want, hand her over to me. I'll take care of it."

"This is where you leave my home."

He turns his back, full of trust I won't blow his brains out.

I watch him carefully, grateful I'm not armed or else it might be quite tempting to shoot.

"You're making a mistake," he warns once again before closing the car door.

I watch as he drives away. Then I step up to the panel and press a button to reach the front gate.

"Let the Rover out, then no one else comes in."

"Yes, sir. Copy."

I flick the screen to activate the image. "Farrow."

"Yes?"

"Were you on when Moore came through?"

"Yes, sir."

"Was he by himself?"

"Yes, sir."

"Have a team do a full sweep of the property."

"You think he smuggled someone in?"

"Unlikely, but possible. There's a camera on the front drive, right?"

"Yes."

"Check the footage."

"Copy."

"When Ash returns, have him come to the house."

"Will do."

I end the call. Scarlet's most likely still in the back. But before I go to her, I return to my office and select a throwaway mobile. I dial a number I've memorized.

Nomad answers on the second ring. "How can I help you?"

When I find Scarlet, she's sitting on a bench, scratching Dog's ear.

"It's a mite nippy. Care to come in?"

I scan the overcast skies. I'm not sure what I expect to see, perhaps a drone. The trouble with antagonizing the syndicate is they have some of the world's most advanced military assets at their disposal. But whatever they choose, they'd lean towards a scenario that evades investigation. Although an aversion to investigations isn't a foolproof deterrent, given they own many investigators and prosecutors.

Clearly, they don't own enough of them. I wonder which of Halston's friends is at risk of getting swept up in an unwanted investigation. There's no doubt the threat stems from Halston.

"What did Dorian want?"

"To be a right prick." I offer her my arm, and she rises, taking it. Dog trots ahead of us. She rests her arm in the crux of mine, and I close a hand over hers. "Did you ever decide, out of all the countries in the world, which one you'd choose to reside?"

Her pace slows, and I slow mine to match.

"Did something happen?"

We're a stone's toss from the back door. Once again, I search the dismal sky. It's the way my mate walked off with languid strides that's irksome. Everything unfolded as he expected. Of that, there's no doubt. So what would he plan to happen next?

"Did he threaten you?"

The green in her eyes matches the shade of a summer aspen.

"You wouldn't be nervous for yourself," she carries on. "He threatened me. Because I'm the witness?"

"He doesn't care that you're the witness."

"What does he care about?"

"World order."

"What does that mean?"

I release her arm and stride to the door. "Let's go inside."

She steps in, and I block Dog from joining us.

"Let him inside," she says. "It feels like rain."

Dog's an outdoor dog, but at the moment, letting the animal in is a simple thing to do for her, so I do. Dog trots past like he knows his way around, hurrying off down the corridor.

Fucking Lina.

I scan the back one more time, close the door, and lock it. Scarlet follows me along the hall to my office. I pick up my everyday mobile and dial.

"Be on high alert. Anything suspicious, call me."

"Copy that. Two patrol teams are out."

"And you're watching the feed?"

"Yes, sir."

"Good. You need me, call this line."

"Copy."

Warmth surrounds my back. and I close my eyes as she envelops me. Her lips press to the back of my shoulders.

"What has you so—"

I flip her around, shutting her up with my mouth. The need to be inside her overwhelms me, pushing everything else to the fringe.

Thank fuck, she's on the same page.

She grinds against me until I've hiked her skirt up and shoved her panties aside. She fumbles with my pants as I finger her. Pleasure shoots through my spine as she grips my cock hard.

"Fuck. I want to be inside you."

"What are you waiting for?"

Time stills for a nanosecond. It's like in an action movie where a droplet of water stills on air. Red strands cascade down, wild and free. Full, lush lips form an *Oh* as I knead her clit, and my finger plunders her velvety smooth pussy. In that second, I'm torn between kneeling before her and devouring her or hiking her up on the wall and plunging inside her sweet heat.

I'm addicted.

The wall wins out, and time ticks on.

God, there is no other place I'd rather be than inside this woman. She's my angel who flies me to heaven.

It's not until we're tangled together on the sofa, panting to catch our breath, clothes askew and half-off, that reality rears in the form of a vibrating mobile.

I stumble off the sofa, pulling my trousers up and buttoning them on the way to answer.

"Yes?" I answer.

Scarlet's gaze follows closely, poised as if expecting the worst.

"Shot a drone down," Farrow says.

"Where?"

"Northwest side of the estate."

"And?"

"Carried some kind of explosives. Possibly ammunition."

"Is there a fire?"

"Damp ground. It's not spreading. I expect authorities will be at the gate before long."

"Don't let them in."

"Might not be a bad thing to let the firefighters—"

"You said the fire's out."

"Explosion was in the air. Ground below is tinged but, yeah—"

"Don't let anyone in. Especially any first responders. You hear me?"

If they expected us to strike the drone, they could have responders on standby.

"Copy. No one enters. We'll say—"

"Shooting off fireworks. Or tell them you don't know what they're going on about. Our closest neighbors grow marijuana beneath the stables. They're not going to call in shit, so don't believe anyone forcing themselves inside. Hear me?"

"Yes, sir. Ash'll be here shortly."

I end the call. Ash took his father to a medical appointment. Bad timing.

Scarlet's repositioned her skirt, but she's topless, and her skin bears fresh marks of possession. Bloody hell. I want to take her again.

"What's going on?"

If I tell her, she'll worry. Blame herself.

"Don't you dare," she demands, standing, her lovely breasts on full display, shoulders arched, with fire in her eyes and her skirt falling from her hips. "Don't play this protection game. Tell me exactly what is going on."

"In exchange for you remaining topless?" Her slender fingers ball into fists. "Wrong thing to say?"

"I'm serious. Is it Massimo?"

"No. That bastard has plenty to worry about." I've been waging a full-out war. He put a hit out on Scarlet. "You aren't top of Massimo's mind. I can promise you that."

"Then what's the problem?"

"It's a different set of colleagues."

"The syndicate?"

"They're right full of themselves. Or at least one of them is."

"Dorian? Your college mate?"

"Boarding school, too." She's losing her patience with me. I can tell from the stern press of her luscious lips. "He stopped by as a messenger."

"They want to kill me?"

"Or me. Seems they're not choosy. I'm going to need to get you to safety."

"Come with me."

"I won't run."

"Why?"

"It's poor strategy."

"I'm not following."

"Because unless I live the rest of my life in a hellhole, they'll find me. And what kind of life is that? Constantly looking over one's shoulder?" I'm an Ivanov. We don't run.

"So, what are you going to do? Fight them? How many of them are there?"

"Eight."

"Not including you? Nine total in the syndicate?"

"Supposed to be an alliance of influencers." I'm speaking more to myself than to her. "The numbers come from those they buy."

"Other mafias?"

"Criminal organizations not too different from your uncle's. On the surface, clean. In the books…"

"Corrupt," she finishes for me. "So you've got a small army of hitmen coming your way?"

"Something like that."

"Dorian plans to kill you? Your friend?"

Can't blame her for asking for confirmation.

"If that's true, why not just kill you when he came here today?"

Because he doesn't really want me dead. He wants to force my hand. Hand over Scarlet. Restore order. It's what the alliance wants. Order over chaos.

"It's me," she answers, sorting it out herself. "He wants you to hand over the witness so the investigation dies. What happens to you…is not of significance."

"You are so bloody brilliant." In this light, her skin shimmers, and those breasts…I haven't spent nearly enough time adoring them.

"How do you know they won't go after Lina?" I lift my gaze from her bare chest to meet a fierceness that if I didn't know her better, I'd mistake for anger. But it's not anger. No, it's concern, caring, and a conviction for righteousness.

"You don't," she says, answering her own question.

And the lass is right. It's only a matter of time before they cave on attacking my estate and shift to forcing my hand through other means.

"I'll go to her. The place she's staying allowed a security presence. They should allow an increase. If they don't, I'll bring her back here."

"She needs to stay there," Scarlet says with a conviction I comprehend.

Lina's in the thick of it with this addiction nonsense.

"Talk with her doctors before you do anything."

I fumble with a desk drawer, searching for a tablet I can connect with a VPN. If I bring Lina back here, I'll just watch her. Hire a round-the-clock watch.

"Listen to me. You think you control everything and everyone, but this is your sister's battle. You can't fight it for her."

It takes me a minute to register what Scarlet's talking about. Of course, she's not the first to share such wisdom.

"Come here. I need you to check out some locations."

"Are these your properties?"

"Technically, no."

Her lashes flutter, and I can't tell if her attention is on the handheld device or me.

"I'm not leaving you."

A dull pain throbs in the recesses of my skull. I should be out the door, on my way to a meeting with my security team, then off to check on Lina, but I'm sinking into the leather sofa and pulling my topless angel onto my lap. I bury my face into the curve of her neck and close my eyes, breathing her in.

"What is this? You're not giving up."

She grasps my chin, pulling me from my haven.

"I've fallen hard for you." She has to see it. "Your safety is paramount. It's everything. *You're* everything." My sternum cracks with the admission. "These people…the men they hire are deadly. Once I deal with them, I'll return to you."

"I'm not leaving you to fight my war."

"After this, I'll let you call the shots for the rest of our lives. But right now, pick your bloody haven. Don't fight me on this. You won't win, love."

CHAPTER 25

NICK

"You're trapped in a den of vipers, mate."

Nomad's voice booms from the speaker. I check the rearview and my side.

"Have you got something for me? Are you risking a trace for the thrill of frisking my balls?"

"I've convened with some experts."

"Members of the intelligence community?"

"You could say that."

Leo? The CIA? An affiliated group? Doesn't matter, I suppose.

"And?" I flick the blinker and pass an elderly driver sitting far too close to the wheel.

"We've got some questions."

"You've got me for ten minutes, tops. Let's hear it."

"Any chance you can smooth things over?"

"Would I have bloody well called you if I could sort it myself?"

"Valid. Obviously, it's a best-case scenario."

"Next?"

"You splinter the alliance."

"As you said, they're vipers."

"Any of them you trust?"

"The one I trusted most served as a messenger." And I would've said Amir, but now he's on a different list.

"Right. So I take it splintering isn't an option because you don't know who you can trust. What are you wanting from us? An escape plan?"

"Not for me. For someone else. And in exchange, I continue as your asset."

Our conversation isn't a long one. Nomad proves his usefulness once again by agreeing to hatch a plan for Scarlet and offering to reach out to some of his local law enforcement contacts about providing additional drive-bys for Lina's rehabilitation center.

When I enter the country house, it's quiet. But Scarlet's here. I received confirmation as I drove through the gate.

She'll leave the country by private jet or boat. Nomad will get back to me on specifics. Given the ease of removing a plane from the sky, I'm leaning toward boat. Although, that's not a surefire winner, given it's conceivable a shipping magnate owns swift boats that hunt with great efficiency. But a boat could get her up the coastline to an area with more options to disappear.

Once again, I wonder which whale the mafia investigation caught in its net. It's someone with pull over a syndicate member. Or hell, maybe an investigation will uncover a lead to a syndicate member.

I find Scarlet in the guest room, sitting on the floor beside an unzipped suitcase.

"Need some help?"

She looks up, and the light glistens in her eyes. "You bought me too many clothes. Won't close." She wipes at her face, fighting emotion.

Fuck this day.

"How's Lina?"

"Better than expected."

I bend down to the floor and tug the zipper. She's right. This suitcase will not close.

"How'd she take the news about the increased security?"

"Didn't fight me on it. Won't make much difference to her." The green in her eyes is so dark, it might be the deepest shade I've seen yet. "Any thoughts on where you want to go?"

"I don't like this."

"I'm not keen on sending you off, but it's the best plan."

"Why?"

With one last look at the suitcase that shall not close, I scoot back on my hands, arse on the ground, until my back's against a wall, and cross one leg over the other. Exhaustion weighs me down, and I need the back support.

"Come now, love. That's pretty clear."

"No, it's not."

"Your darling family has it on good authority you've sold them out, and they'd like nothing better than to riddle your body with bullets. As it turns out, I rather love that body of yours, and I'd like to ensure it remains unscathed."

"It's more than that."

She's not wrong, but—

"You're eliminating my so-called family. That's not why you have a small army patrolling the grounds."

"What makes you think I'm doing any eliminating?"

"I'm not the only one with sources."

"What the hell—Orlando?"

She frowns. "You're not going to kill him, are you?"

"Love, I've no plans to leave England."

"We both know you don't need to."

"I'd like to know more about this source of yours."

"You're not the only one who identified my loyalty issues."

"Your MI6 bloke?"

"Why does it matter?"

"Your mobile was checked. One contact. Are there others?"

"No." She pushes up off the floor and leans against the railing of the bed.

"In Italy?"

"I told you. I didn't trust her. And I don't trust the Englishman. But I am in touch with him."

We're going in circles. I lack the energy for this.

"Scarlet, I need you to trust me. There can't be secrets."

She steps to me, one foot on each side of my thighs, and descends, straddling me. It hurts like blazes so I lift her with a grunt, straighten my legs, and let her settle back down.

Eye-level with me, she says in a tone that brokers no doubt, "You may be the only person in this world I trust."

"What did I do to earn your trust?"

Her gaze lifts to the ceiling, contemplating my question, and she flattens a palm over my heart. "You were patient with me. You love your sister. And you care about my safety."

I fumble with the button on her shirt. "Keeping you safe is rather important to me."

Her shirt splays open, revealing a cream brassiere that's frayed on one edge from repeated wear. I pull her forward until my face rests in the crook of her neck and shoulder, breathing in her light as she embraces me.

"Do you think you could ever trust me?" she asks.

"I'm only alive today because I don't trust anyone." I don't even trust my sister. Oh, I don't think she'd stab me in the back on purpose, but she's an addict. In a moment of weakness, her demons might win.

Scarlet withdraws from our embrace and presses on my shoulders. Our foreheads touch, and she brushes her nose over mine. She's so close I'm a tad cross-eyed taking her in.

"Trust me. I'm an excellent marksman. Skilled in on-the-ground combat moves. Multi-lingual. And I have nothing to lose."

That hurts.

What am I? "If that's true, you'll have no issue leaving."

She pulls back. "I'm not leaving."

"Why?" *Say it.*

"You." With a trick of light, her bright green irises transition and could be mistaken for sky blue.

"Precisely. You have something to lose. We both do."

She places a finger lightly over my lips, and I trap it, kissing her finger, then her palm. My chest cavity floods with warmth and emotion clogs my throat. *No need to get sappy, mate.*

She should go. Every logical fiber in my being screams to force her to safety. But who better to keep her safe than me? Any bastard out there would have to kill me to get to this woman. And they bloody well might.

The smart play would be to let her go. Put an ocean between

her and the vipers. But I've never claimed to be smart when it comes to her.

"Right, then," I say, the words coming out rough. "We'll work together, but there can't be any secrets between us. From here on out, we're a team."

Her eyes light up, relief flooding her features. "And I stay with you."

"God help me, yes." I pull her closer, breathing in her scent. "Though I might be signing both our death warrants."

CHAPTER 26

"If something happened to you…" His eyelids close, and his facial muscles strain. He doesn't need words. I feel what he's saying.

His fingers comb through my hair, and he holds me, inches away. The light brush of his lips across mine raises goose bumps across my skin, and the small hairs rise in the brewing electrical storm.

He seals my mouth with his. What starts as a slow kiss strengthens into a crushing one. Our breaths go from slow to ragged.

He tugs on my hair, pulling me back from him. With his thumb, he dries my lips.

"I can't risk it," he says apologetically, or at least, for him, it's an apology.

"No," I say.

"No?"

"You said you won't run."

"And I won't. I signed up for this. I'll manage it."

"But not alone."

He palms my breast, and his thumb brushes back and forth. I luxuriate in the heat and intimacy.

I won't go so far as to say I love him. I've never been in love, and I need to give myself time to be certain of the emotion. But I care for him. With Willow gone, I care for him more than anyone else in the world.

I don't blame myself for him being in a precarious situation. He approached me. Whatever else is going on, I've no doubt it's thanks to the choices he's made. But I'm not ready to say goodbye to him.

I don't fear death. But I do fear returning to a life without him in it.

"How did you dig yourself into me so quickly?" he asks.

The familiar stretch of a smile crosses his lips.

His thumb pushes my bra lower, and he tweaks my nipple.

My breasts grow heavy and aching. I don't think I've ever been more conscious of my breasts, of my body, of an intensifying need.

"You stay with me, and there's no way out."

"You think they'll win?"

His brows nearly merge. "What? No. The men coming after me will learn lessons. Plural."

His confident smirk is the sexiest I've seen.

"When I say no way out, I mean for you, love. You bind yourself to me, and I'm not letting you go."

"Don't get too cocky," I warn him as I tend to his buttons as he did to mine. "There's always a way out. Have you forgotten my history?"

"If I ever betray you, I deserve your retribution."

He's right. But even as he talks his game, I believe he won't betray me.

I tug at his shirt, and he captures me again, bringing me down until my lips hover over his, so close. Everything bottoms out inside me.

"I never thought I could trust a man. Yet you…" My words trail off as my hips rock of their own accord.

"I'm one lucky bastard."

Hard kisses rain down my throat to my chest. A brief suckling on my exposed nipple makes my entire body twitch. Blood rushes hot and thick through my veins with the desire for him to fill me.

He rolls me onto my back and sits back on his heels. My head lolls, and my eyes snag on the open door as my hips lift, and in one smooth swoop, my clothes are gone.

"The door," I say.

"It's just us."

He says that, but there's a chef, a fire stoker, and more security than I've ever seen, but I don't care much about any of them as I unbuckle his belt and strip him of his clothes.

I grip his erection, and he hisses. Then I'm flat on my back, legs spread, and the burn of his cock fills me, stretching me.

He grasps my hands and holds them over my head, pinning me in place. His hips thrust, and the rug burns my bottom. He stills deep inside me, muscles strained.

"You trust me?"

"Body and soul." It's the truth. My heart squeezes with the

admission, but I don't have time to consider it, because he consumes me.

We writhe like animals on the floor. He brings me close, to the brink, to the point I beg for release, and then he flips us, and he's on his back, with the same intention from earlier, mixed with love.

"Bring yourself there. Use me however you like."

And I do exactly that. It doesn't take me long before my back is arching. My knees scrape against the rug, but fuck if it isn't worth it. He watches every minute of my release.

I run a thumb over his bottom lip and squeeze myself around him, earning a moan.

"What do you want?" He's still hard and deep inside. I need to know what he needs.

He pulls me down and kisses me. It's slow and sensuous, as is the movement of my hips over him.

Then he swats my ass playfully. "Get up."

"Floors not that comfortable, is it?"

He grins. I lift, and we both groan as he slides out of me. But he's up fast, offering me his hand.

He helps me up and spins me around, taking my hands and placing them on the mattress. He knocks my ankle and commands, "Spread your legs, love."

He licks and kisses his way down my spine. His tip nudges my entrance, and I flatten my back, pushing out to meet him. And then he's in, filling me, bringing me to the point of explosion yet again with his fingers and his cock. He reaches around, fondling my breasts, pinching my nipples, his hot mouth on my back, lifting me to ethereal heights. With a grunt and one last, deep thrust, he pulses inside me, and I detonate.

He holds me for long minutes as our breathing regulates, his chest to my back.

"Let's shower," he says into my hair. "We've got work to do."

My muscles are weak, and all I want is to crawl onto the bed. He palms my thigh and nips at my shoulder blade. "If we get on that bed, we'll never get out of it."

An awkward half giggle escapes me because our thoughts are similar.

He groans and pulls me to standing, embracing me fully from behind. His rough beard grazes the side of my face, and he fondles my breast.

"Woman, I believe you've ruined me for all other women."

I curl around in his arms, peering up at him, attempting to ignore his cock, which is miraculously twitching back to life.

His statement makes me inordinately happy.

I push up onto my toes and press my lips to his through my grin, then I reach between us and wrap my fingers around his length.

"Good," I say against his lips. "Because this is mine."

In the shower, I learn he has no issues with my ownership claims.

CHAPTER 27

NICK

UK Terror Threat at Highest Level Since 9/11

The attack in Moscow shows the threat from ISIS is as high as ever

Terrorist attacks "very likely" in the UAE, the foreign office warns

The headlines read like the world is going to hell.

I click on another news article about Turkey tying support for Sweden's entry to NATO to goals on security.

Yeah, right. It's tied to a little something called greed. Everybody wants something.

There's a knock at the door, and I smile because the woman in the doorway brightens everything, even dismal news.

"You've got a visitor."

"Bloody hell. What now?"

"He's at the gate. Don't worry. They followed your rules.

You weren't picking up, so Ash came to the front door. Your guest is peeved. Says he's a business partner."

Interesting. All of those want me dead these days, if I'm to believe the so-called messenger.

One drone sent. Quiet for days. What fresh hell awaits?

I click on a small monitor that's used solely for the security network. I don't use it for anything else as a security protocol.

The dark-haired Asian man in spectacles and a suit chats with the guard. The monitor doesn't offer a crystal-clear view, but it's Jiang Tu.

I ring down to the gate.

"Check the vehicle for explosives. Check under the carriage and trunk. If it's clear, let him in."

In the video, a guard comes around the car with a mirror on a stick to check the undercarriage. The black glass window on the limousine rolls down, and another guard circles the vehicle, peering inside. I can't hear what's being said, but he doesn't appear to be fighting my men. I suppose he wouldn't. He's aware there's a target placed on me.

Now, the question is, did he come here to take me out himself? He's trained in Eastern martial arts.

I open my desk drawer and load my handgun.

"Do you have one for me?"

I stand and tuck the loaded weapon into the back of my trousers and slip on my suit jacket.

At a minimum, there's a driver with Jiang. The retail magnate has an official net worth in excess of a hundred billion, but his unofficial net worth is likely double. If he wanted to end me, he'd hire.

Scarlet stretches her arm out, palm up as if asking for a weapon. I seize her hand and press my lips to her palm.

With her other hand, she fists my cock through my trousers.

"Let's keep this gun safe. Where's another one I can hold on to?"

She is perfection.

"Stop grinning and get me a pistol."

On the monitor screen, the gate opens.

I call down to the gate. "Send a couple of men up with him. And loop a team behind the house, one on the roof."

I step past Scarlet, slapping my palm against her bum as I do, and open a long drawer with a variety of handguns. She's got a wee pistol in her room somewhere, but what's mine is hers.

"Choose your favorite."

She lifts a small Remington and checks the chamber.

"Bullets?"

"The drawer below," I answer, then pause at the door on the way out. "Stay back. Until I understand his purpose, I'd rather he not know you're here."

Jiang resides mostly in Shanghai, but given the government watches over him closely, it's not surprising he'd choose to make a personal visit if he has something valuable to communicate.

She blows me a kiss, and the grin doesn't come off my face as I stand in the front, awaiting Jiang Tu.

The driver opens the door, and Jiang's jet-black, unruly mop appears.

As he exits the vehicle, I ask, "What brings you to my gin joint?"

He looks to the roofline. "You've got protection?"

"Come to kill me?"

He lifts his shaded spectacles and shakes his head. A smile slowly spreads.

"No. But you're the only one on the outs at the moment, and therefore the only one I can trust."

"What do you mean?"

"Can we go in? Logically, I'm aware your property is secure, but I feel exposed."

"The safest place on the property is in the woods. Trees provide cover. Drones can't get through."

"I'm an urban child. I'll take my chances in an architectural structure." He gestures to the stone building. "Nice place."

"You forget I've visited your spot in Singapore." It's not his permanent residence, but it makes my place look like a poverty-stricken hole. "Do you play pool?"

"If I must," he says. "I prefer chess."

"Nah. I want to drink. Chess is a sober man's game."

He follows me through the house to the billiard room.

"You know, Nick, I have a couple of designers in London. I'll send them your way."

"Wallpaper isn't my primary concern at the moment."

When I open the door to the billiard room, I scan the area first, confirm Scarlet isn't in here, and lead him in.

"What's your poison?"

"Sparkling water."

"Seriously?"

"Drink away. I don't care. But I've got thirty minutes and then I'm off to a private tarmac."

I pop the top on a Pellegrino, give it to him with a glass, then sink into the sofa.

"Let's hear it."

"Someone within the alliance is changing course."

"Explain."

"Do you remember the stolen cache of chemical weapons?"

"Did you find out who did it?"

"I've been looking into it since you called me about the theft. Took some digging, but the trail leads back to the syndicate."

"That's not right."

I mentally run through the agendas that coalesced in the syndicate. Finance-minded people, the lot of them. We convened to maintain a modicum of stability and to influence fiscal and regulatory policy as necessary. If a third world war ignites, markets go to shit.

"I have a theory," Jiang says.

"Oh, well…that proves it."

"I flew halfway around the world to discuss this with you. In my car, I have a secure device with the evidence I've gathered."

"Why'd you leave it in the vehicle?"

"Because if I exited with a bag, you'd have held me at gunpoint, and that's not a way to start this conversation."

"Noted."

"What it comes down to is this. What happened in the EU recently? The EMP attack?"

"Right?"

"And the transatlantic wire cutting?"

I nod.

"Tests. Preparing to disable the EU and the United States for an extended period."

"Why?"

"To allow the authoritarian regimes to take over."

"I don't buy it. That's completely against the syndicate's directive."

"No, it's not." He stands and paces back and forth in front of the hearth. "I've thought about this. Think back to Davos. The philosophical discussions between socialism, communism, and democracy."

"We agreed maintaining order would be the best way to ensure stable markets. None of us are pro-Russia or pro-China." I wouldn't have joined the blasted group if they'd been remotely pro-Russia. Fuck Putin and his narcissistic blowhole.

"No. It's not Russia or China."

"North Korea?"

He chuckles.

"Iran?"

"Please. No, I think authoritarian governments may benefit initially from a world adjustment. NATO disbanded. A weak United States government and Western Europe give authoritarian governments free rein for expansion. But I don't think that's the reason for the syndicate's strategic shift."

"All right. Get on with it. What's your theory?"

"I believe a small number with outsized influence are maneuvering the chessboard, and many of our members are too busy to notice."

"Explain that."

"Well, for one, the last several weeks, all of our communications have been about you. By the way, you have a few friends."

"Good to know."

"Geoff Mansueto from the US, Pearson from Canada, and Droga from Ireland. They all refused to approve the initiative to remove you from the syndicate."

"And you?"

"I missed the roll call."

"Why?"

"Because they didn't have the votes to excommunicate you,

and I preferred to keep my stance private." He rests an arm on the mantle. "Xi has requested a meeting."

Right. We all understand Xi will always take priority if Jiang wishes to continue breathing.

"Other than kicking me to the curb, what are they planning?"

"That's the thing. If they were serious about assassinating you, you'd be gone. Someone is looking to get us focused on a noncompliant member while they pull off a plan that would never be met with approval."

"Because an attack like you're describing would kill the markets."

"Precisely. But I believe whoever is behind this has a long-term strategy."

"Does your theory include who these someones are?"

"The Moores. Undoubtedly. Halston led the charge against you. He's constantly messaging. Putting everything in writing. It's unwise. That's another reason I suspect him. He's smarter than that. It's part of his plan."

Bloody bastard.

"Dorian?"

"Absent."

Doesn't mean he doesn't support his father's machinations.

"What about Amir?"

"Amir Nooyi voted to keep you in, but he also voted against influencing the investigation into Titan Shipping. He wants it to proceed."

"They're competitors. He's hoping to swoop in and buy the company at a discounted rate."

"Agree. Amir's allegiance is transparent. His goals are short-term. That's why I don't believe he's the culprit."

After what he did with my sister, he's a rat bastard. His vote is immaterial.

"So, if I'm hearing you correctly, you believe someone has a monstrous plan, and you believe those someones are Halston and Dorian Moore. Two Americans who have a tremendous amount to lose if the United States goes dark. Not to mention, sources claim Dorian is in consideration for the next chief of staff. The current blowhard is at odds with the president, and rumors abound he won't make it through the term. Do I have all that right?"

"Perhaps Dorian cares more about growing Zenith than politics. Think about it. If the world order is disbanded, if existing satellites are wiped and he's prepared, he stands to have customers worldwide with skyrocketing defense budgets."

That's an interesting point. In university, Dorian recoiled at the idea of a political life. But his father harbored hopes for him. If Dorian is in the administration as chief of staff, and there's an attack, martial law could be declared. How would the Moores benefit?

"An attack is imminent. Multiple sources have validated the intel. I believe someone within the syndicate is orchestrating the plan, so I'm coming to you."

"The one member who's clearly not behind it?"

"Precisely."

"What about the others?" His blank expression says he's not following. "Manseuto, Pearson, Droga? Why not go to them? They still have sway."

"Voting against your excommunication means they are less likely to be in on it, but with twisted logic, who knows? They might have voted to keep you in because they wanted to scapegoat you. Until about a month ago, if anyone within our network wanted to buy weapons of any sort, they'd come to you, right?"

"Did someone fill my role?"

"There are obviously arms dealers. No one is offering a syndicate discount. Halston's putting together a replacement."

"And that supports your theory. When we had a master negotiator, we had a handle on the black market. And we're kept abreast of military expenditures from inside sources. If Halston is behind this plan, then he'd want access to the intel?"

He nods. "I might not have it all right. But I'm telling you, my gut says it's one of our own behind this. This business with you might not have been a part of the original plan, but the guilty party is simply playing the hand to their advantage."

"I agree." I'd tell Jiang about the mysterious message alerting me to Leo being a mole, but that would require admitting Leo was a mole.

"There's a limit to what I can do. China reads every email. I get around it, but I'm not immediately available. If you need, I have a couple of squads right here in merry old England. At your disposal. I'll leave you a number."

"I have resources, too."

"Better not rely too heavily on the Interpol chaps. You need someone who isn't bound by laws and directives."

Bloody hell. How does he know about Interpol?

"I've got someone," I say.

"Really? Your name is shit at the moment."

"I've got someone."

"I'm going to be honest with you." Jiang crosses an ankle over his knee. "This one stinks."

"If all your theories are correct, your country comes out ahead if the plan succeeds. Why are you interfering?"

"When I joined the syndicate, I didn't join to make China stronger. Quite the opposite. I don't hold any hope I'll see the regime in China fall in my lifetime, but I can certainly use my leverage to prevent them from growing stronger. If I'd thought the syndicate would veer…" His words trail.

"To quote Thomas Paine, 'No group of men without accountability can be trusted.'"

"It's one or two." He's thoughtful. "And the rest are too oblivious or self-absorbed to notice what's happening beneath their noses."

CHAPTER 28

SCARLET

The scroll at the bottom of the muted screen is both expected and shocking.

With trembling hands, I pick up my mobile. Tiny black spots dot my vision. I focus on deepening my breaths and slowing them down.

It's done.

When I stood over Vincent's lifeless body, calm and tranquility were the dominant emotions. My thoughts ceased, my skin chilled, and I went on autopilot.

Why are my hands shaking? Why am I physically reacting to an event I knew was in progress?

I sit on the floor, back against the bedpost, and press Orlando's name.

One, two, three, four, five rings.

"Scarlet." My name comes out in a growl.

"I saw the news," I say.

"Feeling proud?"

"No."

Yes, I wanted the clan to crumble, but I feel like I might vomit.

"What do you want?" His voice sounds deeper than it has in the past. Angrier, too.

"How are you doing?"

"The lawyers say Papa should work with the prosecutor. You know he won't. He'll die before he testifies against his own. My father will probably die in prison. Titan Shipping is hemorrhaging clients. We may have to fold. We can't sell while it's under investigation. Mama won't leave her bedroom. She asked your mother to leave. If you care, she's not homeless. She's staying with Portofino, an elderly widow who shouldn't be living on her own, so basically she's become a nurse for her. Is this what you wanted?"

My fingers cover my lips. *They kicked Mama out of the Gagliano estate?*

"As if that's not enough, Lupi Grigi members are dying left and right. I'm hearing it's Nick Ivanov's doing. But you know about that, right? Since you're staying with him?" He lets out a deep sigh. "Did you ask him to kill us all? He's hired men that are…they're experts. Bombs. Snipers. Do you have any idea what it's like to be hunted?"

"Actually, yes, I do." Vincent's snarl plays through my mind. He got off on my fear.

"Not like this, you don't. It's like we're all swimming in an ocean, sharks are circling beneath us, and we're treading water, waiting to see which one of us will go down next."

"I suppose," my voice quakes, and I swallow to smooth it, "waiting to see if your husband is in the mood to ignore you or beat you is similar. It's not the exact same, no, but it's not fun to wonder each evening if it'll be a game of dodge the heavy object or be a punching bag."

"One man hurt you, so you go after all of us?"

"The system hurt me. I'm dismantling the system."

"It's a good thing Willow isn't alive to see this. She'd be heartbroken."

The line clicks. He ended the call. I'm hit with an awareness that I likely won't hear from Orlando for some time. He's a minor, and as such, shouldn't be swept up in the investigation. I can only hope that over time he'll forgive me, but maybe he won't. My actions have completely disrupted the life he planned for himself.

A loud explosion rocks me off my feet.

The floors tremble.

I push up off the floor.

Lights flicker.

I rush out into the hall.

"Scarlet!"

Nick's shout echoes through the hall.

I run as fast as I can toward his office.

"Scarlet!"

He comes into view, a gun in hand, eyes wide.

"Drone attack," he says, turning, gun pointed skyward.

What in the hell? This is Massimo's revenge. He'll kill us all.

"Come on. Let's get you to the safe room."

"No." I halt, and he snaps his fingers.

"Now!"

"You're not sticking me in a room. They're here for me."

"This isn't the bloody Grigi."

He grabs my wrist and tugs. I stumble but follow behind, matching his pace.

"You're wrong."

"No, I'm not."

It's the second time in one day a man has growled at me.

"Who is it then?" I snap.

"My old mates."

"They have military drones?"

"They have everything."

Another explosion rocks the house.

The place shakes again.

"What are they bombing?" My voice comes out high and thin.

"Nothing. We're shooting them out of the sky."

Another explosion rocks the house, and I grip Nick's arm. In Italy, violence came with warnings: a look, a word, a chance to make amends. But this? This is chaos. English chaos. Technology. Death from above that gives no chance to negotiate, no opportunity to surrender.

"Won't the police come?" I try to sound calm, but my heart pounds so hard I taste copper on my tongue. The tremors in my hands spread until my whole body shakes. I've faced death before, but never like this—never so impersonal, so mechanical.

"I'm sure they're on their way."

Nick's voice is steady, controlled, but his grip on my wrist tightens. For the first time since Vincent, real fear—not anxiety, not worry, but pure terror—floods my system. Because if Nick is afraid...

Dio mi salvi. God save us; we might not survive this night.

CHAPTER 29

NICK

"You've got company," Ash says into my ear.

"No shit," I mumble, my hand wrapped around Scarlet's wrist like she's hanging off a cliff.

"I mean, a person's here. Says he's here to help."

"Who?"

At the back door, I scan the skies, cursing the day I bought into setting up the garage with the safe room.

It's a new build, they said.

Fuck them all.

"Should I let him in?" Ash asks.

"Who?"

"Amir Nooyi."

Scarlet steps forward, and my arm shoots across her chest. "Stay," I mouth.

I press against my ear. "Is he armed?"

"No."

Amir is a slight man who probably hires someone to cut tough steak for him. He'd hire someone to wipe his arse if it were socially acceptable to do so.

His timing is curious.

"Let him in, but keep men on him. Can't be trusted."

A plume of smoke twists around to the right of relatively clear skies.

"Letting him in. Tommy says drones are sorted."

"Copy," I respond.

I lower my arm and head down the path to the garage, motioning for Scarlet to follow.

"Why do you think they hit in daylight?" Ash asks.

"Testing. Are the authorities on their way?"

"Not yet. It was loud, but I'd bet our neighbors are clueless about what happened."

True. Drone attack won't be the first thing a country person assumes. Emergency response could be part of what they're testing.

"Can you tell what they were targeting?" I ask.

"Based on course direction, looks like the main house."

I reach the garage, open the door, go to the empty bay, lift a mat, and push a button. The trap door glides open.

"Stay with Amir at the entrance of the house. I'll be there momentarily."

"Copy."

"Ash? Whoever you send with Amir, make sure it's someone you trust. Someone who's never met Amir before."

"Copy."

Ash is a good man. He's been on my team for years and

oversees the security staff. He's more of a tech guy, but he's punchy when needed.

"What is this?" Scarlet asks, staring down the stairs.

"Where you're going to be until I come and get you."

"You're not locking me—"

"You can open it from inside anytime you want. But they can't get inside without these babies." I point at my eyes.

I smack my palm against her bum. "Go on."

"You're full of rubbish! They're after me. Not you."

"Scarlet…I don't have the time to debate."

"Absolutely not."

"Scarlet. Go." *Christ, I am losing all patience.*

"No."

She stands there, hands balled in fists, chin up, shoulders back, a portrait of bloody defiance.

"You should breathe. You have blood vessels that look like they might pop," she says, sweet as a lark.

Dear Lord, give me strength.

"I'm skilled. Give me guns. I'll fight with you," she says.

"No."

"Why not? I'm fully—"

"Because I fucking love you, you stubborn, bullheaded woman."

She goes utterly still, the way she does when she's processing something unexpected. Her fingers uncurl from those tight fists, and bloody hell if she doesn't look like I've just handed her the crown jewels rather than shouted at her.

"You love me?"

"Is it that fucking difficult to believe? You are the most resilient woman I've ever met, and I think about you every second of the day. You've gotten under my skin and in my head.

Every molecule and atom craves nearness with you, and if something happened to you…" *Christ.* "It won't come to fruition. Do you understand me? I understand you've trained, but dear heart, we are going up against men who hire men who have spent decades training in situations you can't fathom. I love that you can hold your own in hand-to-hand combat and that your aim is spiffy, but let's not get carried away that you can tackle a small army."

"What about you? You haven't trained—"

"Yes, I bloody well have. And these are my men. I'm not sending them out there unless I'm by their side. Let me figure out what we're dealing with and the best course to take. When I retrieve you, you can have your wicked way with me. Whatever revenge you like, I'm game for. But for now, get your arse to safety. Capisce?"

"Nick."

I press a hand to my ear to hear Ash, all the while glowering at the stubborn love of my life.

"Amir's getting restless."

"What's he doing?"

"Looking around for you. We're following him, but he won't do as asked."

"Get," I demand. *Beg.*

It's those green eyes. So full of passion, life, and grit that do me in. I pull her to me, far more roughly than advisable, and smash my lips to hers. Her fingers curl over the ridge of my hard cock, because yes, all it takes is for her lips to touch mine and my body reacts.

With great reluctance, I break the kiss.

"I'll be waiting."

I squeeze her bum and her eyes smile, but she's too worried

for anything else. The trap door closes over her, and I breathe a little easier.

"I'm on my way," I tell Ash.

"Where the hell have you been?" Amir says, charging through the yard, security on his tail.

"What the bloody hell? You wouldn't wait where told?"

"Are you testing bombs?"

"That's brilliant. I'm testing bombs on my own fucking land."

He has the wisdom to cow. Fuckwad.

"Fair enough. Is it the mafia striking your home?"

"Why are you here?"

"Do you not trust me?"

"Oh, you mean, do I trust the man who told my high-as-a-fucking-kite sister to blow him?"

He runs his hand through his hair and blows out a breath. My security men back up, giving us space. Roger waves a pair of binoculars, a reminder that we're out in the bloody open.

"She told you about that, did she?"

I should punch the fucker.

"I thought she wouldn't remember."

"That's worse, you fucktwat."

"Come now. Be fair. We both mess around. Your sister's not exactly—"

"Think twice before you finish that sentence."

He holds his hand up in defense.

"I… Does this mean you're not going to help me acquire Titan?"

Bloody hell.

"Maybe not the best day to ask," he says, slinking back.

"Amir, go. Leave. Now." I look to the pasture. "You drove today, I see. No chopper?"

"I was in the area." He looks deflated. "Wanted to check up on Lina." He wiggles his mobile. The screen's black, but he says, "Hit one of the rags. The place you've got her is notorious for celebrity leaks."

"She's not a celebrity."

"Eh, she kind of is. The influencer variety, but...the goings on of the lower levels sustains these rags."

"And you read them?"

"Only one or two. It's not a website. It's like alerts. And if you click, you read the article. If you subscribe to one—"

I hold up my hand. *Bloody Christ. Like I want to hear.*

While I'd like to beat him to a pulp and toss him on his arse, I can't exactly afford to turn my back on a member of the syndicate.

"For the record, I support you. What you're doing with the Italians helps me."

"I'm well aware." That's why I read him in in the first place. Of course, that was before the fuck played Lina.

His gaze goes to the sky, then he clocks the men standing around us.

"You can't stay here," he says to me. "You should go...until things calm down."

Curious advice. "What do you know?"

Unexpected visits from two alliance members on the day drones drop bombs... What the bloody hell are they up to?

"Unless you've got a safe house on the premises, you should go. Take a holiday," Amir says.

"Who's behind the attacks? Is it Halston?"

"It's not a singular person. You've awakened the hive."

"Is that a warning?"

He doesn't answer, only shoves his hands into his trouser pockets.

"Amir Nooyi's driver got out of his car and is stretching. He's carrying," Ash says in my ear. "Not unexpected, but letting you know. I've got two crews coming in for tonight. One crew searching the grounds. Woods are not cleared. Repeat. Do not go near the woods."

"You've got a safe room, right?" The fucktwat sounds concerned.

I hold my fingers over my ear, making a show of listening to the piece in my ear, and scan the grounds, pausing on the garage. If she comes out, I will bloody lose it on her.

"I'm gonna go. If you need me, you know how to reach me," Amir says.

"We'll drive up with you," I say.

As we cross through the house, he looks around like he's looking for someone, but he knows Lina isn't here. Is he searching for Scarlet?

We're quiet as we climb into the back of the Rover. Roger takes shotgun and continues scanning the sky with his binoculars.

"How'd they attack you?" Amir asks, breaking the silence.

"They didn't share details on the group chat?"

"Drones," he says, more to himself.

I'm shooting daggers at the traitor when he catches on and scratches his jaw. "Yeah, I knew. I came here to warn you. Mite late. When I told you I'd recommend you leave, I had reasons. There's a bounty on your head. Best to go. If not, bunker up."

How much is my life worth? I don't bother asking Amir.

I trust Ash with my life, but best to minimize the chance that word gets to my security team. I'll search it up later.

Back at the security gate, I leave the team with Ash, taking the vehicle around to the garage.

When the garage door closes, I wait for facial recognition to do its magic and open the hold. The wise move would be to leave her secured. But it's quiet outside. She can't hear crap in the hold. I can show her the security system, so at least she'll have eyes on the property.

My thoughts keep circling to Amir. He might be right. Authorities never came out to investigate. And the bounty bit… that'll send some nefarious talents our way. Now it's me and Scarlet. Racking up to a profitable payday.

"Scarlet," I call, descending the stairs.

Four different gun bags and ammunition boxes are stacked on the coffee table. Two unzipped backpacks rest beside the table, half full of ammunition.

Scarlet comes around from the other room holding two Kevlar vests.

"Ivanov, you know how to stock a safe room. A man after my heart, you are."

"About time you noticed," I say, taking in the sight of her—my scarlet angel turned warrior. She's transformed the safe room into a tactical command center with military precision. Pride and something deeper, something that feels dangerously like love, swells in my chest.

She grins, all fire and steel, reminding me exactly why I fell for her. This woman doesn't need saving—she needs a partner. And bloody hell if that isn't exactly what I plan to be.

CHAPTER 30

SCARLET

"About time you noticed."

I smile like a loon right back at him.

My deep satisfied breaths while preparing to fight for our lives borders on irrational, but it's what he does to me. It's the way he looks at me. With Nick, I feel taller and stronger. With him, I've got a partner.

He curls his index finger, gesturing for me to step closer. He's leaving the choice to me, but his heated gaze leaves no doubt about what he wants.

A sudden flush of warmth spreads. His eyes sparkle. He senses it. Or maybe he sees how aroused I am.

"What's the plan?" I half expect him to stalk towards me, lift my skirt, rip my panties, and bury himself in me. Or maybe that's what I want. It's doubtful he'll actually flip me over the sofa. "Are we staying here?"

There's a bedroom and a bunk room. The loaded pantry holds enough canned food to last months, if not years.

"I considered it," he says, still eyeing me like he's keen to get naughty.

"But?"

"My gut says we're best off getting the jump on things."

The practicality of his assessment disappoints, but I packed the bags because I expected as much. Not to mention the explosions.

"Where will we go?"

He jumps on a computer that's sitting on a desk. It's a desktop with a dial-up I can hear. "How do you feel about Greece?"

"It's lovely," I say.

"I've got a fortified home in Naxos. Off the radar. Owned by a shell company. Tracing it to me would be time-consuming, although not impossible. But if you're game, that's where I'm leaning. I like the idea of lying about naked with you."

"There are lots of places in the world where that can be arranged. You're thinking the Greek mafia might offer us protection?"

"Protection? No." His fingers tap away on keys. I can only presume he's on a secure connection. "There's a bounty on my head."

"On yours?"

"Yep. How much do you think my life is worth?" He holds an arm out and I step into his embrace.

"To me? The value is immeasurable." I don't like where he's going with this. My nails scrape his scalp, and his tousled hair fills the gaps between my fingers. He buries his face in my belly.

The computer screen is unlike any I've seen. It's old, with cursors that blink and green lettering on a black background.

The blinking cursor taps out numbers.

250,000,000

"What is that? Euros?"

He lifts his head to take in the screen. "That's a tidy sum. Yes, I'd say we're going to need to lie low. The Greeks might not be on the syndicate payroll, but there will be some of them who won't care what they're hunting with a fee of that size."

"Who offered that?" The Grigi's funds are tied up.

"The syndicate."

"But they're your friends."

"Some are, some aren't."

"They don't operate as a family?"

"Possibly a lone wolf." *The Prophet.*

"All right, so what do we do?"

He pauses and looks up at me. There's concern in his eyes. The same concern I've too frequently seen these past few days.

"It's best if you stay back, love. This bounty, it's a game changer."

"I don't understand why someone would want you dead. Is it loyalty to the Grigi?"

"They don't give a fuck about one mafia clan. Might be a lesson. Might be a piece in a bigger play. The dynamics within the syndicate are shifting." He taps away. "If it was only you…if the goal was to have a witness eliminated, the exorbitant bounty would be on your head."

He taps away on the keyboard.

A response comes back in the same eerie green text.

Nightfall.

"What does that mean?"

"It means we have some time to kill."

He pulls me onto his lap, and I rock into him as he kisses me, hands tangled in my hair, holding me exactly where he wants me.

Trained assassins the world over are hunting the man in my arms. Morning may not come, but I can't find it in myself to care.

His teeth drag across my lower lip, lazily, as if forever is ours. The rough pads of his fingers press between the gaps in my shirt. I gasp. Tingling and pleasure flood my body.

Our movements are at once frantic and slow. His beard scrapes the tender skin of my neck and jaw. We fumble with clothes, then slow to appreciate touch.

"Fuck, I want you," he mumbles against my lips and throat. His hips thrust upwards, and I ride the ridge of his cock.

The chair jerks, and he's up. His belt flaps in the air, undone by my fingers, as are his trousers. With one shove, his trousers drop to his ankles, and he sits back on the chair. He grasps my hips and pulls me forward, shoves my skirt and panties down, and plants his face against me, lapping at my seam.

"Oh. That feels so good."

My fingers tousle his hair.

His tongue splits me. His large hands knead my ass. I shift my leg, giving him more room, and he takes the hint, closing his mouth around the sensitized bundle of nerves that have been aroused since he entered the safe space. He thrusts a finger inside me, roughly sucking my clit. It's perfect, but it's not what I need.

I push his head away. He looks up at me, lips glistening with my arousal, questioning.

"I want you. Inside me."

"I'm yours," he says, a smirk playing across his lips as his hand fists his cock.

"'Bout time you realized that."

He snorts but grows quite serious as I straddle him, position myself over him, and sink down. We both gasp as I stretch around him. I slow, appreciating the fullness, then push up on my toes, riding him as he embraces me, my mouth over his, tasting myself as our bodies seek heaven.

We're both half undone, shirts asunder, bottoms pushed to the floor, muscles straining, and it's divine. My muscles tighten as I bring myself closer to release, closer to the edge, and then I'm up, feet in the air. He's still inside me as he grabs a pillow from the sofa, tosses it on the floor, and places me on it. His knees are bent, and I'm sitting up, spread eagle on the cushion. The angled position allows him to thrust hard.

It's almost too much. The pillow slides, but he grips it and pulls me back to him. I put my arms behind me, thrusting my hips to meet his punishing pace.

"God damn it, you feel so good. I don't want this to end."

I reach for him, and he catches my wrist and presses his lips into my palm. And then we're kissing. I truly love kissing him.

Tremors wind their way down my sides, over my ribs as my toes curl. He grunts into my mouth as he chases his release.

We cling to each other through our muscle spasms. Long after our breathing has calmed, we're still clinging to each other. He grimaces as he shifts and slips out of me.

I pull back, and we're so close the tips of our noses touch. I rub my cheek against his, letting the coarse strands of his beard scrape my now-tender skin.

"I love you." I back up again so I can see his eyes, needing him to know. He's not leaving without me. If someone wants to kill him, they'll have to kill me first. "I love you," I say again, looking him in the eye, ensuring he hears me.

"I love you so much, my angel. It's terrifying."

He crushes me to him. My chin rests on his shoulder as we sit there, awkwardly wrapped around each other. A moment of peace before the flight.

"What about Lina?"

"The bounty isn't on her head. Those who are after us will go for the reward. The Grigi is too fractured at the moment to seek that kind of revenge."

I pull back, seeking his eyes, the window to his fears. "What?"

"The syndicate won't go after my family while I'm alive. If it's Halston behind this, he knows me well enough to know I'd go after his son if he went after my sister."

"Dorian?"

He gives a curt nod.

"Would you?"

"Nah. He's my mate…but the old bastard will assume I'll think like him. As long as we're alive, Lina should be safe."

"But you still have security with her?"

"Around the clock. When you're playing a chess game, you plan several moves ahead, but you also cover your tracks lest you face an unanticipated move."

His chest rises under a deep inhale, and he claps my ass.

"Up you go."

An hour later, we're showered, dressed, fed, and packed. We're both wearing Kevlar, loaded down with backpacks and totes.

I look to the stairs, but he pushes a button, and a panel that looks like a mesh speaker slides to the side, revealing a plate of black glass.

Nick stands in front of it, and the screen lights up. Then a concealed door opens to a black void.

"What's that?"

"A tunnel. Runs through the back side of the property. Opens up just beyond the property line in the woods. If anyone's watching via satellite, they won't see us leave."

"Nice."

He grins and holds out his arm for me to proceed. "Come on, love. We've got a good fifteen-minute walk ahead of us."

"And then?"

"Ash had his daughter drop off a vehicle for us." The door closes behind us, and floor lights shine along a narrow, winding tunnel. The air is damp, and condensation coats the stone walls.

"Clever."

"It's a backup plan we engineered years ago. A smart man always has multiple exit points from his home. I built this tunnel before moving in."

"You always anticipate the worst?"

"Car bombs breed distrust." He's referring to his parents.

"So it seems. You trust Ash?"

"With my life. And his daughter has no association with me. She's not on anyone's radar. The spot she left the car is on a small dirt road with tree cover."

"And I assume few know about this tunnel?"

"Ash, me, you, a cleaner Ash hired…and the men who built it. But those men built it before the owner was known, and they're from a firm that specializes in privacy."

"Tell me about this place in Greece. Does it have tunnels, too?"

"Bulletproof glass and a safe room, but no tunnel to the sea. But the sea is right out the door."

"I didn't pack a suit. Think it will be safe for us to go into town?"

"You won't need a suit, love."

We grin at each other. In that second, all is right in the world. In a life of fleeting moments, this is one I will treasure.

The ground trembles beneath our feet.

Our steps slow. Nick places a palm on the stone.

The trembling intensifies.

Smoke clouds the light further down the tunnel.

"Run!"

Nick's shout jolts me into action.

"As fast as you can, run!"

CHAPTER 31

NICK

Blackness falls.

The fiery heat singes skin and burns eyes.

The floor lights flicker and die.

Fuck no.

Scarlet screams. Terrified.

I slam into her back.

She stumbles.

I hold her to me, still. Gathering my wits.

It's so dark I can't see my hand in front of my face.

The ground trembles with a muted boom.

"What's happening?" Scarlet asks.

She's winded. I hear it in her gasp and feel it in the expansion of her rib cage.

I fumble with my mobile. The screen light allows me to see my hand, Scarlet's shape, and perspiration along her temple.

For security reasons, the mobile has no apps. But surely there's a light. Please let there be a light.

I find it. The bright white beam lights the floor and the sides of the tunnel.

"Drop a bag."

"I can carry it. Let's go."

"I'll get it."

"No, I can—"

She tugs on a shoulder strap.

"Scarlet, it's not the weight. It's bulky. You can carry the weight, there's no doubt, but you move faster without the bulk."

Stubborn, she grips the strap of my backpack. I grab the handles of the tote she's holding, ignoring her efforts.

"Hold the mobile. Light the way."

With both my hands full of tote straps, I can't very well hold a mobile. She grabs the device and holds it in front. At first, her steps follow a quick pace. I match her, sticking close.

A minute passes, and she shifts into a steady jog.

"Will the fire come through the tunnel?"

"Shouldn't. There's nothing for it to catch. I'm more worried about it stealing our oxygen."

We're getting further away from what I presume is the garage and what must have been a massive explosion.

Is this Nooyi? Was his visit to scope the place out and figure out if my safe house was located somewhere other than the main house? Or did they bomb every building on the property?

The heat increases.

My eyes are watering. The smoke must be getting thick.

A cloudy haze wafts through the cylindrical white light.

"How much further?"

I don't have the answer. I should've marked the tunnel with distance measurements.

"If you need to slow—"

"One foot in front of the other," she says.

Is that what she's been saying to herself for this last stretch?

My lungs are on fire, as is my throat. Sweat drenches my shirt.

Thank god I didn't install a gas line in the tunnel.

"What's that?" Scarlet asks.

I slow, scanning past her. Ready to drop the bags and grab a gun.

The gaping black morphs into a shape. A door.

Thank the gods. We made it.

Scarlet reaches for the latch.

"No!"

She bends over, sucking in air through an open mouth.

The bright white light blinds me, and I hold a hand out, using the tote to block the glare.

"What's wrong?"

The light flits away from my face, and I lower the bag.

"It's too hot in here. The metal may burn your hand."

I drop the bags, unzip one, and locate a pair of leather gloves. They're too small, and I tug at them.

Scarlet snatches them from me and hands me the mobile. The gloves are loose on her, but she can get them on all her fingers.

I pull out my handgun and stand by the door, holding the light so she can unlock the latch. The electricity must be completely gone, as the exit door is on manual overdrive, which is the emergency backup.

She pushes the door open, and a gust of cold, fresh air blows in.

"Wait."

I step past her, gun raised, and scan the surroundings.

The desolate dirt road, lit only by the moon, evokes calm. A night owl screeches. The shadows of the forests blend into an eerie haze.

Down the road, a rusted vehicle sits on the side of the road. Leaves scatter over the hood, and there's one broken limb over the roof, giving it the look of an abandoned vehicle. The dilapidated SUV is all part of the plan hatched years ago. The thought was that if someone wandered by the road, they wouldn't give the clunker a second thought.

I kick the door open wider, and Scarlet grabs the totes, one in each hand. I close the door behind us, careful to kick some leaves back over the disturbed earth in front of the door.

Satisfied it's not immediately noticeable that the door of the long-forgotten shack has been opened, I catch up with Scarlet, lifting one bag from her hand.

A single distant siren pierces the night air.

The explosions were massive. This time, we caught the attention of the authorities.

Scarlet helps me load the back with our bags. She gets into the front passenger seat, but I bend on my knees, checking the undercarriage. It's dark, and the mobile light isn't adequate.

"Get out," I tell her.

"Is something wrong?"

"Being safe, love. Step back over by that tree. The big oak."

I wait until she does as I say, then clamber in and crank the engine.

I've never wished for a remote to start a vehicle more

than this moment. All my daily vehicles start remotely. Typical of electrics. But this gem is of the archaic combustion variety.

The car cranks. I wait a beat.

Press on the accelerator. The engine guns, but with my foot on the brake, the wheels spin.

The passenger door opens.

"Are you kidding me?" she shouts. "You thought it would explode, so you had me sit outside?"

"You can get in now."

"What in the ever-loving hell? You're keen to have me witness your death?"

Her door slams shut, and I check the rearview, then click the headlights on.

The road up ahead is quiet.

I roll down the window with a crank.

"Don't do that," she says.

"Do what? Plan a getaway in a vintage vehicle because we're on the same page. I'm bloody well regretting this bit of the plan."

"Assume your life is worth more than mine."

What is she going on about?

"Get my backpack," I say, focusing on matters of import. "Pull out the mobile. The flip phone."

She bends over the seat, arse in the air, and seconds later, she's got it.

"Buckle up," I tell her, clocking the rear.

It's completely dark behind us.

Up ahead, the dirt road meets a paved one. That's where we turn.

The headlights cast an eerie glow over the narrow road,

with scraggly limbs haunting the space like skeletons cast about on Hallow's Eve.

I repeat a number to Scarlet.

"Should I message them?"

"Call," I tell her. "That phone doesn't message."

"You value artifacts more than I realized."

"Cute," I snap.

"It's ringing. What do I say?"

"Give it here."

I hold the mobile to my ear.

Up ahead, red and blue lights blitz the night sky, and a chorus of distant sirens override the crickets.

"Charlie's Pub," a male voice answers.

"I might have the wrong number," I say. "I'm looking for an old mate, goes by Nomad."

"Nick. Are you safe?"

"In transit."

"Injured?"

"No."

"Alone?"

"The witness is with me."

I side-eye Scarlet. I give her a wink, although, in the darkness, I'm not sure she sees.

I reach the fork in the road and slow. Three emergency vehicles whiz by, lights on.

I turn in the opposite direction on the paved road.

"I'm working on getting a satellite view of your property, but reports coming in are of multiple explosions."

"Haven't seen it myself. We were underground. Any reports on what caused the explosions?"

"Nothing's coming over the wire."

Fuck. Ash and my men. I hope the bombs didn't take out the guardhouse.

In the rearview, two pinprick white lights appear.

"Where are you headed?" Nomad asks.

"Away. Gonna let things calm down."

"Copy that."

The two pinprick lights grow into circles.

"Any reports of drones in the area?"

"It's the running theory."

The circles become disks.

"I think I've got company."

"A drone?"

"A charging vehicle."

Flashing lights and sirens appear up ahead.

The car behind slows.

One, two, three, four emergency vehicles speed by.

"An extraction team is on the ready," Nomad says.

"Scarlet, open the back again. Find my regular mobile. It's an iPhone. The one from the tunnel. Check that it's on."

"Where are you?"

"Can you trace my iPhone?"

"Your common business line?"

"That's the one."

"Yes."

The lights behind me blur the entire rearview and side views.

"Do it," I say.

"Do you trust the authorities? I can get them to you in minutes."

"No."

A shot rings through the air.

"Are you being shot at?"

"Appears so."

Scarlet's arse shoots up.

"Get down!"

Her feet pass my head as she hits the back.

"Keep the line open," Nomad says.

The back glass of the vehicle shatters.

I floor the clunker, and the engine roars.

A burst of air to my left snatches my attention.

Scarlet hangs out the window.

Bloody hell.

Shots ring out.

Bam. Bam. Bam.

The lights behind us swerve to the woods.

Scarlet pulls herself back in.

Bloody hell! "You fucking do that again and I will shoot you myself!"

She sits by the back passenger door, cranking the window up.

"Did you see that? I got the wheels. Do you know what a hard shot that is?" She sounds bloody fucking happy.

"I'll show you a hard shot. What the hell were you thinking?"

"Mate?"

"Yes." I glimpse the rearview. No cars. I turn right onto a major thoroughfare.

"From here on out, you're Falcon. Understood?" Nomad's question lessens my desire to throttle my partner.

"A bird?" I grumble. Yes, he mentioned the bloody code name earlier, but it's not my favorite.

Scarlet clambers over the seat, bopping me in the head with her foot.

"Sorry," she mouths.

"And I've got Angel with me," I say.

"Hold for extraction instructions," he says.

"Are we being routed to a location of your choosing?"

"There's a team waiting to consult with you."

"Consult. Not sure about that one, mate."

"You've got a swarm of assassins hunting you and a two hundred and fifty-million-dollar bounty posted on your head. Are you really bloody taking the piss?"

"Not at all, wayward Nomad. Send those instructions on to Angel."

"She on the line?"

Scarlet's eyes are pitch-black, but with better lighting, I'd be under a glower warning.

"She's watching over us all." I wink.

She snatches the mobile, unamused.

"Angel here."

CHAPTER 32

"Hello again, love."

"Who is this?"

I expected Ash, but the accent's off. It's also familiar.

"No time for Falcon to brief you."

Nick looks at me and mouths the word, "Interpol." Ah, so this is Tristan. The man who gathered my statement and information on the Lupi Grigi.

Out loud, he adds, "Safety precaution. No names…never know who's listening, but also, there are programs with voice recognition searching for keywords."

Ah. And right now, there's no telling how many hackers are running algorithms and malware trying to pinpoint our location.

"We're here to help," Tristan says. "After all, you're going to be a great help to us. The boards are alight tonight with talk of you two."

"Boards?"

"Dark web communities," an unfamiliar voice says on the speakerphone.

Tristan adds, "Someone found the vehicle you dusted. Occupants alive and talking. The world's taking it as confirmation both of you are still sharing our oxygen."

"Did they get tags?"

"Yes, they did," Tristan says. "Which means we need to get you into another vehicle, pronto."

"I've got alternate tags in the back, but—"

"Your vehicle's recognizable. Rust and dents. Tags won't do it, mate."

Nick's jaw flexes in irritation.

"We've located a garage. You'll drive in and we'll have a team waiting for a swap. The mobile you're on doesn't have internet, right?"

"Correct."

"The one we're tracking you on won't do. Too many have the number."

"I suppose that's true," Nick says.

"You've got some of the best black hats out there tracing you. Extreme caution. Angel, is your mobile turned on?"

"Yes," I answer, scanning the back for the bag that I packed it in.

"Throw it out the window," Tristan says.

I thrust myself over the bench seat to dig out the device. Nick's palm flattens on my bottom.

"What're you doing?" I ask.

"Making sure you're stable."

To be fair, we're moving well past safe traveling speeds.

"What about you, Falcon? Anything that should be tossed? I'm about to send you an address, but before I do, let's button you up."

"I've got spares in a bag. Inactive. Never used."

"Brilliant. Angel, dear, light up a spare. We're going to pinpoint a location, and you're going to head in that direction. Bear in mind that if you see a tail, you'll need to correct course. We're going to bring you closer to the city proper. Will limit what they'll do…at least the rational ones. Copy?"

"Copy," Nick barks.

I locate the spare mobile, and while I wait for it to activate, Nick asks, "This team of yours? By chance, is there a Texan on it?"

Seconds go by without an answer.

"The second mobile's on. Shall I message the number you called?" I ask, unsure what Nick's on about, but staying focused even if he can't.

"No. Let's zigzag," Tristan says and repeats a number for me to use.

I message the number and receive a link in return. When I click the link, there's a blue dot on a map.

"Once we've got you, tech won't be an issue," Tristan says. "Looks like you're about twenty minutes out. Could be longer if you get waylaid."

"I asked about who is on this team getting us in because I need to ascertain the trust level," Nick says.

"You've got my word. We're getting you out of there." My breathing slows, and all my attention focuses on the mobile in my hand. The voice is distinctly American. And it's one I've heard before. But it can't be.

The car spins slightly…or it's my head that's off-kilter.

"Gone a split second and you land the world's biggest bounty for your neck," the American says.

"Who—" I begin.

"Let's wait till we're secure," Tristan says.

"Aye, aye," Nick answers.

On autopilot, I hold the mobile up with the map expanded so Nick can see. He takes the device from me and holds it in front of him with one hand, the other on the wheel, studying the grid.

A concrete weight settles over me. My hands grow clammy.

"As you get closer to the city, there will be more cameras and, apparently, about a thousand lookie-loos searching the cams for you. So much for security of the CCTV. I'm going to send you a direct route without cams. If you stray at all, you'll show up," a different English voice says, definitely not American and not Tristan.

"You know, it's the tags most of those cams will be clocking. You said you had a spare?" Tristan asks.

"I do," Nick says.

"Pull over and switch that out. It might buy you some distance. Lots of intersections are wider feed, but out where you are, systems are more limited."

Nick whips the car to the side, onto a dirt road that leads to what looks to be a private residence.

Nick hops out. I've got a handgun in one hand and a mobile in the other. The hum of voices from the team filters through the speaker.

Nick buried Leo and Willow. He buried them. Their deaths made the daily. But the man on the speaker sounds so much like… But it can't be, can it? It wouldn't make sense.

It's just wishful thinking; my brain playing tricks on me. That's it. The stress of bombs and people coming at us. The adrenaline. It's screwing with me. Or…Nick lied. Now's not the time to lose focus.

The car door slamming startles me.

Gravel spins beneath the tires, and we lurch forward.

"Is there a closer location for a switch?" Nick asks.

"We have size requirements," Tristan says. "And we want to do this in a concealed environment."

"Satellites," Nick says, more to himself.

I want to ask what he's talking about, but I'm stunned. And it's not useful to ask questions at the moment.

If Leo is alive, is Willow? If they're both alive, who are these people?

Headlights appear up ahead. The closer we get to the city, headlights will be everywhere.

Headlights from the rear flash in the side view.

"All right. You've got company," Tristan says.

I squeeze the handle on my pistol and undo my safety belt.

"They're going to accompany you on your way. Act as a diversion if needed and defense. Two more in transit. Word from tech is there are no bites. You're in the wind."

"Don't curse us, mate."

"What's that?"

"Save the shite for after we're safe. Keep the bad luck at bay."

"Are you superstitious?" Tristan asks.

"Must be. Once upon a time, he refused to let a groom show up at his wedding without a best man, all because of luck," the American says.

"Yeah, come to think of it, I better toss some salt because that one didn't work out so well for me," Nick says.

My head spinning, I close my eyes and lean my head back against the headrest. It's definitely Leo.

Nick's hand covers mine, the one holding the mobile. I jerk away and tighten my grip on the handgun. My jaw locks as bile rises in my throat. All the sorrow for Willow and Leo—weeks of grief—they weren't just wasted. They were a lie. The metal of the gun grows slick against my palm as my fingers clench. I've never wanted to shoot someone I once loved quite this badly.

CHAPTER 33

I reach for Scarlet's hand, and she yanks it back, out of reach. She's figured it out. Either she recognizes Leo's voice on the line or she's pieced it together from the conversation. Either way, she's pissed.

I can't worry about it right now. We're entering the CCTV zone. Hackers across the world are probably watching like it's live TV.

Two hundred and fifty million euros. The blokes after me don't care why they want me dead. I could be the pope and I'd still have a swarm of fortune hunters after me for a payday that size.

I should've never brought Scarlet with me. But what was my option? To leave her behind in the tunnel and hope they didn't find her? Hope she didn't asphyxiate from the smoke?

My jaw clenches as guilt lashes at my back, striking through to my innards in a way mortal weapons can't. I should've set her up off the grid. Let her live where no one would ever find her, where she could start anew.

"Falcon. Heads-up."

Headlights blink behind us.

"Vehicle coming in hot."

"Christ." I scan the rearview. "Did they get us on CCTV?"

"Unsure. Slow down so the detail behind you can intercept."

The voice on the line isn't Tristan, and it's not Leo. It's a reminder I'm working with strangers.

"Kairi. Get the team to see what's out there. We need to know the exposure."

"On it," a feminine voice says back.

How many people are on this call?

The vehicle zips past us. Shots blast.

It's a pistol. Or a rifle.

I slow, watching as an oncoming car crashes into a parked car. Sparks fly through the darkness, lighting up my rearview.

"Head down." I reach for her on instinct, grasping the back of her head and pushing down.

Shots rip through the air, but from what I can tell, none hit the vehicle.

"Two miles out," a male voice says.

"Friendlies approaching. Going to follow you in. Got that, Falcon?"

"Aye, aye."

A distant high-pitched sound wails.

"Ah, Christ. Have we got the bobbies on us?"

"Someone probably called about shots fired."

"Kairi, don't we—"

"She's off with the crew. I'm on it," another male voice says. "Confirmed. Reports of shots fired. No details."

The street has transitioned to a business thoroughfare. Gone are the trees and driveways and the occasional home. The speed limit has also dropped, but we're blowing through it.

"Map's going to tell you to turn right at George Street. Turn left. Loop it."

I look at the map, studying the grid and the blue dot that's our goal destination. Now's not the time to be pulling some CIA training bullshit. "If you're looking to throw a tail—"

"Do as we say," yet another male voice says.

I grit my teeth. If this goes sideways, I'll know sooner than later to cut links to these blokes.

I'd rather have my team with me, but as it is, I don't know how many of them survived the bombing.

I turn left.

A mass explosion lights the sky.

Shockwaves rock the car.

"Follow the car in front of you. Keep up. Floor it. We're getting you out of there before first responders arrive."

I press the accelerator to the mat, noting the detail behind me is gone.

The car in front of me roars into a parking garage. Scarlet has one hand on the dash and one on the seat.

"Get down."

"Again?"

"Might be an ambush."

The engine rumbles noticeably louder inside the concrete garage.

Four armed men are standing about, one with a lit fag, relaxed enough to take a puff.

The car in front squeals to a stop, and I whip into a spot one over.

I don't recognize any of these men.

"Grab your bags," a voice on the phone says. "Disconnect this call. Get in the van. It's outfitted. We'll connect once you're inside."

The line goes silent.

The men I followed open the back doors and grab our gear.

"Come on," one of them says.

Scarlet's green eyes are clouded with uncertainty, and it's exactly how I feel. But it doesn't appear we have any other choice. We'll play along and hope to land on a safe square.

Four of us hustle down concrete stairs and through a metal door. In my last glance over my shoulder, I see the other men staying behind, the one still puffing on the fag. But they're armed.

"The others, what are they waiting for?" I ask.

"They'll slow down any tails."

"Are any on us?"

"Not that we know of, but it's only the amateurs we'll clock."

Right.

Up ahead, there's a Mercedes van. Glossy black exterior with black tinted windows. A door opens and Scarlet steps up first.

What the bloody hell is she thinking?

I push past her, but it's safe. It's a fucking control station. Screens, computers, seats. In the back, it looks like a small sofa bed.

"Welcome aboard," a woman dressed in black says. "I'm Sophia. Up there, behind the wheel, is Fisher."

The totes hit the floor of the van with a thud.

"There's ammunition in there," I say. *Who the bloody hell tosses a gun bag around?*

The driver says something to the man outside and the door slams shut.

"Sit down. Once we're a block away, we'll connect and plan."

"Who do you work for?" I ask as the van's headlights flick on.

"Sit," Sophia says. "We're doing a favor for Arrow." Her gaze locks on Scarlet, and she extends her hand like she's at a networking event. "You're Scarlet, right?"

"Yes."

"What's Arrow?" Scarlet asks, looking as wary as I feel.

"It's a group that takes on projects governments won't touch." Sophia sits in a chair that's bolted onto the floor in front of a computer terminal. The tinted windows dim the passing streetlights. The driver appears to be having a conversation.

The man's either off his rocker or he's got an earpiece. He's got a rough, full beard and an American accent.

I'd guessed Leo was CIA. Who are these bastards? The private group Tristan referenced?

"Might as well sit. Our plan is to drive south," Sophia says.

"South?"

"From the channel, we'll get you out via ship or air. You can sit back. The vehicle's bulletproof. You're safe. For now."

She taps on some keys, and a screen comes to life.

"You doing a bloody Zoom call?" We'd had a shit ton of folks on the call earlier.

"No. I'm pulling up a few forums to track things. We'll loop back with the team in a minute once I get us up and running. We've got an escape plan to hatch, right?" She smiles with the nonchalance of a woman who does this shit for a living.

Scarlet sits as far away from me as she can in the vehicle. She doesn't want to be here, but she, like me, has no choice.

There's a sliding door in front of the sofa bed in the back. "Do you mind… Can we have a minute?" I ask.

"If you pull that door closed, we won't hear you."

I don't buy for a second that anything we say won't be listened to, but at least we'll have the semblance of privacy. If Scarlet will let me explain.

She pushes past the narrow center alley.

That's good. Maybe with all the stress of getting shot at and such, she'll overlook the bit about Leo being alive.

I fumble with the door, closing us in. It seals us shut, and I knock a finger against it. It might really be soundproof.

"How could you?"

So much for letting it pass.

"Is Willow alive, too?"

Thanks to raising Lina, I know a helluva a lot better than to tell a woman to pipe down, but it would be lovely if she'd lower her voice.

"I believe so," I answer honestly, voice hushed.

"And you let me cry? You let me believe she died. You orchestrated a funeral." She's practically screaming.

"I'm not actually certain this is soundproof, love."

"Don't *love* me!"

"I'm going to sit back here." It's awkward moving around. It's a high-ceilinged van, but it's not tall enough for my frame.

I squeeze into the back corner and study the black leather upholstery, collecting my thoughts. *Lead with the important bits.*

"I care about Leo. But I should mention, Leo isn't his real name." She opens her mouth. "I don't know what it is." I hold her gaze so she hears me. "I could find out if I wished. But I don't. And that's because it's best if I never know his identity. It's best if all those around him—and Willow—believe they are dead and, most importantly, behave as if they are dead."

"Why?"

"Leo was an arms dealer. Let's just say if word got out he was a leak that double-crossed some of the most dangerous men—and governments—in the world, he wouldn't live long. Neither, quite possibly, would his family members."

"Why take Willow?"

That's an uncomfortable point. "In the end, he didn't have a choice. And…with what you know of your family…would she have been safe in your world?"

Those green eyes turn thoughtful, taking me in.

"Are you planning to do the same? Fake your death?"

"It's not an option for me," I remind her. "Lina is my family. I can't… She needs me."

"Does she? You are such a control freak. You control every-thing. Fake deaths. I bet you decided to send Willow to her fake grave, didn't you?"

"You're yelling, lo—" I wisely bite back the word.

"Has it ever occurred to you that your sister would be better off without you always standing there to clean up her messes? You probably fucked her up by solving every single problem she's ever had. If she needs money, you give it to her. By controlling every bit of her life—and by the way, filling every need is a form of control—you never let her come into her own. You clipped her wings before she flew."

Yes. I cocked it up. That's why I owe her.

Scarlet leans down. She's holding her head in her hands, and a curtain of silky red covers her.

When she rises, tears streak her face. "I'm sorry. That was harsh. I'm just…"

"We've had a rough day, what with being bombed and shot at."

She sniffles. She looks more vulnerable than I've ever seen her appear, and while she's breathtakingly beautiful, the vulnerability is an illusion. She is the personification of enduring strength.

"I won't leave Lina. As you said, I owe her. Faking a death isn't an option for me. I'm going to regroup and fight. I'm an Ivanov. We don't hide." I swallow and force out what I know to be the truth, but one I don't want to face. "But you…it's not the same for you."

I am a selfish bastard. She's right about that. If I weren't, she'd be off the grid.

"Were you ever going to tell me about Willow?"

"No." The Aspen green transitions to a terrifying, warmongering green. "I gave my word to keep Leo and Willow safe."

"Who did you give this word to? Leo?"

"No. Myself."

"You let me mourn her, and you knew… The entire time, you knew."

"You'd have done the same if our situations had been reversed."

She wipes her cheeks. I think she hears me.

"She's safe?"

"You can ask. These blokes out there…I believe they're

protecting her. Or, hell, maybe they work for them now. I'm…
Leo deceived me right up until the end."

"But you trust them?"

"Fair question," I admit. "Jury's out. My gut trusts Leo. He's
with them. He also lied to me for years. He could've put me
under and didn't. Left a lifeline if I needed it. I'm choosing to
trust him. There are loads of others attempting to off the two of
us right now, so there's not much of a choice."

CHAPTER 34

I love him, but do I trust him?

After Vincent, I trusted no one. I couldn't fathom trusting anyone who bought into organized crime. It went beyond the crime, of course. How could a trustworthy person believe a man had the right to beat his wife? How could a family member sell a daughter in a business transaction, not caring for her well-being? Greed is a sin for a reason. Greed leads people down amoral paths. And one thing motivates those in organized crime—greed.

But here is a man with more money than he can spend in his lifetime. His motivation has evolved. He wants his sister to be healthy. He wants her to beat a demon that he's furious he can't fight for her.

To me, he has been kind. I trusted him to touch me, the first man since Vincent. And right or wrong, while the rational part of my mind says he wasn't honest with me, I believe him when he says he did what I would've done in his shoes, because Willow was the one person in my world I trusted. She hated our family's culture and what we represented as much as I did. I would've done anything to assure her safety.

My soul trusts the man before me. But still...he lied to me.

There's a rap at the closed door.

"Hate to interrupt, but we need to convene. We've got to finalize plans before we exit England."

"Aye. Give us one more minute." Nick's index finger brushes against my cheek. "Your eyes have softened. An Aspen once more."

How poetic.

"You okay?"

"You let me mourn her." That's the bit I can't let go.

"She's still dead to you. Don't you see that?"

"No. She's alive." Can't he see that?

"Is it so different? If she's living in another country, and you can't see her ever again, or if she's up on a cloud, living in heaven?"

I close my eyes. It's different. Christ, it's different.

"Can you forgive me?"

"Forgive, yes. Forget, no. From here on out, I need honesty. Absolute. You're the one who said no secrets."

"Quite right. Understood."

We stare at each other, gazes hard and firm, only his burns through my skin and singes my heart.

I nod confirmation. *We'll be all right.*

He pulls me to him, pressing my face to his, one hand on the back of my head and one on my back.

"I love you, Angel."

Just as quickly, he releases me and slides the door open.

The man behind the computer says, "If you're ready, I'm going to dial in the team. Won't mess with video, as we're in transit."

The driver of the van remains focused, intent on the road.

"Works for us," Nick says.

Nick's strong hand nestles into my lower back, and the warmth eases the tension. He guides me to a bench that runs against the side of the van opposite Sophia and her computer terminal.

There's a click and then Sophia says, "I've got Angel and Falcon here. Ready to chat."

"Excellent. Angel, let's talk about your options first."

"Why me?"

"Sounds like a plan," Nick says, practically speaking over me.

I shoot Nick a glare, but he unwisely ignores it.

"Angel, this is Nomad. I'd like to move you into protective custody."

Ah, Tristan. "What about Falcon?"

"If he's game to walk away from his businesses—"

"No," Nick says. "I'm not running from this. But it's a good idea for Angel, temporarily, if you can do it right. Like we discussed."

"No," I interject. "And don't talk over me as if I'm not a human being with value."

"You have a tremendous value, and that's why we're talking about you first. You are the highest priority," Nick argues, the blue in his eyes icier than I've ever seen. It's like we didn't just have an argument and make up.

"All right, you two. Good to see you've bonded. But we've

got some decisions coming up. Need to decide which direction this caravan is going and need to get teams in place to assist."

I recognize that American twang. "Leo?"

"Hi there, Angel. Might as well tell you now that we heard your discussion. You're in a souped-up van. You'll do well to keep that in mind later tonight. As for the one you were asking about, she's good, and I want to keep her that way, so from here on out, if you ever need a name for me, it's Saint. Alrighty?"

"She's nodding," Sophia says. "There's no video. You've got to use your voice."

"When this is over, can I—"

"Let's discuss that later. You two open to new identities? It would mean leaving everything you know behind," Leo says.

"What're you offering? Greater protection than what Nomad can provide? Or are you speaking for his employer?" I ask, careful to avoid saying the word Interpol lest that be a keyword that's being searched.

"Until the case, WITSEC is an option."

"WITSEC isn't the worst idea," Nick says.

"I never imagined an ending where I floated to the clouds unscathed." I scowl at Nick. "Let's stop circling. I'm staying with you."

Nick's jaw clenches.

He blinks. Rubs his eyes.

"I dare you to fight me on this."

His face softens. Resigned. "If I believed these blokes could keep you safer than I can, I'd fight you tooth and nail on that, love. As it is, there are too many parties here. I'll keep you safe."

"And you won't consider a new start? There's a lot of shit going down, Falcon. We could use you. You and I both know you don't give a flying fuck about your businesses." Leo's voice comes through strong.

"Disappearing's not an option," Nick says.

"Copy that," another male American voice says. "So, what's the plan? Where do you want to go? You're tracking due west at the moment."

"And to confirm," Leo breaks in, "it's the two of you? You're not separating? Safest option—"

"We're not separating," I cut Leo off and meet Nick's gaze dead on.

"Seems I can't shake my angel," he says, the corners of his lips tugging upwards.

"No, you can't."

CHAPTER 35

NICK

"You heard her, mate. Seems you're not the only lucky bastard."

"The world's changed mighty fast," my old friend says.

"Yeah. I'd say so." I smash my lips against Scarlet's and grin. I have half a mind to carry her into the back space and give the ops team an earful, but there's no time.

"Where are you thinking?" Leo asks.

"My original plan had been to holiday until the controversy died down. I've got a spot that shouldn't be connected to me."

"How secure on that are you? The explosions launched a press field day. Lots of speculation. BBC has a quote from the Ministry of Defense saying terrorism has not been ruled out. A zealous reporter dug up your Russian connections."

A female voice weighs in. "So far, we've only picked that up on fringe media sites."

"Only a matter of time before the networks validate it," I say.

"I didn't hide my ancestry. My last name's Ivanov, for Christ's sake. It's the Russian equivalent of Smith. What's the casualty count? Have they said?"

"Hasn't been released. If terrorism is on the table, they'll be tight-lipped as long as they can," the woman says.

"And what did you say your name is?" It's unnerving to speak into a void and not know all the participants. These damn Americans are bloody informal.

"Kairi. I'm with Arrow Tactical. Everyone on the line except for Nomad is with Arrow Tactical."

"Right. And you are the US government?"

"No," Kairi says. "We're a private operations group. We take on odd jobs. And right now, helping you is one of those jobs."

"And you're helping me...why exactly?"

"You helped us," Tristan says.

"I owe you for my life. And my wife," Leo pipes in.

"And now you're a goddamn rhyming poet," I say.

He snorts.

"All right. Can you let me know if Ash made it?"

"We're working on our end to get an accounting," Tristan answers. "Have a man attempting to gain access to your estate, but it's a bit of a mess with the bobbies at the moment."

"I'm sure it is. Can you get me a secure line? I have some calls to make."

"That van's about as untraceable as you'll get," a woman says.

"Who are you thinking you want to reach out to?" Leo asks. "Based on the intel I'm gathering, I don't trust any of your so-called friends."

I do love a man with brutal honesty. "Need to get my PR team spinning as it seems my reputation's at stake."

"Glorious as it is," Leo says.

"Piss off," I say, but I'm grinning. I've missed the bloke.

The guy sitting at the computer types away.

"I also want to reach out to Ash. See if he—"

"His mobile's out," Leo says. "We've tried to track it. It's not on. Area hospital hasn't released names yet."

Shite. His mobile went up in the blast. Please let Ash not have gone up with it.

"Okay," Leo says. "I'm getting reminded we need to strategize. Do you have a definitive location, or are you planning on contacting someone first? I wasn't shitting you. I don't think you can trust any of the folks I'm privy to."

"Nooyi's likely working against me." I tug on my jaw, thinking it through. "He stopped by and was looking about.... I think he was a designated scout."

"He knows your property. You think he stopped by to collect intel on security levels?"

"They could've gotten that from a satellite, no?" One of Dorian's companies has over 6,000 operating satellites in the sky. "Of course, tough with the trees to get a good satellite view. It's one of the reasons I bought the estate. I'm thinking he was scouting for a safe room location. Don't trust the bastard. I trust Jiang Tu."

"Interesting you say that," Tristan says.

"Why?"

"We suspect Xi is currently detaining him. It's not public knowledge yet, but he hasn't been seen since returning to Shanghai."

"Damn."

"If he follows the course of Xiao Jianhua, we may not hear from him for months."

"And when he returns, he won't be the same Jiang," I say. Even if he seems the same, he couldn't be trusted.

"Droga? Do you trust him?" Leo asks. "We could leverage his resources to ship you off from Ireland."

"Jiang said he voted for me. He's solid."

"What about Mansueto?" Leo asks.

"Track what his news network says about me. If it's blowing up with conspiracy rubbish, that'd be a no."

"I'll set my team on it," a woman, I believe Kairi, says. "He's got strong connections to the social media sites, too, right?"

"He has influence," I answer. It's all about influence. "The one I want to call is Dorian."

"And you know you can't trust him," Leo says.

"Eh, true enough. If I stand a chance of getting that bounty on my head dropped, it's Dorian. We have history."

"All right," Kairi says. "Use one of the lines Sophia gives you. You can count on Moore tracing the call. We'll run it to Iceland."

"Brilliant."

"Do you have his number?"

"Got it memorized in this head of mine, right along with eighties song lyrics."

Scarlet rubs my back, comforting me. She's a mite younger. Does she like old eighties tunes? Are they familiar to her? We have so much to learn about each other.

Sophia passes me a handset. The rectangular device connects to a base with a cord.

"Type the number in using the keyboard. I'll handle connecting the call."

I do as she says and wait. It takes a minute or two and a lot of clicks and clacks cross the line. I wink at Scarlet as I wait, letting her know there's no cause for concern. This is a negotiation.

The Moore men are bright ones. They'll be expecting my call. Or at least, Dorian will. Halston prefers to be a step removed. I've not got a good read on the man, and it never bothered me before, as his son is my mate. A lesson for the future. Know everyone with power well.

"This is Moore."

"Hello, mate."

"Nick?"

"How many Brits call you in a day?"

"Thank god. You survived. I was concerned."

"Were you now?"

Silence falls on the line.

"How disappointed are you to learn they won't be pulling my body from the rubble?"

"I didn't want this. I'm not responsible, if that's why you're calling."

"Who is?"

"Someone you pissed off."

"Who?"

"I honestly don't know."

"You threatened me."

"The rules stand, whether we like them or not. That's what I said. I didn't plan to wipe you out."

"The rules? Are you really going on about that?"

"You became a problem. For many, it seems."

"Rules of the syndicate," I say, mocking the man who used to be my mate.

"Death solves all problems. No man, no problem."

"Quoting Stalin now? That's an interesting philosophical evolution."

"It's not my philosophy. It's the philosophy of whoever put the bounty on your head. Whoever you pissed off most recently. I'm guessing you're not in Iceland."

"No, Dorian ol' boy, I'm not."

"Who are you working with?"

"Nope. This is my dime. Did your father place the bounty? Are you protecting him? That Stalin bit is classic Halston."

"My father isn't behind this. He also doesn't need my protection."

"Quite right. Then I need you to relay a message to him."

"Why not call him directly? You believe I did this, not him."

"We both know your father's a stubborn arse. And a narcissistic one, to boot."

"We all possess a degree of narcissism."

"Defensive. No doubt you've evolved, mate. University Dorian could've written a dissertation on the negative effects of narcissism on logic and decision making."

Static crosses the line. I lean closer to the computer screen to confirm he hasn't ended the call.

"What do you want, Nick?"

"Well, I'd like to share oxygen a mite longer. And I've no desire to spend the rest of my days in a secluded, third-world location deprived of takeaway."

"I'm not the one who placed the hit. And for the last time, I don't know who did."

"Well, that's unfortunate. Because you've opened Pandora's box, friend."

"Me?"

"Unless that bounty is rescinded, I'll administer a kill order of my own. And I'd like to remind you you're in the United States. I have access to greedy bastards who purchased powerful weapons perfectly primed to earn a quick five hundred mil."

"You're off on this. We want you out. Not dead. You broke the rules. But we're not the ones looking to terminate you."

"Your father didn't consider he's going up against an opponent with means, did he? In this situation, you nor anyone else knows where I am. And I've got a tracker on your father. And people watching your compound. How confident does your father feel he can escape without the locusts descending?"

"That's your game? Assuming you've got the right guy, the two of you outbid each other until someone somewhere figures out a way to claim the bounty?"

"It's a ludicrous situation, no? Talk with your father. Call this off. I'll back out. My excommunication will be my punishment for breaking the jacked rules."

"And the Lupi Grigi?"

"Oh, that arrow's flown, friend. They're good and fucked."

"If you sacrifice the witness—"

"No. She stays out of this."

"You give her up, you can stay in the syndicate. I'll fight for you."

"Let me be clear. If anything happens to Scarlet, I will scorch the entire state of Colorado and every yacht on the sea in my hunt to personally decapitate you, your father, and every single member of our so-called alliance. Capisce?"

"I'll devise a more diplomatic manner of communicating your agreement to exit the syndicate."

"As you wish."

"For the last time, though, I do not know who placed that bounty. If you go after my father," he half laughs, "you'll only be creating more enemies."

"Oh, I trust you to sort it."

"You're crazier than my father ever was." His huff piques my interest. "How do I get in touch with you?"

"If the bid isn't withdrawn within an hour, I post my counter bid."

"Let's say a syndicate member is responsible for this order. What does he get if he rescinds?"

"To live, Dorian. Your father gets to live."

━━

"Are you really going to walk away?" Leo asks after I end my call with Dorian.

"The syndicate is one alliance. An idea born from a place of naïve idealism. It's gone belly up."

I wink at Scarlet, and her soft smile shoots a fission of warmth through my chest cavity. This mess will wrap up shortly, and I'll be wrapped up in my angel soon.

"I disagree," Leo says.

"What's that, mate?" Yeah, I unleash the argumentative tone, but the bastard left my world, literally. Weasel's got shite to say about it.

"Falcon, this is Jack Sullivan."

"Ah, nice of you to announce yourself."

"I got looped in when you were on the call with Moore."

I've met Jack a handful of times over the last decade. As the CEO of a weapons manufacturer and the brother of an innovative weapons developer, our paths were bound to cross. "There are reasons we need you to maintain contact with as many syndicate members as possible."

"You might've missed the bit where relations have soured."

"We're aware. If you're open to it, I'd like to brief you on the intel we've been gathering."

"I'm not a useful asset anymore, Jack. Not with these blokes."

"That depends on how you play your hand," Jack says. "Just hear me out."

"I'm not teaming up with the bloody CIA. MI6. Any of the devious scoundrels."

A light touch on my forearm grounds me and pulls me away from the crowded van and electrical displays. Evergreen irises claim me. For seconds, she becomes all I see.

"Listen to them," she mouths.

This woman. She's full of beauty and surprises. Although I should've expected she'd see the intelligence blokes as friendlies.

"What've you got?" My gut tells me I'll regret this maneuver.

"We have reason to suspect an attack is imminent on the United States and its allies."

"That's broad." It's also what Jiang Tu went on about, and I have every reason to believe he's right.

"Great Britain and European Union at a minimum. Canada, Mexico, and India likely. Australia and New Zealand, less likely. Russia or China are likely the culprits. One. Or both."

"You think they're aiming to instigate the Third World War?" I shake my head because they are so off. "If such an effort by China or Russia were underway, we would've picked up on it. Even without the syndicate, my Russian sources would've notified me."

"The intel is inconclusive. Might not be the effort of a nation-state," Tristan says.

I laugh out loud. "You think the syndicate is attempting to start World War III? You are way off, mates." People get these visions of an evil syndicate, but that's not what we were about. Business and legal interests were our primary concerns, and peacetime aids our interests.

"I've studied the intel," Leo says. "And communications we've captured between syndicate members."

"You hacked them?" I ask. "You Americans listening to everyone?" I grit my teeth, but once again, Scarlet's hand on mine calms me right down.

"Like you, we have sources," Jack says as calmly as if we're sitting at a fine-dining establishment.

"All right. Let's hear it. I concur. Something's off. What've you got?"

"Attacks against the electrical facilities in the United States have increased."

"Terrorgram. Been going on for years." That really hasn't been on my radar.

"Right," Leo says. "By white supremacists and alt-right groups fostered mostly through Terrorgram messaging. The alliance member leading those fringe groups is Halston Moore."

"Correction. He has influence because he donates to their causes. He's not sharing a pint with them." Yes, I believe he's the one wanting to kill me, but he's been a two-sideser for decades.

"Agree. But the nature of the attacks has changed in the last month. They more resemble exploratory scouting, and there's the occasional hit to a transponder, as if capability and impact are being measured."

I roll my eyes because there are at least a dozen parties interested in taking out the US electrical grid. "Is that all you've got?"

"The gas line cutting exploratory," Leo adds.

"That is Russia." We're all clear on that point.

"The Russian fishing boats made us think that," Leo says, "but we dug deeper, and the boats are owned by a shell company."

"Likely Russian," I say.

The Russians would theoretically love to damage the connection to the West.

"And there's the theft of the gas from North Korea."

"You determined who did it?"

"Private entity. And we've located a lab that's producing more of it, following the same formula."

"Why haven't you shut them down?"

"Can't get to them. They're in China."

"And they've got Jiang isolated, so the alliance is blind at the moment."

"There's buzz that an EMP attack is imminent, too," Kairi adds.

"You think it's all going to happen at the same time? An electrical grid attack, an EMP attack, and chemical warfare?" I shake my head and cross my arms. I don't trust Halston, but Bedrock Advisory, his pride and joy, controls funds worth trillions. Halston protects his self-interests. "That would destroy the financial markets. No one in the syndicate would take part. It goes against our mandate."

"My theory," Leo says, "is that the syndicate has fractured, and the mandate and vision have changed."

"The syndicate has fractured, I'll grant you, but you're talking about a massive ideology change." I'm fighting Leo just like I fought Jiang Tu.

Of course, even as I say it, Dorian quoting Stalin comes back to me...and then another quote from Stalin which would appeal to Halston: "The only real power comes out of a long rifle."

CHAPTER 36

SCARLET

I didn't leave one organized crime family to join another. Nikolai Ivanov might bend some laws, but he's not inherently evil.

When my hold on his wrists tightens, he turns. Confusion reigns in his gray eyes, but there's lightning on the horizon. He's feeling attacked, and he's ready to fight. *Semper paratus.* Always ready.

Listen to them.

I silently plead with my eyes and my touch.

"You want me to work with these blokes?"

I nod and lick my lips. My mouth and throat are dry. He's got to do this. But he's not alone.

"I'll help, too," I whisper.

The muscles below his cheekbones flex, and his lips flatline.

My grip on his wrists lowers to his hands, and I squeeze, holding his hands in mine, my thumbs grazing his knuckles.

His jaw clenches, but then he softens.

"What exactly do you want me to do?" Nick asks the room.

"Work your connections," Leo answers.

"You heard me tell Dorian I'm out."

"Yes, but you've still got your contacts. Mansueto, Droga, Pearson… They won't alienate you. You have aligned business interests. Plug them for information. Besides, I'd bet they aren't buying into this shift in direction. Best case, they can give you insights. Worst case, you fracture the syndicate further," Leo says.

"Angel stays out of it," Nick says. "She doesn't need more enemies."

"They won't trust her anyway," Leo says. "Best to keep your relationship with her on the down low."

"Can I get a look at this intel you're working off of?"

Nick avoids my gaze, but he lifts one of my hands and presses his lips to my fingers before releasing them and moving closer to the computer.

"He did it. The bounty has been rescinded," Sophia announces.

"That was fast," says Leo, or maybe it's Jack. The two men sound similar to me. "Would you have really posted a bounty on the old man's life?"

"To end the madness? Yes," Nick says without an ounce of remorse.

My mobile rings through one of the bags. Nick's eyes narrow accusingly. "You have your mobile on?"

I scramble for the bag, searching. "I thought I turned it off."

"I thought you threw it out," Nick grumbles.

The weight of my mistake settles heavily in my chest. One careless oversight could have led them right to us. After everything Nick and the others risked to help me, I'd nearly compromised our safety over a mobile.

By the time I locate the device in my backpack, the call has gone to voicemail. There's a string of messages, all from Orlando.

Are you ok?

The news shows a terrorist attack near the Ivanov estate. Are you okay?

You're scaring me. Respond. Pls.

The news says it was on the Ivanov property. Scarlet?

I show the screen to Nick, my hand slightly trembling. "I'm going to call him. Okay?" I need to make this right, starting with using proper security protocols.

"Should she call on her mobile or yours?" Nick asks. "She's calling her cousin. Apparently, news of the explosion traveled to Italy."

"BBC has been covering it. It's everywhere," Kairi confirms. "You should be fine in the van, but to be safe, use our lines."

Sophia opens a drawer, pushes some buttons on an odd-looking mobile, and hands it to me. "Here you go. And you should be fine, but let me disable that mobile."

I take the device Sophia hands me, give her mine, and head to the back of the long van. Nick catches my eye and gives a reassuring wink as I press the mobile to my ear. That small gesture helps ease some of my guilt. He understands that in the heat of the moment, even trained operatives can make mistakes. I'm as far away from the others as I can be. There are no windows back here, and I can't see outside other than a distant view through the windshield up front, but we're traveling at a quick clip.

Nick sits in the seat beside Sophia at the computer, and from here, it appears he's in an intense conversation with the Americans.

Orlando doesn't answer. It's an unknown number, and I've no idea what area code shows for my number, or if it simply says unknown number.

I shoot him a message.

It's me. Pick up.

This time, when it clicks and rings, he answers right away.

"Scarlet?" He's mystified, understandably.

"Yes. I'm okay."

"Oh, thank god. The blast…were you close by?"

"Closer than I'd wish. But I'm okay."

"You're not injured?"

"No. I'm good. How are you? I've been wanting to reach out, but I wasn't sure you wanted me to."

"Straight up, I didn't. But, seeing the explosions…you know, there's video of the blasts. Looks like a nuclear bomb went off."

"It can't have been that bad." The ground shook sure, but nuclear?

"It didn't mushroom, but it could've been a movie set. Lots of locals caught the explosion through the trees. It's all over the news. I'm just…I immediately thought the worst, and…thank you for letting me know you're all right."

"How are things there?" I soften my voice, not because there are listening ears nearby, but because this has to be a difficult time for Orlando.

"I'm being sent away to boarding school. I leave this weekend."

"Really?" It's not unheard of for mafia kids to get shipped off to boarding school, but now he's one of the men.

"Sixteen arrests last week. The rival mafia clans smell blood. They've been attacking locations under our protection. We're spread too thin. I want to stay and fight, but Papa believes it's only a matter of time before the Ombra come down, and…his priority is Titan Shipping. Willow was right. She always said that, and I told her she was wrong."

Uncle Alessio built Titan Shipping from a small shipping company to a worldwide force. He served as a blood member of the Grigi, not out of desperation for funding but out of loyalty. Ironically, the fallout from the investigation may free his son of his misaligned allegiance.

"I'm relieved he's prioritizing you. It'll be good for you to get away from this."

"You know, I think I understand why you did it."

"Oh?"

"Forgiveness is hard."

My mouth drops. "You think…" I can't quite say the words.

"The irony is that if Papa had forced Willow into a contractual marriage, she would've forgiven all involved. Forgiveness is intrinsic in her nature. And it's ironic because Papa saved her only for her to die."

There's no response to his warped reasoning.

"But between the two of you, I think I'm more like you, Scarlet. It's truly hard to forgive."

"You mean it's hard to forgive me? You understand that the family is a criminal organization, right? They traffic drugs and murder people."

"You'll never understand. It's Aunt Catarina's fault. And maybe my parents. You and Willow spent too much time on your own, watching television and TikTok. You've been indoctrinated."

"Who has been filling your head with this nonsense?"

"Let's not argue. You want to know what it's like these days? Papa only cares about protecting his sole heir."

"That's a good thing, Orlando."

"He was arraigned, you know? The only reason he's not sitting in a cell right now is because he's got some of the best lawyers around. He still has to stand trial. And the case against him will be a tough one because of the evidence you supplied. It's not too late, you know. If you refuse to testify, he can throw the case."

I'm silent because what can I say? Orlando refuses to accept it, but his father ruined my life. And yes, with time, perhaps I can forgive Uncle Alessio. But forgiveness and absolution are not the same. He still must suffer for his sins, against me and against all the innocents his crimes have hurt. If forgiveness cleared one of all sins, there would be no hell.

He sighs as if my silence pains him. I glance up and meet Nick's concerned gaze, his blue eyes alert and protective.

"I hope one day you'll understand my position. It's my hope you'll go on to university, and when you take the helm of the business, whatever business that might be, that you do good." I swallow down the emotion threatening to erupt. "That's what Willow would want."

Guilt swirls in the shadows, threatening me for the lie of

omission. His sister is alive. That knowledge might be all he needs to change course, but I can't risk her new life. If Orlando is going to find his way, he needs to do so on his own.

The screen on my phone lights, and I read the message.

Unknown number
Your death day is here.

"Orlando, did you just text me?"

I hold up the mobile for Nick to see. His eyes widen with alarm.

Nick grabs the phone from me and taps out a response.

Me
Who is this?

"I'm on the line with you. Why would I message you?" Irritation laces Orlando's words through the handheld speakerphone.

Unknown number
Your friendly prophet.

Nick carries the mobile to the others.

"Orlando, I'm going to need to go."

"Wish I could say—"

A loud crash explodes in my ears.

My body lurches.

Gunshots ring out.

Pain shoots through my knees and hands.

A cupboard opens.

I scramble for the mobile on the ground.

The men grab guns.

Chambers click.

Crushed circles mar the windshield.

Fisher announces, "Don't shoot. The glass is bulletproof. I'm going to back up and drive around this car."

Up ahead, there's a small van that's pulled in front. Four men with guns stand in the back of it, shooting away at us.

"Clock what they're carrying," Fisher shouts from behind the wheel. "This baby's fortified, but it's not invincible. That first strike may've been a drone. We need cover."

CHAPTER 37

NICK

Two men with assault rifles splatter the van with a spray of bullets. The windshield won't last forever.

"Where the fuck are we?" I shout.

Fisher slides the van into reverse, and I scramble to the front. We need a bloody strategy.

"Nick!" Scarlet cries.

"Stay back," I yell as she steps forward. "Get her back," I yell at Sophia.

A man carrying a military-grade assault weapon joins the others. Unlike the other blokes, he's not wearing a balaclava, and he grins an eerie, slow grin.

We crash into something, probably a car. Fisher grinds the gears, and we lurch forward.

I study the weapon in the lunatic's hands.

"That's a bloody bazooka."

A spray of bullets shoots from the side, sending the armed men to our front diving for cover.

The wheels screech as we take off.

"As fast as you can," I say to Fisher, probably quite unnecessarily.

Scanning the surroundings, I recognize where we are.

"Let's head to the wharf," I say, directing the driver, on autopilot.

I point in the direction we should head. I don't know the street names, but the area's familiar.

"Shouldn't they know the bounty's been dropped?" Scarlet asks.

That's an interesting question. Could these be some zealots who've ignored the updates? Perhaps hoping a kill will still be honored?

No. That text. No coincidences. This is Prophet.

She's huddled on the floor, but she's clutching a handgun—Atta girl.

"Did you recognize those men?" The question comes from behind me. Sophia's got a phone to her ear.

"Negative. Could be bounty seekers, but chances are they're hired." I shoot my love a wink as she's gone quite pale. "We'll need to nab one. Find out who hired them. My bet is, they'll lead us to this Prophet bastard."

Up ahead, the wharf comes into view. It's late. Warehouse workers will be off-shift. We can nab a fishing boat if we can lose the cocksuckers behind us.

"That way," I say, pointing to a loading dock.

The back of the van explodes into a burst of flames and skids onto its side.

"We're hit," Sophia exclaims.

Well, fuck. So much for outrunning the bazooka.

Metal on asphalt screeches across the pavement.

"Where are the fucking bobbies?" I yell to no one in particular.

I swear to god, spend a lifetime skirting the blokes and when you need them, they're nowhere to be found.

Gunfire rat-a-tats outside the vehicle.

There's a hole in the back of the van big enough for us to exit through if it weren't for the flames lapping the edges.

"Where's the gas tank on this thing?" I ask.

Fisher kicks out the door, rises up to eye level, and scans the grounds. The van's on its side, and he's peering out the door like it's a tank.

I pass him a gun.

"Help the women out, one by one," he shouts. "Bring up the rear."

"Arrow, can you hear me?" Sophia asks. She's shouting toward the speaker as she arms herself with a rifle, two hand-guns, and a blade.

There's no sound from the speaker, not even static.

"Blast disconnected us," I tell her.

Nearby gunfire from our backup team means we're not alone.

When we climb out of the rubbish, we'll need to run. Hope-fully, the others are in position to give us clearance.

Rapid-fire gunfire mixes with smoke.

This shit isn't going according to plan.

Fisher taps me, guns strapped on, and I crouch to assist.

Fisher shoves off my back, climbing out of the hole with a spray of bullets.

"Clear. Move it!" he shouts with the boom of a drill sergeant.

Sophia is next, reaching one arm up to Fisher's protruding hand. Her foot's on my shoulder for a brief second before she's gone, practically airlifted by Fisher out of the hold.

Gunfire splits the air.

The smoke has grown so dense it's a challenge to see through the back of the van.

Scarlet steps up and I stop her, pulling her close.

"If shit goes sideways, stay with Lina. You'll be taken care of."

"Nothing's going to happen." Evergreen eyes pierce the shroud. "Believe."

"I love you."

"Now's not the time, Nikolai. Tell me when we're through this."

I want to believe. But from inside this tin can, it's sounding like we got stiffed.

I flatten my lips against hers, memorizing the feel and the pulse through my body. All too fast, it's over.

I watch as she stretches an arm high above, and I hold my breath, searching for Fisher.

His hand reaches down, and I breathe more easily as I push up on her bum, helping her rise out of the vehicle.

Given the intensifying smoke, this rig could blow any second.

Gunfire returns, and I send a prayer to the heavens that Scarlet's taken cover and then haul myself out of the hole.

My arm muscles burn as I pull. Fisher's on the edge, shooting, giving clearance.

I don't see Scarlet. Nor Sophia.

I roll out of the hole, scrambling down the side.

Both Scarlet and Sophia are crouching on the ground, guns out, firing back.

"How many?" I ask, boots landing with a painful crack on the pavement.

"SITREP unclear," Fisher shouts. "Visibility zero."

"SITREP?"

"Situation Report," Sophia says. "Fish, they aren't military. You lead, I'll cover."

"Negative," he argues.

Looking over my shoulder, I estimate we've got a football field's length to reach cover. Unless these blokes are shit shots, they'll fill us with lead before we reach the warehouse.

A boom sounds, and the van shifts, throwing us back against the pavement.

My ears ring.

Smoke's everywhere.

I swipe my eyes and blink.

High above me, Scarlet takes aim, her hair flaming, a vision in marred white.

Bap. Bap. Bap.

I push up, coming to her side.

To my right, a rifle aims at my angel.

Time stills.

All my senses heighten.

I sail through the air, feet leaving the ground.

I pull the trigger and answer with a barrage of gunfire.

And he's down.

Sirens ring.

It's about bloody time.

CHAPTER 38

Blue lights flash, and sirens scream.

Slowly, realization dawns. I've felt this before. The adrenaline rush, the fight for survival, the beating of my heart so loud it pulses in my ears.

Deep breaths.

Blinking.

A forced swallow through a tight, dry throat.

The pounding whoosh dims as the danger abates, and the present bleeds through a clear, unfiltered lens.

"Over there," a man shouts, and I glimpse one shooter rounding the corner of a building.

Officers take off in pursuit.

A river of blood streams along the pavement from the man Nick shot right in front of me.

Did I take more lives?

"Are you okay?"

Nick stands before me, rubbing my arm. I see him touching me, but I don't feel it as much as see it. The scene of destruction, much like when I killed Vincent, is observed through an out-of-body experience.

"Scarlet?"

With a whoosh, I snap back to the present. "You threw yourself in front of me? Are you mad?"

His grip on my arm tightens, his expression severe. "I couldn't let him shoot you."

"I should shoot you for doing something so stupid. What were you thinking, you stupid man?

"I was thinking that you're the love of my life, and I'd rather die than let that bastard shoot you."

I blink.

Anger and relief and repulsion at the bloody scene before me blend.

I focus on Nick, on his concern, on his love.

"When you say it like that, I can't stay angry at you."

He pulls me into his chest. I turn my head to allow for oxygen. I'm still holding a handgun and consider dropping it, but instead, I keep hold, careful to remove my finger from the trigger, and lean into Nick.

Fisher approaches. "You two okay?"

He's shouting to be heard over the shrill and constant sirens.

There were none. Now they're everywhere.

"We're good," Nick says over my head.

"Let's get you out of the open," Fisher says.

"Is Sophia okay?" Nick asks.

"She's taking point with the authorities. We're making

arrangements to transport you once we get clearance. Any idea who these men were?"

"No," Nick says.

I'm fairly certain he's already told them this, but we're all rattled. If it's like it was with Vincent; he'll be asked that question a thousand times more. We both shall.

"They're not Italian," Fisher says, holding an arm out to usher us into the warehouse.

He's acting like we're still at risk, but we're surrounded by police.

"Could be bounty seekers that didn't get the cancellation memo. I'd say it's far more likely they're mercenaries."

"Hired by?" Fisher probes.

Nick doesn't respond, seemingly lost in thought.

"It wouldn't be the Moores, right? Dorian's the one who canceled the bounty," Fisher says.

"Which only means he posted it," Nick says. "And there's that message. If Halston's the Prophet, why would he cancel the bounty? Unless it was to give a false sense of safety."

"He's your friend," I say, sounding stupid.

"Did any of these blokes live?" Nick directs his question to Fisher.

"Ones who got away. We'll see what we can get from their vehicles. As we ID them, we'll get more information."

Sophia steps into the archway and waves for Fisher to join her.

"I'll be back," he says and heads out into the open with the authorities.

Nick rests his chin on top of my head, holding me close against him. "Seems our little escapade dug up a few enemies, eh?"

I pull back so I can get a better look at him. I rub my hand over the side of his jaw and dig the edge of my thumb into his goatee. He grasps my wrist and places his lips against my palm.

"Churchill said that it's good to have enemies. It means you stood up for something."

"Is that right?"

"You're a brave man. You don't fear enemies."

"No, never did. World's richest bastard took my family, and I survived. Prospered right under his nose. But that was before you."

"Me?"

"Yes." He's circumspect.

"You're afraid of losing me, is that it?"

"Terrified."

"You don't need to be. Your enemies are my enemies, remember? They're the ones who need to be afraid."

"God, I love you."

He presses his lips hard against mine, then breaks away, holding my shoulders.

"Where shall we go? I've got a place in Copenhagen. If we're leaving by ship, that's a mite closer than Greece. I could probably scrounge up a yacht from there that'll deliver us to Greece undetected."

"Is that it? We go into hiding?"

He half chuckles. "Do I look like the hiding type? No. We duck out and regroup. Study. The syndicate fractured. To be expected with any self-serving, fluid group. I need to figure out who's behind this madness."

"And then?"

"We stop them."

"I like that plan."

"Good. After we've knocked that out, you and I are going to ride off into the sunset and shag like bunnies."

"I love you, you know?"

"Oh, that's been sorted for some time now."

"Has it?" I'm grinning. This man, he's always making me smile.

"Oh, yes. You're my angel. Seems I can't shake you."

"Nope. You're stuck with me."

"Thank the gods."

EPILOGUE

NICK

The Next Day

Scarlet circles the Christmas tree, fingering ornaments as she inspects the noble fir. I relax into the sofa, content to observe my angel.

Outside, the wind howls with an incoming storm. Inside the cozy cottage, the fire crackles. With each passing second, I slip deeper into relaxation.

Jack Sullivan and his partner, a man named Ryan Wolfgang, argued against lying low in Greece. They said that given I'd done extensive construction work on a sizeable home on a small island, the owner would be known, discreet paperwork be damned. In truth, they're probably right. Besides, I had to bribe a few in the Greek mafia to get it built, so right there sits a weak link.

It worked as a hideaway when I didn't have experts searching for me.

There's also the likelihood the Greek mafia won't take kindly to hosting a witness for the upcoming drug trafficking trial. While the Greeks and Italians aren't besties, there's a code of honor amongst thieves, and turning a brethren in violates said code.

Drago insisted we stay at one of his remote homes. Claims the estate is difficult to get to and so remote that while someone might see a helicopter traveling over the islands, they won't care who's in it, and the locals, of which there are few, will assume it's Drago. The flight manifest doesn't list our names. And he swears the staff he has on-site will see to our every need.

I'm not fond of leaving Lina behind, but I'm assured she's in good hands. And this little respite is temporary, a moment to regroup.

I said I trusted Drago, and we'll find out if that trust is warranted. If I'm right, it's a good job. I'll have insight into the frayed syndicate while I sort this mess.

Ash survived the bombing, but he nearly lost an arm. Miraculously, no one lost their lives. The authorities are combing the estate under my team's oversight.

Drago and his staff are helping to control the narrative. At the moment, all is hush-hush, and in theory, my enemies don't know if I'm dead or alive.

We couldn't trace the message from the so-called Prophet. I'd bet my last pound it's Halston. Dorian may or may not be aware. At this point, coming at me is a game for the demented prick. Drago isn't convinced the Moores are the culprits, but he agrees it's a conceivable scenario. He's convinced it's Russia. Maybe Putin himself.

Drago's place in the Shetland Islands is one that he keeps under a trust. It's difficult to get to and hours from any urban center. If all goes as planned, we'll spend the holiday here and return to my London flat in the new year.

Our allies are much more concerned with the disparate attacks and this idea that it's all testing for a much larger, coordinated attack. According to Jack Sullivan, the world's intelligence agencies are convening, working around the clock. We'll work together.

The European authorities want to find this Prophet as much as I do, given the use of militarized drones has the public up in arms.

I've agreed to use my resources and contacts to stunt any coordinated attack and to determine who's guilty. No one wants to blame the wrong party, especially a country, and bring us into war. Right now, we need more intel.

A satellite phone sits on the coffee table. Reception for cellular isn't present where we're located. In another room, there's a hardwired computer with access to the world. Drago, like me, is a tech guy, and we'll be good here. I'll weigh in as much as I can.

The one bright spot? The case against the Lupi Grigi's smuggling business will proceed. The authorities have unearthed enough evidence and witnesses that the famiglia's leaders will be locked up with or without Scarlet's testimony. Massimo is being held without bail. Pearson's media conglomerate will run a series on the affair, and within a week, every major news outlet will follow suit. The investigation is unstoppable.

"Are these Drago's family ornaments?" Scarlet asks.

"I've no idea. Could be his staff's."

"Did we kick someone out of the cottage?"

"No, love. The caretakers live not too far away. Keeping this place up is their whole job, plus I think they have sheep or something. Work options are slim out here, so they're grateful for the year-round work. I don't think they're bothered too often."

They've stocked the kitchen and promised to be by every three days with more supplies. Other than that, Scarlet and I are on our own.

Whoever came after us are lucky bastards. If they'd harmed Scarlet, I'd be ensconced in a sky-high flat in London daring any fuckwit to come after me, and I'd be drafting a terminal list. Instead, I'll wait to see what the police, the intelligence blokes, and Arrow dig up. Then I'll draft that bloody list.

In the meantime, Scarlet's safety remains my concern. No one will stumble upon us out here in this remote spot in Shetland.

"This is really nice," Scarlet says.

"You like it?"

The best attribute I see to the place is that it's secluded. If it weren't so bloody frigid, we could fuck outside by the cliffs.

She abandons the decorated tree to stand before me and cocks her head to the side.

"You worried about being bored?"

"No," I answer honestly. "I think we'll find plenty to do."

"Are you planning on hunting?"

"No." I'm not big into hunting. Although that is a reason people travel here.

"I didn't see any golf courses." She smiles a teasing, flirtatious smile.

"I don't golf," I say.

"I thought that's big in Scotland."

"It is. Not here."

"You're exhausted, aren't you?"

She straddles me on the sofa, and my hands fall to her hips.

"I'm a touch knackered." I barely slept last night, what with getting reports, answering questions, and ensuring my staff had been taken care of, and today's been a travel day.

"So, how do you envision us spending our days?"

The firelight casts a halo around her, and I reach for her, cupping her cheek in my palm.

"Shagging. Eating. Every once in a while, maybe we'll brave the elements for a hike."

"And what about when this is over? When the holiday is past?"

"Whatever you like." It's an honest answer. "Would you like to live the life of a digital nomad? We can travel. Go wherever you wish. What is it that you want, my love?"

"Do you know you're the first person to ever ask me that?"

"That's criminal."

My back muscles ache, and I pat her thigh. She intuitively understands and rises. I reposition a few pillows and lie back, gesturing for her to join me, and pull a blanket over us. She rests her head in the crook of my shoulder. A sense of peace washes over me.

"What about you? What do you want? Oh, god, I just had the worst thought."

"What's that?"

"I bet you're impossible to buy a holiday gift for. You probably have everything you could ever want."

"I suppose I do always get what I want. After all, I got you."

She playfully slaps my chest, and her leg curls over my thigh. *This. This is what I want.*

"Do you want children?"

The shift in her tone isn't lost on me.

"We've never talked about it, and if we're talking about the future—"

"Never made it to my wish list. You?"

"Can't have them, remember?"

"If you want them, there are ways. I'll give you anything you want."

She lifts her head and rests her chin on her balled-up hand so she's looking down at me.

"You mean that, don't you?"

"Yes, I do. I mean, I mucked up royally with Lina, but if you want to give it a go—"

"You didn't muck up with Lina."

"She doesn't fly straight. Don't know if she ever will."

"And you'll never know. It's her demon to fight. You can't hold yourself accountable."

Easier said than done. But each time this one tells me Lina's future isn't my responsibility, I feel a tad lighter.

"I don't think I want children."

She's bouncing around, going from topic to topic.

"I'd like sheep."

"What?"

Her lips spread into a dreamy smile. "Don't you think Dog

could use some friends? Maybe I'll be a dog breeder. No. I'll create a rescue."

"We'll fix up the country house. There's lots of land."

"Chickens. Kitties."

I close my eyes and stifle a groan. "You're going to bring the cats inside, aren't you?"

"A sanctuary for animals that have had a crap lot in life." She's completely disregarded me, but her eyes are sparkling, and that's everything to me.

I loop a silky strand around my index finger and twist. "If that's what you want, that's what we shall do, love."

BONUS EPILOGUE

SCARLET

Six Months Later

Vehicles line the road straight to the fountain. The sound of hammers and mechanical saws slice the spring morning with signs of renewal. The garage and the underlying tunnel were destroyed in the explosions, and a fire that ripped through the mansion left the stone façade and little else.

In true billionaire fashion, the way only someone without a budget could do, Nick set about restoring the estate, remaining true to the period of the home. The progress the restoration team has made is awe-inspiring, a testament to the power of a team motivated by the prospect of a substantial financial bonus.

Given most of the walls burned, the furniture and art destroyed beyond recognition, the interior was a blank slate. Nick wanted to hand the reins over to me. After resolving the issues with his global partners, he became obsessed with drones. He bought up a small drone start-up and sees the tech as an important component for ensuring European independence and stability.

As there's a good chance many of my days will be spent in this country home, I've weighed in on plans. But at my urging, he let Lina loose with the interior design, and she's found a passion. She's enrolled in an interior design program, and she's enthused.

"Is Lina meeting us here?" I ask Nick as he weaves around the parked cars and trucks.

"She said she's got too much on her plate this weekend. A project of some sort due. But she wants us to message photos."

I study him, searching for anger or concern. With his sister, he always anticipates the worst, but I've told him he's got to believe in her and let her tread her own path. He can be near and help her if she falls, but he's got to give her the space to conquer those demons.

"Are you worried?" I ask, choosing the direct approach.

Bright blue eyes meet mine for a brief second as he parks the SUV in a location that will block other vehicles from looping the circle.

"Not at all. Her sponsor says she hasn't missed a meeting. She's got one this afternoon."

"Don't park here."

"Why?" He opens his mouth to argue, and I swat him.

"It's my place," he mumbles. "I can park where I bloody well like."

"Won't hurt you to be considerate."

"I'm always considerate."

I toss him a soft glare, and he half chuckles.

"To someone other than me."

He pulls up and shifts to park.

"Your wish is my command."

I roll my eyes as he comes around to my side of the vehicle and opens the car door, offering me his hand.

"Watch where you step," he warns. "Nails."

I do as he says, meeting the gaze of one of the security guards on the perimeter. I give the stern man a curt nod.

I'm uncertain if the abundance of security has to do with the upcoming trials where I will serve as a witness, or if it's simply an ongoing precaution, but I've grown accustomed to their presence.

Shall we go inside? The sound of hammering and power saws fills the air. The front-facing facçde will largely remain unchanged, but inside it's a thoroughly modern home.

"I'm going to go around back," I say.

Ash approaches with four dogs hot on his heels, tails wagging. Ash survived the explosions, but not unscathed. His hearing took a hit, and he's still in physical therapy. He recently returned to his post as head of security and lives in a neighboring home Nick purchased for him.

The three additional dogs with Ash are mine, and when I bend to greet them, I'm nearly plowed over by their exuberance.

Nick surprised me at Christmas with an abandoned litter of curly-haired puppies. He read about them somewhere, or so he told me. Said he set up an alert for any mention of puppies in the area and, he read about these being left near a Cotswold pub. I'm not sure I completely believe his story, but I could hardly pass them up, especially with the red bows tied around their necks.

Sometimes they stay with us in London, but they're getting quite big and prefer it out here where there's room to roam. Plus, they hate their crates.

While Ash and Nick chat, I rub them down and lead them away from the hub of activity to the small barn. Lina's horses are currently boarded nearby until the completion of the stables. The small barn adjacent to a paddock is where we keep the dogs when they stay here. It's fine for summer, but we hope to be in the main house come fall when the weather turns.

Lina's horses may return, or she may choose to stay in London and possibly sell her horses. It's her choice to make.

Orlando and I speak about every fortnight. He's summering with a friend's family in Turkey and sounds like a teen once again. Overall, I'd say boarding school suits him.

The sun beams overhead, and the dogs run in circles. I lift a stick and throw it as hard as I can, and all four head off on a chase.

Nick approaches, mobile in his hand, speaking into it to message someone. I'm not sure if he's always been like this or if his preoccupation with work is due to his drone start-up, but I suspect it's the former.

When he slips the mobile into his pocket, I arch an eyebrow. "Work?"

"No." He smirks. It's a familiar look I've grown to adore.

"What are you up to?"

"Scheduling a time for a private shopping excursion."

"I do not need more clothes."

He lifts my hand and caresses my fingers with his thumb. "But you could use some diamonds."

I withdraw my hand from his and bend to greet Daisy, the

black curly-haired dog. The other three boys are off grappling with the stick.

"Thought it might be nice for us to make it all official before we see our friends across the pond."

I haven't yet spoken with Willow, but I've been assured that soon, we'll go on a private holiday and meet up with her. She goes by Lily now, and he goes by Sam. They've been quite cautious, as they should be, but Jack Sullivan promised us he'd find a way for us to safely meet. Nick assured me that it would happen. And now the designated holiday is a few short weeks away.

"Should it concern me that you don't fancy the idea of wearing my ring?"

Daisy licks my face, buying me time for a response.

"Do you not want to be my wife?"

I push up off the ground, brushing my hands on my thighs.

"I'm already yours. I don't need a ring or a document stating it."

His eyes cloud, and that's not what I want.

I interlock our fingers. "I have a proposal."

He's been dropping hints for weeks that he'd like for us to marry on our upcoming holiday.

"Let's get tattoos."

His face contorts, and I can't suppress my laughter.

"You can't be serious."

I point at my ring finger. "On our ring fingers. You can take a ring off. You and I, we're not traditional. That's not what we're about."

"You did traditional. Didn't fancy it," he says, thoughtful.

"That's a fair assessment. But that doesn't mean I plan on

walking away. Let's do a commitment ceremony when we're on holiday."

He won't tell me where we're going, but I'm envisioning a private tropical island.

"Your mate can be your best man."

"That needs to happen," he says, quite serious.

"Why?" I'm fascinated by the machinations of his brain.

"Luck. We need the good luck."

"No. We make our own luck, you and I."

"I suppose that's true." He lifts my hand to his and presses his lips to my knuckles. "After all, I'm one lucky bastard."

"You warming to the tattoo idea?"

He chuckles. "Well, yes." With a grin, he adds, "My angel committed to spend the rest of her life with me. Keep me treading the right path forward. If that's not luck, what is?"

His strong arms loop around me, and I rest against him as we watch our dogs race around the English countryside. The sun warms my face as I think about how far I've come, how much has changed.

Once, men feared me for the blood on my hands. Now, this man calls me Angel.

Keep Reading. Dorian's story continues in Blind Prophet...

BLIND PROPHET

PROLOGUE

CAROLINE

The day ran its course like any other September day.

It might have been rainy or sunny, but the weather was immaterial. Life around me continued. The lights flicked on and off. The occasional siren sounded, punctuated by horns. Pedestrians passed along the sidewalks. It was an unremarkable September day.

Yet my fractured insides struggled with insufferable pain.

My fingers trembled as I zipped the last suitcase. I didn't want to leave, but I couldn't stay.

I stared at the door for hours. A weak voice begged to leave a note, but I couldn't be that person. I'd like to think I sat there, sitting beside my luggage, remembering our past, but that wouldn't be true. I chanted to myself, in a near-meditative trance, wearing a crisp, white blouse and navy slacks that would garner Gwyneth Paltrow's approval. Makeup lightly done for a natural glow, hair glossy and smooth, gold Cartier bracelets on one wrist, and a diamond-encrusted Rolex on the other, pale pink freshly manicured nails.

If the paparazzi lingered outside, their photographs would show a well-put-together woman leaving for a brief trip.

My nerves churned. I hoped for luck, to exit unobserved. The last thing I wanted was to have my photograph circulate with rumors about marital strife.

An unnamed source might say they've sensed issues for months. A writer would speculate Dorian and Caroline Moore haven't been seen together since the MOMA exhibit two months prior. And a body language expert might decode a photograph from two years prior to one snapped when we'd been ducking paparazzi. *"See how she's changed? Her arms are wrapped around her middle, she's crouching forward like she doesn't want him touching her, and they aren't making eye contact."*

I could write the articles myself.

The lock clicked. I swallowed.

My spine stiffened. My chest ached.

The doorknob turned.

His gaze tracked me and the two suitcases.

Wordlessly, he closed the door and locked it.

When he faced me again, his shoulders sagged, I think. Time may have painted that flicker of emotion in the recesses of my memory. His freshly shaven jaw held no discernible emotion.

"So, this is it."

It wasn't a question, rather a statement of an expected event. "Where will you go?"

"I'll stay with my parents." In Connecticut, the paparazzi would be less present. At his insistence, I quit my job after we married. Ironically, if he'd let me keep it, I might have thrived. Well, thrived is a strong verb. It's possible I wouldn't have suffocated.

Anger surfaced with those thoughts. If I recall correctly, I made no attempt to conceal the emotion.

"You won't get a dollar more than the prenuptial agreement allows, you know that, right?"

His accusation sliced like a scalpel, deliberate and strategic. When he chose to speak, he did so with intention.

"I don't want a fight."

I want my sanity. My confidence. My sense of worth.

He stood there by my suitcases. Unreadable. Silent.

I don't know what I expected or why I waited for hours for the awkward interlude. It was a marriage no one wanted, and it ran its course.

When I stood, I swiped my palms against my trousers and noticed how cold my hands had grown.

Are photographers outside? The question died on my tongue. It didn't matter.

A thousand regrets weighed down my chest, and a singular hope kept it functioning.

If he had nothing to say, neither did I.

My hand fell to the luggage handle, and his covered mine.

He cupped my cheek and forced me to look up into his cloudy eyes.

Silent tears leaked from eyes that hadn't truly seen me in months.

And then his lips covered mine, and I splintered. Our kiss stemmed the tearful tide. I clung to him, leaning on his strength.

When he broke the kiss, he breathed into my ear, "One last time?"

That's what he wanted. Sex.

His last words to me.

As feared, when I exited the townhome, I faced a flash of lights.

One photographer with a long-range lens across the street. Two others hovered closer to my left. My good side. Almost as if he planned it.

He could have. We had a security video in our living area accessible by his phone. He could have seen me and my suitcases and known exactly what was coming.

I held my head high.

"Where are you going, Mrs. Moore?"

"Are the rumors true?"

"Caroline, are you separating?"

I forced a cold, cordial smile. A barely there smile that straddled the line of detached model and wealthy philanthropist with a disdain for the media. A parting gift for the three photographers, strategically positioned for maximum coverage. Just like a surveillance operation, except their target was emotional devastation rather than intelligence gathering.

Newspaper photographs often struggle to capture nuance. In the articles about that September day, the captions spoke of a tear-streaked face, but the photographs, especially those printed in black and white, didn't show tears. My stoic expression concealed the evidence of heartbreak.

Social media, however, was full of commentary filled with

vitriol. How could it be otherwise? After all, I walked away from the golden boy, an American prince, a billionaire. Stupid, crazy, cheating slut, ice cold, plastic, full of filler, greedy, social climber: they didn't know what exactly I had to have done to be thrown out of the gilded castle, but one thing was certain: In the court of public opinion, I held the blame.

GRATITUDE

To my husband and daughters, thank you for putting up with late dinners and deadline weekends as I chase my dream.

To my doodle, thank you for being my ever present office companion and home protector.

To my writing friends, thank you for serving as my sounding board and support group. To the "blue ladies," thank you for helping me keep my sanity during trying times—your friendship means so much.

To Damonza, thank you for all the care you put into cover designs and marketing elements.

Karen Cimms, thank you so much for stepping in as editor and adding your finesse. Jaime Ryter, thanks so much for your final coat of polish.

To my advanced reader team, thank you so much for reading, reviewing, answering my questions, and sharing my books on the vast web and beyond. You are the loveliest! Pure gold!

To my readers, thank you for taking a chance on me. There are millions of stories out there, and I'm grateful you chose to read mine.

ALSO BY ISABEL JOLIE

Arrow Tactical Security Series

Better to See You (Wolf and Alexandria)

Sure of One (Jack and Ava)

Cloak of Red (Sophia and Fisher)

Stolen Beauty (Knox and Sage)

Savage Beauty (Max and Sloane)

Sinful Beauty (Tristan and Lucia)

Gilded Saint (Sam and Willow)

Scarlet Angel (Nick and Scarlet)

Prophet (Dorian and Caroline) - Releasing June 12th

The Twisted Vines Series

Crushed (Erik and Vivi)

Breathe (Kairi and David)

Savor (Trevor and Stella)

Haven Island Series

Rogue Wave (Tate and Luna)

Adrift (Gabe and Poppy)

First Light (Logan and Cali)

The West Side Series

Blurred Lines (Jackson and Anna)

Trust Me (Sam Duke and Olivia)

Finding Delilah (Delilah and Mason)

Forgetting Him (Jason and Maggie)

Chasing Frost (Chase and Sadie)

Misplaced Mistletoe (Ashton aka Dr. Bobby and Nora)

Standalone Romances

How to Survive a Holiday Fling (Oliver Duke and Kate)

Always Sunny (Ian Duke and Sandra)

The Romantics (Harrison and Zuri)

ABOUT THE AUTHOR

Isabel Jolie, aka Izzy, lives on a lake, loves dogs of all stripes, and if she's not working, she can be found reading, often with a glass of wine. In prior lives, Izzy worked in marketing and advertising, in a variety of industries, such as financial services, entertainment, and technology. In this life, she loves daydreaming and writing contemporary romances with real, flawed characters with inner strength.

Sign-up for Izzy's newsletter to keep up-to-date on new releases, promotions and giveaways. (**Pro-tip** - She offers a free book on her home page…just scroll down after arriving at her site.)

Buy ebooks and signed paperbacks direct from Isabel at www.isabeljoliebooks.com

Want to say hi? Email her through her website or reply to her newsletter…she loves to hear from readers.